JUST ONE LOOK

P.J. Womack

Spicy Contemporary Romance

New Concepts   Georgia

Be sure to check out our website for the very best in fiction at fantastic prices!

When you visit our webpage, you can:
*Read excerpts of currently available books
*View cover art of upcoming books and current releases
*Find out more about the talented artists who capture the magic of the writer's imagination on the covers
*Order books from our backlist
*Find out the latest NCP and author news--including any upcoming book signings by your favorite NCP author
*Read author bios and reviews of our books
*Get NCP submission guidelines
*And so much more!

We offer a 20% discount on all new Trade Paperback releases ordered from our website!

Be sure to visit our webpage to find the best deals in e-books and paperbacks! To find out about our new releases as soon as they are available, please be sure to sign up for our newsletter (http://www.newconceptspublishing.com/newsletter.htm) or join our reader group (http://groups.yahoo.com/group/new_concepts_pub/join)!

The newsletter is available by double opt in only and our customer information is *never* shared!

Visit our webpage at:
www.newconceptspublishing.com

Just One Look is an original publication of NCP. This work has never before appeared in book form. This work is a novel. Any similarity to actual persons or events is purely coincidental.

New Concepts Publishing, Inc.
5202 Humphreys Rd.
Lake Park, GA 31636

ISBN 1-58608-723-1
2004 © P.J. Womack
Cover art (c) copyright 2004 Kat Richards

All rights reserved, which includes the right to reproduce this book or portions thereof in any form whatsoever except as provided by the U.S. Copyright Law.

If you purchased this book without a cover you should be aware this book is stolen property.

NCP books are available at special quantity discounts for bulk purchases for sales promotions, premiums, fund raising, or educational use. For details, write, email, or phone New Concepts Publishing, Inc., 5202 Humphreys Rd., Lake Park, GA 31636; Ph. 229-257-0367, Fax 229-219-1097; orders@newconceptspublishing.com.

First NCP Trade Paperback Printing: February 2006

Chapter One

Lauren liked him. He wore his male persona with casual proficiency, nothing flashy, just plenty of smoldering seduction. She liked his looks and the fact he didn't bother hiding his gaze, which lingered on her like a deep kiss, touching her almost intimately.

She hadn't expected to see someone like 'Mister Sexy' her first night back in New York. But there he stood, looking at her from across the room. His warm gaze torched her libido. Funny how a gorgeous man could make her forget jet lag, cigar smoke and being dragged here by her sister.

Raini insisted she attend the weekly cocktail party without giving Lauren a chance to recover from her coast-to-coast flight. Get her back in the swim, Raini said. *Some swim. I'm on the edge of a tidal wave thanks to Mister Sexy.*

He looked familiar, but no. A woman wouldn't forget him. All other males were relegated to the title of 'poor seconds' after seeing him. He stood head and shoulders taller than the collection of men gathered near him. Her curiosity was piqued.

He made direct eye contact with her and made it clear she interested him with a lift of his head. Maybe she shouldn't encourage him. She smothered a sarcastic laugh, admitting to herself she was intrigued with him. *But no need to let him know I'm swallowing my tongue.* If she didn't get herself under control soon, she was going to do something tacky--like drool.

Caught up in flirting with him, she was unaware of the absence of her ex-fiancé Justin at the gathering. It must have been a hard choice for the host to make. This crowd loved her ex-fiancé. Justin was a rising star in the medical profession, a top flight surgeon. She remembered him as a low-down cheat.

Until the moment he'd suggested they see other people, she'd thought she loved him. He'd left three days after her father's funeral exactly one year ago.

Already past the post phases of being dumped: hurt, anger, sorrow, her only current feeling toward her ex-fiancé was intense disgust. The fine looking guy across the room looked capable of soothing any pain she felt.

Did he know she was out-and-out ogling him? He'd have to be

completely blind not to know.

There was no way to be sure, but from across the room his eyes appeared to be stormy-blue. Perfect. Her gaze touched his dark hair, which he wore a bit longer than that of his companions. The difference suited him, emphasizing his masculinity.

Mister Sexy flashed her a warm smile. Her staring had been officially recognized, and he was probably trying to figure out just how far his newest admirer would go. That's all he did, smile at her and then resume his conversation with his friends. She wanted more, to hear his voice and touch that muscular frame. *Take your time. You'll scare him off.*

"I've been without a man too long," she mumbled to herself. Her snide inner voice had been taunting her a lot on that very subject lately.

She openly assessed the collective group of attorneys, writers and doctors. Which was he? Alpha wolf out hunting alone? Whatever his occupation, the man was the Chief of the clan. She was deeply curious about him. *Damn, you're beginning to think like someone with a fatal attraction. You're just window-shopping remember.*

Lauren made a face of distaste after taking a sip of her warm martini and then looked for a place to discard the drink. At the front of the room she caught sight of her sister and brother-in-law, Adam. They were waving, a signal for her to join the crowd around the piano and listen to one of Broadway's darlings belt out his latest song. She touched her temple to indicate she had a headache, a ruse she used occasionally to get out of something she considered unpleasant. Her sister hurried through the crowd to offer first aid.

Raini's smile of sympathy hit Lauren with a twinge of guilt for her deceit.

The look of motherly concern vanished from Raini's face. She had apparently figured out the recipient of her sister's undivided attention. "I see why you didn't budge from this corner." She looked across the room. "You've noticed Victor Raven."

Lauren's mouth opened slightly in genuine surprise. "That's Victor Raven?" Her sister's expression said she had been caught doing something tasteless.

"Yes it is." Raini gave Lauren an arch look. "You met him at father's funeral."

"Oh, I don't think so." Lauren tried to place a time she would have met this man. "That can't be the same Victor Raven you and your girl friends used to giggle about."

"We were comparing notes." Raini looked at her watch as if she were anxious to change the subject. "Actually, there's no reason for you to remember him. He was in college when you were in high school."

"Your age, huh?" Lauren teased. "You didn't have an affair with him, did you?" Her gaze sped back to him and a hint of a smile tilted her lips. "He looks just about the perfect age to me."

"Lauren. He's a lot older than you in a lot of ways."

"What's wrong with him?" Lauren handed her drink to a passing waiter. "Why hasn't some woman got him on a leash?"

"If you mean, is he married, no. Involved, probably." Raini lowered her voice and glanced at Victor. "His marriage ended in a bitter divorce and now he's sharing custody of his little girl with his ex-wife."

"That doesn't make him untouchable." Lauren grinned at her serious-minded sister. "Victor and I have something in common. We've both been dumped. Maybe we can help each other over the rough spots."

"I didn't say he was unhappy, Lauren." Glancing over at the man in question, Raini sighed. "Women haven't been too kind to him. He just doesn't get deeply involved in relationships."

"Is this some kind of warning?" Lauren wanted to know everything about Victor. "I suppose the divorce made a pauper of him." Her eyes widened in mock horror. "Please don't tell me he's a doctor."

"He's hardly a pauper, Lauren. He's made the millions he inherited look like pocket change with his business savvy." Raini smiled at her curious sister. "And no, he's not a doctor. And I wasn't issuing a warning."

"Sounded like it." Lauren tilted her head from side to side, looking at Victor from every angle. She liked him more with every passing second. "Well, since he's not a doctor, I think I'll go introduce myself."

"Lauren." There was no playfulness in Raini's voice. "Victor has his own set of rules. Be warned he is a charmer and a nice guy, but he is immunized against the long term relationships you enjoy."

The urge to remind Raini to stop lecturing her battered against her teeth. But Lauren kept the remark to herself. She didn't remember her mother and Raini had stepped in to keep her in line since their father had given them free reign to explore. Grudgingly, she admitted that if not for her socially conscious sister, she might be living in a commune in the mountains. On the other hand, she was twenty-six and it was time Raini realized it.

"I suppose you know that statement made him absolutely irresistible." Lauren squeezed Raini's hand. "You worry too much, sis. Anyway, aren't you the one who said I needed to find a new love interest?"

Draping her arm about Lauren's shoulder, Raini seemed to be in a quandary. After a moment, she lifted her hands in a small show of defeat. "I did say that, didn't I?" She started to walk away, pausing to add a last comment. "But does it have to be Victor? I'm not meddling, Lauren. It's just that you seem vulnerable right now."

"I might have been a year ago, but I've learned never to believe a man, no matter how great looking he is." Lauren turned her head to search the group of men for Victor, but he was no longer there. She shrugged then winked at Raini. "See. Nothing to worry yourself about. Seems he's already lost interest."

"Your eyes tell me you're plotting something, Lauren." Sighing, Raini looked at the noisy group that had begun singing again. "After you've found out what you have to know, come join Adam and me at the piano."

"Promise."

Lauren was disappointed that Victor had left. She had enjoyed their brief game of silent flirting--a first for her. Justin hadn't liked flirting. Too childish, he'd said. Childish was scarcely what she'd call the art of flirting in relation to Victor; it was more like a prelude to spontaneous combustion. That would be a first for her too.

Taking a minute to scan the crowd on the chance of catching another glimpse of Victor, she laughed at her sudden infatuation with a stranger. Coming back down to earth, she checked her appearance in the bank of mirrors lining the wall, smoothing the short skirt of her slip dress and brushing a stray wisp of hair from her cheek. All preening stopped when a smooth baritone voice wrapped itself around her.

"Everything looks perfect from here."

Lauren couldn't help the little smile of delight that lifted the corners of her mouth. Like some quiet hunter, Victor Raven had found her. His rich voice stoked her ear, exciting her. She didn't turn to face him but observed him in the mirror. She liked the way he had let her know he was behind her.

"Everything's exactly where it should be." He moved effortlessly and stopped just short of touching her. His gaze traveled the length of her body in a leisurely fashion.

He stood so near that his jacket brushed against her body. She didn't move but involuntarily arched her back slightly in delicious expectation. Heat bloomed through her blood, the power of what was happening too pleasant to describe. He was seducing her without a touch, without speaking.

Victor took a long, unhurried look at her hair and caught a few strands in his fingers. "You have incredible hair. Dark mahogany and silk."

She gave him a wry smile and turned her head slightly. "Are you saying I'm a block head?"

"Hardly. I'm saying you're beautiful." He chuckled and leaned over until his cheek brushed hers. "You're an intriguing woman. Sexy and exotic." He drew his fingertip across her nape. "You make me think of warm beaches and soft night trade winds." His touch teased light as a feather when he traced the line of her jaw. "What are you thinking?"

Lauren shivered under his light touch. A tiny but powerful little flame skittered down her spine. This was way beyond flirting, bordering on foreplay. She should end the encounter. But why? The way he made her body sing was too wonderful not to experience. *Stay*, her woman's voice crooned. Breathe in his male scent of wild heather and warm moss. She blinked when her hair swung free of the heavy silver clasp that had held it. *Wake up, ninny. He's undressing you.*

She tried to sound unconcerned while pushing her hair behind her ear. "And I worked so hard to get it that way."

"It wanted to be free." His fingertips were at the neckline of her dress, branding her skin with his touch. He leaned nearer. "You're unsnapped."

She felt his fingers brush her skin and her pulse raced dangerously. "You have very good hands, Mister Raven."

"Mister Raven?" He arched a dark eyebrow at her comment, not bothering to ask how she knew his name. "And what is your name? I can't just keep calling you fantastic." His finger skated intimately over her wrist. Somehow his hand slid to her waist with the unhurried ease of a man bent on seduction.

"Lauren. Lauren Rose." Gripping his wrist, she moved his hand from her waist. The heavily seductive expression on his handsome face had changed to one of deep interest. She liked that. Flirting wasn't something she did on a regular basis, but Victor made it so easy.

"Lauren. A beautiful name." He leaned forward again, inhaling her scent like a jungle cat seeking a prospective mate. "Of course you would have a sexy name."

Lauren's knees threatened to buckle. Everything about him made her remember the long ignored yearning to be desired and touched in a sensual way. She had to say something that wasn't suggestive or her blood pressure would send her to the hospital.

"I don't remember seeing you at one of these parties before. Did you crash this one?"

"Maybe." An incredibly soft growl tumbled over his lips. "I'm glad as hell I decided to drop in here tonight. Otherwise, I might never have found you."

She let him turn her to face him. Captivating, midnight blue eyes were gazing into hers and she knew it would be easy to become lost in their warm depths. And yes he was tall, but not too tall for her to fit comfortably in his arms. There was a scar at the corner of his mouth, an inch long lightning bolt that looked terrific on him. Damn, she wanted to touch it. Oh dear, what was he doing to her now?

He moved her hair aside to brush a kiss against her earlobe, smiling easily at her. "There isn't a lover lurking about is there, Lauren?"

"Not yet." She felt her nipples tense and become painfully sensitive. What was wrong with her? That was a singles bar invitation for sure.

"That sounds promising." He tilted his dark head to an angle that would have been perfect for a slow, deep kiss, but his mouth only hovered above hers. "Do you keep promises, Lauren?"

The way he said her name stroked the most secret parts of her body. Somehow, she had expected there to be a soft burr to his words. It didn't matter. She liked everything about him and the feeling of being melting wax in his warm hands. She didn't know if she liked his ability to bring out the vixen in her. *Why lie to yourself. You love it.*

"I don't believe I know you well enough to answer that." Her fingers slid over the silk of his tie.

"I hope to change that," he said. He took her hand, lightly squeezing her fingertips. "After we have dinner, we'll satisfy our mutual curiosity about each other."

She wasn't surprised by his suggestion and let her senses enjoy the maleness of him. His presence was overwhelming, and the power of his sexuality pushed her into a satin bed of erotic fantasy. An indescribable flare of desire quickened in her body, ending up in her tense thighs. "Are you asking me to leave with you?" Lord. This was going way beyond flirting.

"Of course." He took a moment to study the hair clasp in his hand. "I thought we were in agreement."

Lauren knew her lips were forming a quivering O while she tried to think of something to say to him. "What would we tell our hostess?"

"Goodnight." He laughed, the sound rich, warm and all male.

He was confidant and she was enthralled. But not so much that she had completely lost her head. At least not yet. How was she going to refuse without sounding like a frightened mouse? The word slipped out of her mouth in a whisper.

"No."

"No?"

She smiled sweetly up at him. "Raven, how would it look if I waltzed out of here with no reasonable excuse?" Was he as strong as he appeared? The breadth of his shoulders said he was.

"You need to know more about me," he coaxed. "I have to know everything about you." His thumb brushed her lower lip.

"Have to?" She leaned against the surface of the cool mirror, breathing in the heady aroma of the sexiest man alive. "Are you sure you want to?"

"I can't believe you're asking me that after I plowed through a hostile crowd getting to you." He braced one hand against the mirror, leaving her enough room to walk away if she chose to. He ran his thumb over her knuckles. "We need to be together on a steady basis. You can question me night and day."

"Night and day?" Not snapping up the idea went against everything she was feeling. It would have been heaven to escape to whatever exciting and sensual place he would take her. *Stop it. You're suffering temporary insanity. Show some class if you're still able. Say something sensible.* "Aren't you employed?" She had managed to regain some decorum.

"Self-employed," he said. Cupping her chin in his fingers, he leveled a warm gaze on her lips.

She blurted out her reply without thinking. "Gigolo?"

Victor seemed to delight in her resistance and playful wit. He renewed his effort to keep her with him as long as possible.

"Lauren. Of course Laurens always have cherry lips and mysterious dark eyes." He drew back a fraction to smile at her. "What does someone as incredible as you do with her time?"

At last, she thought. Something to talk about that wouldn't make her sound like a complete pick-up. "I dream up horribly expensive fashions."

He pressed the hair clasp back into her palm. "That sounds interesting." He watched her replace it in her hair, grinning when he noticed she had missed several strands. "Have lunch with me tomorrow."

Lauren hesitated, unsure if he was serious or simply looking for a way to leave. "Will this be a power lunch?" She hadn't said yes or no. It was up to him now. Oh damn. He eyed the small points of her nipples, and she wanted to rub them into a respectable flatness. He smiled at her as if he wanted to assist her.

His gaze lifted to her mouth. "It will be whatever you want it to be." He caressed her wrist with his thumb. "Anywhere you want it to be."

Lauren hadn't meant for their banter to drag a luncheon date out of him. Or had she? Did she really want to share any part of her life or put her emotions at risk yet? Of course she did. He made her feel what she hadn't for a very long time. Sexy. She plunged ahead.

"All right. Trent's Garden Café."

The sidewalk café around the corner from Raini's apartment building was perfect. Nothing dramatic. And not too expensive.

"Trent's it is." He let her step away from the nest he had created for her.

Lauren moved several steps away on unsteady legs, pausing long enough to look back at him. "Two o'clock. I'm very prompt."

"I'm patient, Lauren. You'll never have to hurry anything for me."

Chapter Two

Lauren was glad Adam wasn't accompanying them as she and Raini got into the taxi that would take them back to the apartment. An emergency call from the hospital had sent him hurrying off into the night, leaving his wife to go home without him. She was hoping Raini wasn't in a talkative mood. She wanted to think about Victor and what the next day would bring. She bit back a groan of irritation when her sister nudged her arm.

"Lauren."

"Yes, Raini."

"Everyone was happy to see you tonight." Raini began rummaging in her handbag, searching for the taxi fare. "But they were disappointed you didn't mingle a little more."

Lauren gave her sister a tired smile. "You and I both know they don't give a fig about me. Fodder for the gossip mill was what they wanted. I'm sure Justin has told the story enough for both of us."

"I don't know why you take that attitude, Lauren." Still searching through her bag for the fare, Raini continued talking. "They're simply interested in your welfare."

"Oh, I know they think I left New York with my tail between my legs, beaten and shamed, but nothing is further from the truth." Lauren had taken money from her bag, handing it to Raini who looked frustrated. "Sure, I was a little embarrassed, but the real reason was financial."

"What?" Raini was in an obvious state of shock. "You're hardly in financial need."

"You forget dear sister, that I studied to be a fashion designer and that's what I do." Searching for a job with the design houses in New York had been nothing short of demoralizing. "No one here took me seriously. The offers I got came from Dad's friends and they only wanted me for a receptionist or a gofer."

Raini's sigh was dramatic. "You didn't have to leave New York. This is your home. Malibu, of all places."

"Hey. When opportunity knocks, you do what you have to do." Lauren put her arm around Raini's shoulders. "You're just wanting me to say I'm homesick."

"Well. Aren't you?"

"Yes, but not enough to give up my job. The Swanson Corporation appreciates me. Besides, that was the only legitimate job offer I got."

The taxi pulled up in front of the apartment building, ending the conversation briefly. It resumed in the elevator.

Lauren grinned mischievously, bringing up a subject that made Raini uncomfortable. "Do they still talk in hushed whispers about my vow to avenge Dad's death?"

"Hardly, Lauren." The keys in Raini's hand jangled musically as she fumbled with the lock. "Everyone knew you were overwrought and stricken with grief."

"Yes. I was. But I meant it when I said some faceless corporate raider killed my father." A year later, Lauren still experienced grief for the vibrant man that she thought would never have simply thrown in the towel.

Inside the spacious entryway of the apartment, Raini softened her attitude and tried to reason with her sister.

"Lauren, our father died of a heart attack."

"He died of heartbreak."

Raini tried logic. "Did Dad ever tell you he was heartbroken? Or sorry he gave up the business?"

"No. He didn't tell me he had heart trouble either." Lauren did something her sister hated. She kicked her shoes off in the entryway then walked off toward the living room. "I'll get those in the morning."

Scooping the slinky little sandals up, Raini tossed them toward Lauren's rear. "I'd hate to see your house, Lauren. I'm sure it's deplorable." Seeing Lauren wasn't going to claim her footwear, Raini picked the sandals up again.

"A pig sty," Lauren tossed back over her shoulder. "Night sweetie." Peeking around the door of her bedroom, she added one last comment. "By the way, when Adam gets home, try to hold down the sounds of ecstasy. I need to catch up on my sleep."

Lauren laughed when she heard the thud of her shoes hitting the bedroom door.

* * * *

Oh Lord, Lauren groaned. Not house cleaning at this hour, please. From the thumping and bumping sounds coming from the den, she knew her sister had the cleaning bug. Giving the clock a bleary glance, she couldn't believe she had slept until twelve-thirty, or that Raini had let her. Groaning again in resistance to whatever Raini had cooked up while she had been sleeping, Lauren rolled off the bed. Slipping on her house slippers, she clomped out into the hallway, yawning audibly. No use letting Raini think she was in the mood for domestic duty. Coffee. She needed it fast and in great quantities. Making a half-hearted check around the spotless kitchen, she looked in the refrigerator. Bean sprouts and plain yogurt were out of the question.

After pouring herself a generous mug of the steaming brew, she ambled to the den. Raini was kneeling on the floor, fiddling with stacks of papers that she had taken great care to place in tidy rows. Squatting down beside her, Lauren gestured toward several boxes that were lined up in a neat row.

"What's all this?" Lauren didn't know or really care what the boxes contained and hoped she wouldn't have to deal with their contents.

"Papers from Dad's desk. The realtor gave them to me."

"I really don't want to do this, Raini." Tossing a wadded up piece of paper into the empty box between them, she lightly smacked her sister's arm. "Why did you wait until I came back to go through this stuff?"

"I didn't want to dispose of anything you might want to keep." Raini continued making neat stacks of the envelopes and papers.

"Give me those," Lauren said. "At this rate we'll never finish." She chose several stacks, sorting through them with little interest. "Gibberish. Why did you save this stuff again?"

Raini retrieved what Lauren had flipped into the empty box. "You're not being very helpful." She tapped her finger on a small scrap of paper to emphasize her words. "See this. This is a list of dad's golf buddies."

"Geez." Lauren flopped onto her back, huffing loudly. "What would we do without that?"

"Piker." Raini was at her task again. "The sooner you get back to work, the sooner we finish."

"You're obsessed." Lauren sat up, taking a handful of what she considered trash. "Junk. Junk, junk, keep, junk and this is...." Her voice trailed off as she reread the words on the paper she held.

"What did you find?" Raini put a rubber band around the items she was tossing out.

"I'm not sure." Lauren waved a sheet of paper under Raini's nose. "Isn't this a copy of a sales proposal for the Rose Corporation?"

"What makes that so interesting?" Raini reached for the paper in Lauren's hand. "Toss it. The original and final contract is in a bank lockbox."

"I'll tell you what's so blasted interesting." Lauren stared at the neatly penned proposal. "No signature. Just the initial *R*." Her eyes narrowed as familiar anger filled her heart. "The initials of the raider." She folded the paper, shoving it into her pajama pocket. "The animal didn't sign his name."

"Lauren. It's a proposal and a hefty one at that." Raini got to her feet. "Men make offers like this all the time. It means nothing." Not wanting to stir Lauren's anger further, she moved the boxes out of reach. "I'll finish up here."

"Fine with me." Lauren couldn't shake the image of those bold initials from her mind until she noticed the time: one o'clock. She had to shower and dress to keep her appointment, and nothing was going to chill her anticipation of being with Victor.

"You go ahead, Raini." Getting to her feet, she patted her sister's head. "I've got to change."

If Raini had made a comment, she didn't hear it. She was in a hurry to meet the man she hadn't stopped thinking about. Never one to fuss with clothing, Lauren dressed casually. New York was locked in a heat wave, and she dressed accordingly, pulling on a pair of white silk pants and a sleeveless white T-shirt. She was giving her hair a final brush when Raini peeked around the doorway.

"Going out?" Disappointment registered on Raini's face. "I thought we might get in some shopping this afternoon."

"I have a luncheon date." Lauren didn't volunteer her date's identity. "I'm game for tomorrow though." She stepped into a pair of white strappy sandals.

"Lauren." Never verbose, Raini managed to speak volumes with minimal words. "Be careful."

"That sounds ominous." Lauren gave her sister a look of wide-eyed interest. "What am I supposed to be careful of?"

"Not what. Whom." Raini straightened the pillows on the chaise lounge. "You're having lunch with Victor, aren't you?"

Lauren heard the ring of parental authority in her sister's voice. She wasn't accustomed to being quizzed about her personal life, and she didn't like it. But she also didn't want to spat with her sister. She chose to ignore the question while dabbing perfume behind her ears.

"You hardly know him, Lauren."

Damn. Raini was going to force the issue. "Unless he's an axe murderer, I think I'll be okay." Lauren picked up her handbag. "Anyway. It's not like he's a complete stranger. You know him."

"Yes, I do." Raini crossed her arms at her waist. "He won't settle for lunch. Are you prepared to be a trophy girl?"

Lauren bit her lip then slung her handbag onto her shoulder. "I hope he's half as exciting as you seem to think he is." She kissed Raini's cheek before heading out the door. "It's just lunch, sweetie."

* * * *

Walking a straight path to the restaurant, Lauren was still mystified by Raini's attitude. They were in complete disagreement about Victor. What the heck. In a few days, Raini wouldn't have to worry about her baby sister. Her vacation would end all too soon, and she would be heading back to California. Until then, she planned to wring every moment of fun out of her time left in New York.

Her stride lengthened as she rounded the corner and caught sight of the sidewalk café, her heart racing a little as she searched the crowd for Victor. Where was he? Of course she had arrived too early. But what was wrong with that? Let the guy know you're happy to see him when he gets here. *Listen to yourself,* her woman's voice crooned. *You can't hide your feelings from him. You're wearing the face of a way-too-anxious woman.*

A touch on her elbow startled her, causing her heart to hammer with excitement.

"Would you like a table now?"

She hated the fact her cheeks were flushed as she turned to find herself face-to-face with a young waiter. A poor substitute for the man she had thought it was.

"Yes. Thank you." She lowered her gaze as she followed him, checking out the crowd from beneath her lashes. After ordering a glass of iced tea, she discreetly scoped out the lunchtime crowd. After ordering her second tea, she began to feel embarrassed. He had forgotten or simply stood her up. Stop it, she ordered herself. Yes. He's late. But you know New York and traffic is horrid sometimes.

One hour later, she sat staring at the seafood salad she'd ordered, grimacing with disgust. She checked the time again. Where was he? Idiot, you've been dumped again. With a shrug of her shoulders, Lauren paid her tab and left the café to hail a taxi. She wasn't about to slink home in a demoralized state. Fifth Avenue offered a wealth of ways to tickle a woman's fancy.

By late afternoon, her credit cards were practically melting. Clothing was no bargain in New York, but she didn't care. There were times a woman needed to indulge in the finer things of life.

And had she ever, she mused, looking at the charge slips in her wallet. When she finally got tired of the crowds, Lauren headed home. It was after six when she walked into the apartment. Raini was working on a floral arrangement and greeted Lauren with a sweet smile.

"I'm glad you're back, Lauren." She gestured toward the sofa table. "The tickets arrived while you were out."

"Tickets?" Lauren dropped her shopping bags onto a side chair. "Tickets for what?"

"A special Beethoven concert." Raini picked up a package that had fallen off the chair. "I know you favor his music. It's my way of saying I'm sorry for butting into your life."

Lauren put her arms around her sister, relieved she wouldn't have to explain or lie about the days disappointing outcome.

"You're entitled," she said. "And thank you." Her mood brightened when she made a suggestion. "But really, I would rather stay in and order a couple of super fattening pizzas."

"Sounds good to me," Raini said. She eyed the mass of shopping bags meaningfully. "Did you have a nice time today?"

"Splendid." Lauren knew she sounded cheerful, but she couldn't quite shake her let down feeling. It would never do to let Raini in on that little secret. "Let us prepare for a night of debaucherous gluttony."

"It will be just the two of us," Raini said. "Adam will be tied up at the hospital for hours."

"Good. We'll have more fun without him," Lauren teased. "After we eat, we can go for ice cream and eat all we want without Adam giving us dirty looks."

When the pizzas arrived, Lauren threw pillows on the floor where they lounged to watch a Bette Davis movie. After a few minutes, Lauren couldn't ignore the snickering of her pesky woman's voice taunting her for being a real twit. Okay. So I'm not watching the movie. I'm thinking about the man that almost was. Damn it. It wasn't her nature to brood over inconsequential events. But this was different. She had experienced something new and powerful with Victor Raven. No other man had ever elicited a feeling of such magnitude in her. Certainly not Justin.

Lauren sighed heavily, trying to remember exactly what she had felt for Justin. Whatever it had been, it paled in comparison to the thunderstorm that had burst over her in a mere few minutes of flirting with Victor. There had never been fireworks between her and Justin, more of an agreement they would marry and be like the rest of their crowd. Well. That just wasn't good enough anymore. Not since she had been touched by fire. She hugged her pillow with another sigh. She reacted to Raini's nudge by tossing a pillow at her.

"I hear your deep sighing, Lauren." While she gathered up the debris from their meal, Raini gave her sister several sidelong glances. "Something on your mind?"

"Not a thing." Lauren lounged back on her pillows, patting her stomach. "There's still room for ice cream if you want to go out."

"I think we could both use the exercise after what we just consumed." Raini stopped policing the area, snapping her fingers as if she had thought of something clever. "Book passage on the cruise with us, Lauren. We haven't been on a trip together in ever so long."

"Raini." The suggestion made Lauren laugh aloud. "Don't you think Adam would rather I wasn't hanging around on your second honeymoon voyage. Really now."

"Nonsense. He loves your company." Raini handed Lauren the shoes she had kicked off under the coffee table. "Ice cream. Remember?"

"Yes to the ice cream and pass on the cruise." Lauren slipped her shoes on. "I have a job waiting. Send me some postcards."

"Are you certain you won't change your mind?" Raini grinned. "A cruise is the perfect place to meet someone special."

"Not that again." Lauren couldn't blurt out she had already met someone special and wasn't likely to meet his equal again.

* * * *

The next day, Lauren had the apartment to herself with Adam at work and Raini out finalizing last minute details for the cruise. She whiled away the time, lounging on the terrace, basking in the solitude until she got hungry. Knowing the kitchen had nothing she needed to whip up a big pan of lasagna, she decided to run to the neighborhood market to get the ingredients.

While she was grabbing her handbag, the doorbell chimed softly. She hoped it wasn't the sweet little lady from across the hall. She was constantly borrowing one egg, but Lauren knew it was just an excuse to talk about her grandchildren.

She opened the door and automatically looked down, expecting to see the petite woman. Instead, a pair of size twelve, black British Walkers and knife pleat trousers was in her line of vision.

She looked up, mouthing the word first then managed to speak. "Raven."

Chapter Three

"Lauren." He was smiling down at her with measurable amusement in his eyes. "Did you forget?"

Forget the way she had tripped merrily off to be with him? She almost laughed at the absurdity of his question. "How did you find me?" She clutched her handbag, withholding the urge to throw herself into his arms. Her attempt at sounding gruff came off in a wimpy mew. Telling him she was ecstatic he stood at her door would have made more sense.

"Luckily I happened to run into Adam. He told me you were here." Victor looked at the handbag she was choking to death in her grip. "You stood me up."

Lauren opened her mouth to deny the charge, but laughed instead. His smile had wormed its way into her female needs area. *Easy, you pathetic woman. He knows you're shamelessly attracted to him. Just look at that posture of complete self-confidence.*

Lauren countered with a question. "Stood you up?"

He didn't need to know she had waited for him for an hour and a half. He didn't need fuel for his ego, and she wasn't about to feed it anything but a few choice cuts of baloney.

She started to close the door, slowly, just to see how serious he was about wanting to see her. He caught the door. She arched her brows in a ridiculous attempt to look innocent.

"Raven. Is there something else?"

"Plenty." He smiled ruefully at her. "It became pretty damn clear you weren't going to show when the waiter at Trent's suggested I order dinner instead of lunch."

He glanced inside the apartment and then looked down at her with a heat wave smile. He wanted to be invited in. It wasn't going to happen. She thought the situation over. Could she have missed seeing him at the restaurant? Impossible. There was no way she could have missed seeing Victor Raven. He was playing with her.

"Well, I'm sorry you underwent such severe trauma." She knew any sane woman would be telling him to hit the bricks at that moment, but she couldn't. And damn. He did smell so good and look so ... so sexy?

"No. You're not sorry," he said. He caught her hand. "You're evil to the bone. But I like that."

He was working on her sense of humor again. "Since you put it that way, I forgive you." She shushed her snide inner voice, which tittered at her caving in.

Why would she send him away when her veins were pumping hot blood after being virtually flat for a year? No. She wanted to feel the zing of life with him. Before her stood perfection in a white linen shirt and black slacks. Anyway, a guy with hair that gleamed with that just showered look was worth another moment of her time.

"Want to try again?" He gave her mouth a lingering study. "I have the day off. I'd like to spend it with you."

"Sorry, but I'm on my way out." *It's not that easy, bub.* She held her bag behind her back. That pesky female voice screamed, yes, but she wouldn't fall all over him. "Some other time. Maybe."

His attempt at a forlorn little smile was ridiculous. He seemed to be able to do nothing to temper her desire to know more about him. He was silent for a moment and then said something that amazed and amused her.

"I'll go with you."

She laughed. "That won't be necessary."

He tried a new approach. "I just heard on the news there's a mugger in the area, and it's dangerous for a woman to go out alone."

She gave him a wry grin and stepped out into the hall to lock the door behind her. "I think the danger's right here in this hallway."

"Okay." He had offered a new prospective on the situation. "You can protect me."

She didn't think he was being humble or sweet, but he was amusing her. No harm in letting him hit on her. She needed the ego boost. "You may as well walk with me as far as the market. Since you're already on your way out."

He gave her a crooked grin. "My thoughts exactly." He leaned around her to push the elevator button. "You're even sexier than I remembered."

"Stop it. I'm mad at you." Lauren turned her head to hide her smile. She would let her sensory glands guide her actions: tease him and leave him. Too bad the elevator was coming.

"And I'm crazy about you, Lauren Rose." His gaze was leveled on the tortoise clip that held her hair back. He reached out to touch it.

"Don't even think about it, Raven." She shook a finger at him.

"It's too hot to wear my hair down."

He chuckled, letting her enter the elevator first. That soft rumble of male pleasure skewered her heart. She nearly melted into a steaming pool on the floor. How long was she to remain aloof to this guy? A while longer, maybe. He deserved some punishment for bad behavior.

Outside in the bright sunlight, Victor tucked her hand into the crook of his arm.

"You know you're an exquisite woman."

"Keep talking." She found herself checking out places to maybe stop and have a make out session.

"I'm glad you're not the coy type."

"A complete waste of time." She tightened her thighs against an unexpected rush of erotic longing. Everything he did touched her intimate places and she didn't mind.

His laugh zipped straight to her breasts and made tight circles around her tensed nipples. He kept up the flattery while she stared straight ahead. "You have the most exotic, sexy dark eyes I've ever looked into."

She raised her brows and shook her head, pulling her hand away. "You're staring. I'm surprised you haven't fallen off the sidewalk."

"You've been sneaking looks at me too," he teased. "Why don't we just stop and really take a good look at each other?"

"I never sneak." she denied easily.

"Yes, you do." He touched the small of her back. "I'm curious as hell about what you look like in the moonlight, sans clothing. Aren't you the least bit curious about me ... in the nude, I mean?"

"Control yourself, Raven." She could hardly keep her feet from tangling together while he touched her. "I haven't forgotten yesterday."

His grin told her she was a miserable washout in giving him the heave-ho. He eased her back to the present when he took her arm, stopping her in mid-stride. He looked smug.

"Lauren. Is this the cafe where you waited for me?"

"This is Trent's as the sign will tell you."

"Well, damn." He gestured to the neat building. "Lauren, how did I know you meant this one?"

"Because, Mister Raven. This is where we agreed to meet." She wasn't ready to give in to defeat. "And I didn't wait for you."

"Well, I did wait for you at Trent's. Just not this one." He rubbed her lower back as if the matter were closed.

"Oh brother." She moved a few steps away. "Now I've heard

them all."

"Let me explain." He caught her hand. "Would you believe there's another café with the same name near Central Park?"

"No."

"No, you don't believe me, or no you don't want proof of my innocence?" His attempt at a serious expression evaporated when he looked into her eyes. "I have to redeem my good name." He hailed a cab, ignoring her arch look. "I'm taking you to lunch. At my place."

"Raven." She tried to pull his arm down. She didn't need a taxi. "It doesn't matter."

"It matters more than you'll ever know. I won't have this doubt standing between us."

"*You* won't have it? There's nothing between us." What a liar she was. There was plenty between them. She exhaled noisily, shrugging as if she were going along merely to pacify him. "Okay. If you're going to be such a big baby about it."

"I promise you won't regret it."

"I probably won't." She smiled like a cat with sweet cream on its whiskers. "But you may."

* * * *

So this was his lair. It was perfect in a masculine way with large, inviting chairs and couches for a man who knew how to relax. He also was a man with expensive taste if the rare Persian area rugs meant anything.

"Make yourself at home while I get things started." Victor looked around the kitchen doorway to smile at her. "That is, unless you'd rather skip lunch."

"What's on the menu?" She was pretty sure he had more than lunch on his mind. Victor was coming back into the living room. Should she bolt for the door before becoming a trophy girl? Of course not. She would be getting quite a trophy of her own.

He spoke to her in a conversational tone. "Want a drink?" He went straight to the beautifully mirrored bar. "I have some decent champagne."

She went to the bar and leaned against it. "Truth is, I don't like champagne."

"You're right," he said, pouring two glasses of chilled Chambord. "Champagne isn't good for anything but to bathe in."

He came back around to her side of the bar, sitting down to look at her. While he drank his wine, she found herself completely infatuated with his big, well-defined hands. He caught her hot study of him and smiled at her.

He moved her glass out of the way. "You don't talk a lot, but your eyes say plenty." He took her hands, holding them gently. "And you really didn't want that wine."

"Not really." The man was attuned to her feelings. Just one more reason to stick around. She smiled at him. "I really don't want lunch either."

He caught her hand and teased the soft skin of her wrist with a slow caress of his fingers. Up and down, swirling like licks of a tongue. She jumped when he spoke.

"I hear the dessert in this establishment is hard to forget."

"Is that firsthand knowledge or something you just made up?"

"I think you will be glad as hell you stayed." He got up and went to the refrigerator, pulling out a bowl of crimson cherries and strawberries and a tub of whipped cream. His smile was sexy as hell, and she wanted to tell him to hurry.

Not wanting to seem too eager, she looked around at the sparkling clean chrome and stainless steel. "I love your kitchen," laughing a little when she thought of how seldom she cooked. "It's probably cleaner than mine too."

"Can't take any credit for that." He washed the berries in a steel colander before pouring some in a small bowl. "Annie takes good care of us and the house." While he grabbed the tub of whipped cream, he explained the abundant supply of food at his disposal. "All of this is Annie's idea. She makes it a point to package up meals that we can prepare with no trouble while she's on vacation."

"Annie?" Lauren didn't want to sound curious, but she was. She wanted to ask about his daughter too, but she didn't.

He walked around to sit next to her. "The lovely lady that cooks and cleans around here." He dipped a berry in the frothy dessert. "Now, I want to take good care of you." Holding the fruit to her lips, he gazed warmly at her. "I don't know about you, but I'm starving."

She watched the color of his eyes deepen into darkest sapphire while she bit into the berry. Never having reached climax with foreplay or during sex, she nearly fell over from the powerful quake of delirium skittering through her body.

"What do you do when you're starving?" She dipped a berry and brushed it across his lower lip. "I think I'm ready for the house specialty."

The gleam in his eyes said she was thinking about exactly what he wanted--a long round of unbridled sex. Unbridled? All she knew was hurry up and finish. But this would be different. Go ahead, that sneaky voice urged. She picked up on his tremendous sexual vibrations.

Above it all, her sensibility warned her to be careful, that she wasn't ready for intimacy with a man like him. Not yet. But when? She pushed doubt away. Now, she was ready now.

He leaned nearer to her and murmured. "I hope I'm tantalizing you." After dipping another of the succulent red strawberry into the snowy whipped cream, he touched it to her lips. "Close your eyes. It tastes better that way." His grin was crooked and his gaze went to her breasts.

When she moaned in pleasure, he leaned over to lick her lips. She laughed but kept her eyes closed.

"Lauren, I want to take that berry from your mouth with my tongue and then kiss you until the taste is gone."

"Do you do everything with such intensity?" She hoped he did.

He groaned when she licked her lips and made sensuous sounds of pleasure. She looked at him and nearly melted under his hot gaze. He was taking in every little thing her mouth did, and she loved his look of pain when she slowly ran her tongue around her lips. He seemed mesmerized. When she touched his mouth with her fingertips, he took them in his mouth and sucked. She smiled seductively.

"Mister, you're not trying to feed me." She pressed her palms to his thighs. "I think you're trying to seduce me."

"That's right. See anything that tickles your fancy?"

"Oh yes," she said. "You're tickling it with amazing ease."

"I can do better."

"You're doing so well, what more could you possibly add?"

He touched her lips. "For you, baby. I bring out the big guns."

The first touch of his lips shook her to her toes. A tingle of pleasure slipped up her calves to caress her inner thighs and settle between her legs. Sexual desire was a sensation she hadn't experienced for a long time. She had missed it.

He pulled her onto his lap, taking her will to do more than be in his arms. He stood and gazed into her eyes, his silent message promising an inferno of playful sin. She could hardly breath and hoped her voice flowed in a sultry tease.

"Are we going to check out the big guns now?"

He buried his face in her neck and laughed. "We're going to pull the trigger."

As he carried her to his bedroom, she knew this was the most impetuous thing she had ever done, planning to have sex with a man she had only met once before and now, he practically had her panties off. Was she nuts? No, she wanted him and nothing could change that.

He kissed her hard, pulling her lower lip into his mouth to suck greedily. She liked it, liked the way he held her in his arms. He was big and strong and breathing hard. He wanted to have sex with her, and she wanted to make him happy.

The bedroom was dimly lit by a bedside lamp, giving her a look at his huge bed and its puffy down comforter. As he let her slide down his body to stand in his embrace, she gave in to the scent of wild heather and sage that were so much a part of him.

Tipping her face up to his, he coaxed in a husky voice. "Kiss me again, Lauren."

She loved his eyes of twilight blue, seeing herself in their inner light. He was an incredibly gorgeous man whose mouth was a masterpiece of warm chiseled male seduction. She wanted all of him.

Not willing to wait for the perfect opening, she drew his head down to cover his mouth with hers, sliding her tongue between his lips to savor the taste of him. She liked the way he tightened his embrace to pull her hard against him, cupping her rear in his strong hands. He drew her forward, letting her feel the heat of his pulsing length.

She clung to him, lifting her leg to grip his thigh as he pressed his fingers to the crotch of her slacks. His touch created a delicious fiery pleasure in her sensitive flesh and she sagged against him. He buried his face in the curve of her throat, kissing and nibbling the tender flesh while working her blouse up to cup her breast. She forced herself not to buck against his erection, letting him squeeze her breast and tease between her legs. He pushed his leg between hers and held her on his hip, plunging his tongue deep into her mouth, teasing and probing in and out while caressing her into a near orgasm.

She let him take her breath away with the passion of his kiss, let him move her to his bed only to hear a tiny voice of sensibility. Sighing with resentment at being brought to reality, she leaned back to smile up at him.

"Protection is required with this dessert."

His voice weaved a warm veil of seduction around her. "Got it covered." He inclined his head toward the nightstand.

With her blood on fire and her body quivering, Lauren nodded and looked around the room. "Powder room, please."

He turned her around and walked her down a short hallway. "The first door." Touching the buttons of his shirt, he smiled at her. "Hurry back."

Lauren laughed at herself when she noticed that her hands shook while she washed her hands in the lavish marble bathroom. She was in a rush to be in Victor's arms and she didn't dally around checking things out. As she dried her hands, something on the floor next to the massive tub caught her eye. Panty hose.

She saw red. Furious with herself, she thought of Justin's infidelity. Victor Raven was just another Justin and she wasn't setting herself up to be used again. Her snide woman's voice was making tsking sounds. It angered and embarrassed her that Victor hadn't even respected her enough to get rid of a previous lover's underwear before taking her to bed.

She went back to the bedroom where Victor waited and tossed the fancy lingerie at his feet. She wanted to strangle him with them for the look of confusion on his face.

"I hope these aren't yours." Thinking there was nothing more to say, she grabbed her handbag off the coffee table. "It's been an enlightening afternoon."

"You're not leaving, are you?" He kicked the damning evidence aside.

"Now you're acting simpleminded." She gestured toward the knot of fine, tan silk on the floor. "Of course I'm leaving. I don't want to be around when the owner of those comes back."

He caught her hand. "I can explain." He grinned at her. "I've been on my own here for three weeks and I'm not the best housekeeper in the world. I'll do better." He tried charm. "Will you stay, Lauren?"

She gave him an incredulous smile. "You're kidding."

"That item of clothing belongs to my daughter." He tried to pull her to him. "I'll have to speak to Rachel about her habit of tossing things into my bathroom."

Lauren grimaced "Sure, and she's wearing bras too I suppose." She pushed away from him and walked smoothly from the room, going to the entryway door to open it with a flourish.

Victor followed her, offering a snippet of an explanation. "She filches stuff from her mother's stash." He held his hands out, palms up in an attempt at supplication. "You can see that happening, can't you?"

She shot a withering glance in his direction. "No. I see no sign that you even have a child, and what's worse is you have the nerve to blame her for your careless habits."

Looking first at the ceiling, then at the man she had planned to sleep with, Lauren could faintly see the funny side of the moment. Forget it. He was a tomcat and she wanted no part of him. At the moment anyway.

"Lauren?"

"Raven. You are pitiful."

"That's why you should have mercy on me." He put his hand over hers and gave her a heart-stealing grin. "Desperate men make stupid comments. Another chance?"

She shook her head in dismay. "You're pitiful."

Chapter Four

Lauren tried to have fun while revisiting all the old haunts she remembered in New York. She convinced herself there were a million things to see and do here, and she made a heroic attempt to do it all. Adam did manage to spend several evenings with her and Raini, taking in a play and attending a wedding reception.

There were moments she completely forgot Victor, only to be jabbed by his memory if a scent similar to what he wore wafted by. Raini didn't mention his name, but Lauren caught her quizzical glances if she thought Lauren wasn't happy or not having a good time.

During one of their many shopping trips, Lauren had almost shouted out to a tall dark man that stood in line at a bagel shop because he looked like Victor from behind. She had sagged with disappointment when he turned to look at her. Nice, but not the right man. *Knock it off sister,* she had scolded herself. *You're going home in a couple of days, and you are not dragging a bad attitude along on the trip.* She thought about her vow to keep a tight rein on her emotions. No way a man was going to send her off with a fresh load of self-doubt.

Her stalwart attitude lasted until the evening before she was to go back to California. She tried to stifle the heavy sigh that hit her each time she looked at the luggage stacked on a chest outside her bedroom door. She wished she could stop the nonsense, but she couldn't. Leaving New York meant leaving something special behind--Victor. Oh sure, she had left him in a huff and was living to regret it. Maybe she should have given him another chance. Even felons get a third time.

She laughed at herself at that point. You just wanted to see if he had a tan line, you ninny. No, that wasn't quite all. It was leaving something she would never experience again. She wished that she had never met him, and then she wouldn't be so unhappy about leaving.

Screwing up her reserve of common sense, she dismissed her pining as being in need of some tender attention, which she had figured Victor could slather her with. The feeling must not be mutual. He hasn't bothered contacting you, and this is your last night in New York. Damn him and his silk pantyhose.

Stop being a dying calf and paint on your best party smile. Lauren wanted the evening with Raini and Adam to be pleasant. They were taking her to the country club for dinner that evening, and she wasn't going to let her bruised feelings ruin it.

"Such deep thoughts." It was Raini, looking at her from the doorway of her bedroom. "You look lovely."

"Thanks, sis." Lauren did a slow turn, holding her arms out for Raini's inspection. "I know I made this, but do you think this gown makes my butt look big?"

Raini tilted her head to one side, watching Lauren model her claret red gown. "It's perfect, but your breasts are in danger of spilling over the brim."

Lauren gave her sister one of her trademark wry grins. "No danger." She ran her palm down her hip, liking the feel of the caviar beading. "Susan Hayward would have loved this and not worried about her boobs falling out." She worked her shoulders to check the motion of her breasts. "Perfect. And when did you become a prude?"

"Not prudish at all," Raini said. "That's just a bit daring for the country club."

"Well, maybe those old codgers need something to look at that will open their arteries." Lauren winked at her sister who was trying to smother a giggle. "This will give them something to talk about."

Raini went to the closet, pulling out a fancy black lace shawl. "I know it's hot outside, but the club can be extremely cold sometimes." She handed the shawl to Lauren.

"Ladies." Adam poked his head around the door. "If we're having dinner at the club, we'll have to leave right now."

"Yes, dear." Raini waited until her husband had left before whispering to Lauren. "He can't wait to discuss his latest medical triumph with his friends."

"Oh wonderful," Lauren said, tossing the shawl on the bed. Why should she cover up what the gown was meant to reveal? Catching Raini's grimace of displeasure, Lauren pointed to the doorway. "Tut tut now. No time for arguments." She followed her sister down the hall, admiring the white silk of her gown. Lauren had designed that gown specifically for Raini and the woman did it total justice.

* * * *

When they walked into the country club's dining room, Lauren felt a surge of vindication as the men in the crowd reacted to their arrival. On a scale of one to ten, she figured her gown was a twelve.

True to her fashion, Raini appeared cool and untouchable. In contrast, Lauren emitted the look of heat. The exact aura she was hoping for.

They were shown to a table near the French doors that opened onto the golf course. As was customary, Adam left the table to chat with several of his physician friends despite Raini's piercing stare of disapproval. She smiled at Lauren and seemed to be making an excuse for his actions.

"That's Doctor Meyers he's talking to, the most respected proctologist in New York." Raini made a gesture of resignation. "If you do marry a doctor, get used to taking second place to a beeper."

Lauren laughed at her sister's wry humor. Never in a million years would she have the temperament to put up with him, the notorious schmoozer. He was pure New Yorker and never turned down an invitation or the chance to throw a big bash, even though nine times out of ten, he had to hurry off to care for a patient.

"Shall we order?" he asked, rubbing his hands together before kissing Raini on the cheek.

"The conversation must have been stimulating," Raini said.

"Very." He leaned over to take her hand. "Waiter." As usual, he set about ordering for Raini and himself.

Lauren touched his arm to stop him when he asked for three house steaks. "I'll have a fruit salad and tea." Seeing Adam's look of disbelief at her lack of appetite, she quickly explained her choice of meals. "Saving room for dessert."

The moment the waiter left, Adam was hailing someone he knew in spite of Raini's admonishment to stop drawing attention to himself.

Lauren's smile of amusement disappeared when she saw whom the big greeting was for. It was Victor. He would probably think she had prodded Adam to get his attention. Damn his gregarious nature. She tugged on her brother-in-law's jacket to get his attention. "Adam. For heaven's sake. Sit down and have your drink." At that moment, she felt like having a stiff shot of something.

"In a second, Lauren." He was smiling broadly, evidently looking forward to a good conversation with someone he liked. "I'm going to invite Victor to have dinner with us."

Lauren couldn't keep quiet. "Adam, he's probably not alone." She wasn't sure she wanted to be that near Mister Raven.

But then again, why not? She mumbled her last comment. "And if he is, chances are he won't be for long."

"I'll ask him to sit with us." Adam was oblivious to the meaning of Lauren's statement. "We were partners in the last tourney. Did quite well too."

Trying to speak with disapproval was hard for Lauren. "Raini, can't you do something with Adam?" She couldn't take her eyes off the impressive man making a beeline for their table. "I was hoping for a quiet, family evening."

Before she could denigrate him further, Victor stood at their table, looking like a million bucks in his Armani and knowing it. It seemed to her he purposely left her for last to speak to. *Get a hold of yourself,* her feline voice whispered. He's looking at you, or your breasts, with a hearty appetite. What harm in teasing the bounder for an evening? Straightening her spine, she made certain her bosom was in his line of vision.

The small talk started easily enough, Adam asking Victor how the business world was treating him. Victor was pointedly explaining that he had been in Europe on a business trip. Lauren figured that was his attempt at an excuse for not contacting her and gave him a scornful look of doubt beneath her lashes. A couple of eyeball rolls gained her a crooked grin from him.

Lauren and Victor communicated with long gazes and light accidental touches. He appeared deeply interested in what Adam had to say but his attention was for her alone. She smiled at his expression of surprise when she brushed her foot against his shin. That little gesture seemed to ignite his libido into a blast furnace. She grinned evilly when he tried to reel in the conversation with Adam like a cat with a ball of runaway yarn.

"I had a disappointing week after some hostilities arose with a highly respected acquaintance." Victor swallowed a hefty portion of his drink while returning Lauren's caress, gently sliding his foot along her calf. "I was afraid we could never reconcile our differences, but I hope that isn't true."

"You're awfully poetic this evening, Raven." Lauren leaned forward to let her bosom fill her bodice to overflow. "I hope you and your friend have kissed and made up."

"Not yet, but I'm going to try my damnedest to erase the memory of what ended our time together." Victor smiled at Lauren's miniscule raspberry, eying the pink hue of her tongue that slipped out of her mouth to tease him. "That is, unless that friend is too angry to talk with me."

"You must have done something pretty despicable." Lauren tapped his ankle firmly with the toe of her slipper.

Raini looked aghast at her sister's comment. "Lauren, I can't believe you."

Victor grinned at Lauren while she was being chastised. "Lauren's probably correct." He rubbed his chin, appearing to search for the proper wording for his explanation. "I'm sure I was a heel and all the other titles that friend gave me."

Adam had been listening and watching without saying a word until the orchestra began to play. "Raini. They're playing our song." He stood up, drawing his wife with him. "I'm in the mood to dance." Adam led his wife away to the dance floor.

"So," Lauren graced Victor with a syrupy smile, "you left Lucy Lacey panties at home?"

"I'm afraid you're confusing me with someone else, Lauren." He reached out to touch the underside of her wrist. "And what about you? Want me to question you about Joe Shmoe? There has to be a Shmoe in your life."

She allowed him a few seconds more to caress her wrist. "You won't find his underwear laying around like a GQ advertisement." Not likely. There hadn't been any shorts in her bedroom lately. She wondered what kind he wore.

"Good one," he said, leaning closer to her. "Lauren. I don't know about you, but I'm still curious."

"I'm curious about one thing," she purred. "Are you here alone or is there a person waiting for you on some barstool?"

He caught her thumb in his fingers, squeezing gently. "I'm on my own tonight." He closed his hand around hers. "The plan was to play a few hands of poker in the back room." He grazed her cheek with his chin. "I would forgo the card game for a crust of encouragement from you."

"Sorry, Raven." She tried to quiet the clatter of bells ringing in her head, but she was helpless to do anything about the rosy flush he started in her body. She wanted to squirm in her chair. "All out of crusts." She wanted to give him the whole loaf.

"Listen." He made sure his arm was touching hers intimately. "Do you think you could stop being mad at me for just one night?"

"I'm not mad at you." Lauren was mad all right. Mad with wanting to sit on his lap and kiss him until he begged her to stop. She tried to sound sophisticated to cover her heady thoughts. "You know women too well to think that. I simply don't trust you."

His grin was accompanied by a chuckle. "I don't believe you trust yourself." He lifted her hand to nip her fingers between his teeth. He gazed at her warmly before issuing his next comment. "We want each other. I say we make each other happy."

She drew her hand back, trying to stifle her woman's voice chirping giddily that she was so in need of doing exactly as he said. "I say this subject is closed. Adam and Raini are coming back to the table."

Little conversation passed between them for the remainder of the meal. It wasn't necessary. Lauren couldn't resist the dare in Victor's smile, answering his nudge to her knee by stroking his leg beneath the table. She slipped her shoe off, slowly inched her foot under the cuff of his pant leg and worked her toes up the muscled length of his calf. She slid down in her chair to press her foot to his crotch before straightening in her chair.

While she calmly gazed at him, Victor smiled at her in amusement. That smile spurred her on to more daring deeds. Pretending to drop her napkin, she gripped his thigh, inches from his sex. She squeezed the firm flesh beneath her fingers several times before removing her hand.

Victor leaned near her, a wolfish smile on his firm mouth. "You missed."

"I never miss." Lauren brushed her foot against his leg for emphasis.

Adam had been watching the couple with a bemused expression, finally asking, "What are you two talking about?"

"World problems," Lauren answered drolly. She ignored Raini's hard look of question. Since this would be the last time she saw Victor, damned if she wasn't going to leave him with something to think about. "And dessert."

The rattle of a serving cart was the source of a new subject.

"Ah, here it is," Adam announced.

"Cherries Jubilee." Raini sounded as if she were counting the calories.

Victor smiled at Lauren, and then looked at the chafing dish. "Cherries. That brings back a fond memory."

"What a memory you have, Raven. No wonder your friend is irked with you." Lauren nudged his ankle again. "Sure you're not thinking of something lacey?"

* * * *

Victor was delighted Lauren recalled at least part of their time together. Would she be in a receptive mood to being alone with him again? Don't rush her like a charging bull. Miss Rose has to be wooed in a subtle way. No matter how hot you are she won't be yours until she's damned good and ready.

Watching Lauren as the flames licked over the cherries, Victor saw a definite likeness to dessert. Like that flaming dessert, she was hot and delicious to look at, but not ready to be touched. He figured there was no ceiling to the heights her passion could go. Leaning back in his chair to gaze at her, he decided to make it his quest to fire her passion to its fullest.

"You go for blood," he said. "I'm a changed man, and I really was in Europe." He grinned when she moved her hand out of his reach.

"I didn't ask where you've been." She sipped her tea eyeing him over the rim of the glass. "Some advice though. Don't change too much. You don't want to disappoint your stable with drastic changes of conduct."

Victor's eyes twinkled with mirth while he began to savor talking with Miss Rose. She was twice the woman he had been fantasizing about, and the top of her gown kept sagging lower each time she took a breath. Why did her shoulders look so smooth? More importantly, was that a tiny vein on her left breast?

He would stop playing with her. She knew what he wanted and was making it damned clear she was ripe for the plucking. He would have her.

Chapter Five

She was driving him crazy and he loved it. Victor thought of the birthday cake his adoptive mother had made for him on his fifth birthday. What a concoction it had been. Swirls of white frosting loaded with colored candies and stacked three layers high. His mouth had been full of juice, tasting that manna long before his first bite.

Lauren was having the same effect on him. If he read her actions correctly, he was going to experience the same mind-boggling sensation once she was in his arms. A pager startled him out of his lusty thoughts.

"Excuse me," Adam apologized while checking his pager. "I'll check in with the hospital. Everyone, please go ahead and enjoy your dessert." He hurried off toward the bank of phones near the entryway of the dining room.

"I'm sorry, Lauren." Watching for her husband's return, Raini smiled and shrugged, seemingly resigned to the situation. "It goes with the territory."

"Don't worry about it, Raini." Dropping her napkin in Victor's lap, she grinned impishly. "Doctors and corporate heads guarantee a wife plenty of time alone."

Raini patted her sister's arm, pinching a little as she defended her husband. "Adam's devoted to his patients and his work. I can't complain when he gives up his free time to help someone in need."

"Pshaw. I'll bet it's nothing more than a hangnail." Lauren's remark earned her a glance of exasperation from Raini and a crooked grin from Victor. "Well, I know Adam and he never let's anyone take over for him no matter what. I think he considered making you wait at the alter while he took care of a sprained ankle on your wedding day."

"You're exaggerating. It's called dedication, dear." Raini took her purse off the table, turning in her chair to watch Adam as he made his way back to the table.

Appearing worried, Adam began making his excuses. "I'm afraid I have to leave. A patient has taken a turn for the worse this evening." He held his hands up when Raini got to her feet. "Please. Everyone stay and finish your dinner."

"Drop us off at the apartment darling." Raini was ready to leave and her hard-edged stare at Lauren made it clear she expected her sister to go with her. She picked up Lauren's evening bag and pushed it close to Lauren's face. "I have a splitting headache." She leveled an unwavering gaze on her sister. "Coming, Lauren?"

Victor seized his opportunity. "I can take Lauren home later," he offered. "That is, if she's agreeable."

Lauren sat back in her chair, mulling over the situation. Go with Raini, or stay and have the time of her life. "I have cab fare. I'll be along in a while. And," she smiled benignly at Victor, "you don't have to stay just to entertain me, Raven. Run along if you have to be somewhere else."

"I want to entertain you Lauren, and I have all night." He seemingly forgot Adam and Raini were present. He stood up, wisely shielding the front of his pants with his napkin to conceal his erection. He touched Adam's arm. "Please. Go ahead with your plans. Lauren seems to be enjoying her meal too much to be dragged away."

He stayed on his feet until Adam led Raini away before looking back at the woman that smiled knowingly up at him.

"I'd sit down if I were you, Raven." Gesturing toward the napkin dangling from his hand, she laughed. "Your pants seem to have gotten a bit snug." She took a cherry from the chafing dish, giving it a lingering once over.

"You wouldn't be aware my problem if it wasn't your doing." Victor took the chair next to hers and positioned it close enough that he could see the fine detail of her eyebrows. "Are you going to eat that or torture it?"

"What a nasty thing to say." A hint of a grin softened her lips before she popped the cherry into her mouth. She didn't chew immediately but slowly slid her tongue out to show him the fruit. Like a thief in the night, her tongue slipped back into the depths of her mouth. With deliberation, she crushed the cherry between her teeth.

"Are you always that rough with everything?" Their knees touched and a tremendous jolt of pleasure shot up his leg to his groin.

"Only if it becomes necessary," she murmured. "What exactly are you worried about?" His laughter seemed to spur her on. She continued her seduction, dipping a finger into the cherry glaze and then sliding it into her mouth. She closed her eyes and fluttered her lashes in an exaggerated demonstration of ecstasy.

Victor couldn't take his eyes off the seductress by his side. The woman taunted him with the expertise of a courtesan. He couldn't think of anything but how he was to get her in his bed, and it had to be damned soon. He was near vaporizing. Lord, she had moved on to a slice of mango, slipping it in and out of her mouth while making little sounds of happiness. God help me if she enjoys sex half that much. *Get on with it man. She's probably tired of you staring at her like a dunce.*

"Would you like anything else to play with, Lauren?" He almost grimaced at his slanted question. "Your robust appetite has made me hungry."

She laid the slice of mango on her plate, eyeing him with astonishment. "What are you suggesting, Raven?"

She shivered when he boldly pressed his hand to her leg and began working his way up her thigh.

"What are you doing?"

"You're privy to my condition." He didn't blink as he slid the skirt of her gown up to her knees. "It's time I brought you to the same dilemma." Slowing his forward motion, he gripped her thigh. "Want me to stop?"

Their gazes locked, and he saw the promise of unbelievable adventure in her eyes when she murmured her answer. "Don't you dare."

She had closed her eyes, seemingly not conscious of the soft sound of pleasure spilling from her lips. He knew she would never have admitted it to him, but she was aroused to fever pitch. Like him, the hormones were raging. Lauren was enjoying herself and placed her hand on his while he moved it deliberately up her leg. They were being reckless, but the urgency wouldn't be shut down. They had to have completion.

"Lauren." He pushed her gown up several more inches. "I could try to flatter you with pretty words, but you would see right through that." He pressed against her, warming her with his body heat. "I won't take the chance of losing you again with innuendos. I want you and I can't think of a better way of telling you other than straight out."

Lauren touched his hand, breathing deeply and pressing her quivering thigh to his. "Just one of the reasons I like you Raven. You don't try to sweet talk me." He held his glass to her lips and she took a sip. She tasted the red wine as it seeped into her mouth. She moistened her lips.

"I'd rather use that energy making love to you, Lauren."

He felt the tremor of delicious anticipation, which slithered up her spine when his progress reached the juncture of her legs and pressed the critical point. She met and held his gaze, communicating with him through sheer emotion. "Touch me... Yes, there." She exhaled sharply, near the brink of explosion when his fingers slipped under the leg of her panties.

Her chin lifted and she shivered as if she were taken by a storm of lightening and fire. Turning to him, she reciprocated his sensual touch, sliding her hand over his flat belly and down to his hard length. She smiled dreamily at him, her smile telling him she relished his sharp intake of breath at her touch. To his great pleasure, she gripped his hard sex.

"I told you I was rough at times." Her voice had taken on the texture of warm fog.

"Have you ever seen the spa in this place?" He cupped his hand to her and pressed her fully ripened mons. "It's quite impressive and private at night."

"I might be coaxed," she murmured, arching her back as if to capture every drop of the honeyed heat he built in her. She blinked her eyes and offered one last bit of resistance.

"I really shouldn't go with you. All you want is in my panties." She fluttered her lashes and grinned mischievously. "What the heck. I want in your boxers."

Victor almost swallowed his tongue. She was incredible. "So, you and I are going to make skyrocketing love?"

She tightened her thighs and murmured. "I expect it. In fact, I'm extremely anxious."

What had she said? Victor couldn't believe his infernal stroke of luck. Taking her cue, he quickly straightened her gown and his shirt. His hands seemed to be all thumbs as he dug in his wallet and managed to slip several bills into the folder the waiter had left on the table. *Hurry, you idiot.* Knowing Lauren's penchant for rapid mood changes, he had damned well better hurry. Before helping Lauren out of her chair, he pressed a kiss to her ear, growling deep in his throat. He took her hand, thinking they were like a pair of cats at the height of the mating frenzy.

"Come with me, little kitten." He rested his palm at the small of her back, letting his hand slide down until he felt the rise and fall of her hips as she walked.

Lauren looked up at him with pure invitation, flexing her buttocks before whispering to him. "You've just made the biggest mistake of your life, Raven. I'm a full grown cat."

"All the better," he laughed, cupping his fingers at the curve of her waist.

He skillfully guided her to the elevator that would carry them to their long awaited rendezvous, following her into the plush interior of the car. Before the doors slid shut, he had her in his arms, crushing her lips beneath his in a hungry kiss. He couldn't seem to kiss her deeply enough, touch her enough. His hands seemed to be everywhere, capturing every curve of her voluptuous little body.

She smacked his hand as it worked on the zipper of her gown, laughing at his look of anguish. "I wasn't supposed to be showing you anything, Raven. The spa, remember?"

"Would I forget?" he murmured against her ear. "Aren't we going to play show and tell?" He cupped her breast, bending down to kiss the smooth mounds of golden satin.

"But you haven't shown me anything yet," she teased. Her voice was a bubbling spring of seduction. "We'll talk about it when we get there."

"I'm counting on it," he said, moving her to the back of the elevator. Fitting her between his legs, he caught her arms to lift them above her head, kissing her with such intensity she sagged against him. She would have slipped to the floor if not for the strong prop of his body.

Victor trailed a scorching path of quick kisses from her wrists to the sensitive skin of her underarms, nipping gently at the soft flesh of her shoulders. He was dizzy with excitement, caught up in the firestorm of heat that imprisoned him in its powerful grip. He groaned loudly when she gripped his buttocks to pull him close.

Lauren was reaching for the legendary experience just like him, clasping his neck to hold his kiss. There wasn't time to ease into the next scene. Lava hot passion had caught him up, and he carried her toward the ultimate pleasure he wanted to give her.

Matching his raging desire, she pressed her face to his neck, sucking until her lips parted in a gasp of ethereal pleasure. When her hair fell free of its bonds to caress her shoulders, he dropped her silver hair clasp into his jacket pocket.

Victor steadied her when the elevator came to a stop, not letting go of her until the doors slid open. Lifting her high on his chest, he hit the hold button before carrying her out into the deserted hallway. It was as natural as breathing, locking her legs about his waist, putting his hands beneath her hips to hold her fast.

"It's always going to be like the first time with you, Lauren." His voice was raspy with urgency. "I'm trying to be all debonair so you'll have to overlook it if I stumble. But just in case, I apologize now." Oh yes, he conceded seeing through a neon halo of light. *Don't stumble while you're carrying the most sensuous woman you've ever met.*

Stumbling was forgotten while he delivered his fragrant burden down the hall, oblivious to the fact her fancy slippers fell from her feet, one by one onto the floor. He watched her slender fingers work at loosening his tie, his heart pounding harder with each button she released on his shirt. He touched her cheek, encouraging her. "Everything you do is right and sending me right over the brink."

Her hands locked behind his head to draw him close enough to kiss the scar at the corner of his mouth. She pressed her lips to his, probing the warm interior of his mouth with her tongue in a provocative kiss of hot encouragement.

When Victor stopped walking, Lauren gazed into his eyes in a dreamy fashion. He smiled at her, inclining his head toward something behind her.

"What?"

"The door," he murmured. "We do want to go in, don't we?"

She leaned down to push on the fancy brass door handle, and then wreathed his neck with her arms. "Just try to keep me out."

"I wouldn't go in without you."

"Me either."

"Wouldn't be any fun."

"Is this our first argument?"

"I think so."

"So why are we standing out here?"

"I don't know." He squeezed her a little tighter. "I think I lost my mind for a second there."

He carried her into the dimly lit room where the scent of soap hung in the air. She felt herself sliding down the length of his body. Her most intimate part rubbed against his sex and sent her into a furious quest for release.

"Victor." She reached for his belt buckle, working to release it with one goal in mind. "It's time." She tugged his shirt from his slacks, licking the warm flesh of his chest with each button she freed, mouthing his nipple, biting in her excitement.

He couldn't believe how clumsy his hands had become. This may as well have been his first time with a woman. The damned zipper of her gown resisted and then slid to her waist. He touched her face, awed by her incredible beauty. Her seduction of his senses was complete.

"Victor," she prompted softly. "You're still dressed?" The glow in her eyes mirrored the heat in her blood.

She lifted her arms and let her scarlet gown fall in a sensual puddle about her bare feet, leaving her dressed in nothing more than a pair of white silk panties. She felt no constrictive bonds of modesty, eagerly helping him remove his jacket and shirt, observing him closely while he shucked off the rest of his clothing.

Victor had no desire to hide himself from her. Being nude with a woman wasn't new to him, but the treasure standing proudly before him was. Looking at Lauren was something he would not tire of. The olive smoothness of her skin held his attention until he noticed the way her softly rounded hips miraculously melted into slender incredible legs. He pressed his hand to her taut belly and pulled her close to breathe in her sweet scent. He wasn't convinced he was really a part of the scene swirling about him.

She ended his doubt, gripping his sex with audacity. There were no longer secrets between them, not when she moved closer to him, placing him in the warm nest between her legs.

For a brief span of time, Victor regretted there was no comfortable bed to take his prize to. The thought was brushed aside in his eagerness to have Lauren. Picking her up, he carried her across the room to place her on the soft squabs of a padded massage table.

She stroked his chest and smiled wantonly at him before boldly gazing at his sex. "What are you offering, my magnificent lover?"

He teased her knee with his fingertips. "Only the finest and the best are yet to come."

"Show me," she murmured, leaning back to rest her weight on her elbows to watch as he kissed her breasts, then suckled her tight nipples. Her stomach muscles jerked spasmodically in the wake of kisses he trailed down her stomach and thighs to find her center, which pulsed with an indescribable ache.

He straightened, pulling her legs up to dangle over his shoulders, bending to her again to taste her, probing, inciting her into delicious madness until she gave into the flow of hot lava that consumed her.

Her hands were in his hair, pulling, demanding, and urging him on. She gasped, and then freed an outcry of exhilaration.

She peaked several times before pulling him down to cover her trembling body, to end his raging need. Arching her back to take him all in, Lauren gripped him between her thighs, whispering to him of his incredible lovemaking, how he filled her completely, touching her with strokes that were driving her over the brink of ecstasy again. She heard his voice from somewhere in the licking flames that wrapped around them.

"Lauren." He rasped out, struggling to hold back his final moment. "What else do you desire?"

"I want you to come with me." She slid her hand between their bodies to encircle him with her fingers. "Make me purr again, you tiger."

He gathered her close to his heaving chest, his strokes deep and sure, pleasuring her until the moment she toppled over the abyss. He spun out of control, following her to the sun.

* * * *

Long moments passed with no word uttered between them. Lauren lay in Victor's embrace, seeming content just to feel him pressed to her. Gentle play between them became intense, sending them back to the bed of embers they had created.

The massage table was abandoned for a comfortable leather sofa where they made love once more, slowly and completely. In sublime weariness, Lauren lay on top of Victor, sprawled in exhausted splendor until she heard the chiming of a clock somewhere in the distance.

"I think that's our signal to get our clothes on." She hung one leg off the couch and playfully tangled her fingers in the coarse hair surrounding his sex.

"Much more of that and we'll be locked in here for the night." He kissed her chin and helped her to sit up.

After she was partially dressed, she sat on his lap, quietly studying his face.

"What do you see?" He worked on the zipper of her gown. *Now, of course you work like greased lightening.* The damn zipper moved with no effort.

"I see one tired, very satisfied man." She touched the unexplained scar by his mouth.

"You're right," he said. "But I'm not tired." He held her firmly against his chest. "You know this will never be enough. Come to my place tomorrow."

She made a soft sound of distress while weaving her fingers into the depths of his damp hair, apparently lost in some secret world.

"Lauren?" He leaned his head to one side, waiting for her to answer. "Where were you?"

"Here." She smiled at him while making a huge bow of his expensive tie. "About tomorrow. I can't do it."

"Is that definite?" He didn't try to hide his disappointment. "I'll humble myself. How about the day after tomorrow?"

She laughed a little, and he figured he'd sounded ridiculous.

"The day you're humble, the sun won't set." She looked into his eyes, seeing incredible promise. "I'm catching an early flight out in the morning."

He slapped his thigh as if he'd hit on a great idea. "When you come back, we'll have a hell of a party." He smiled at her with unabashed happiness.

"Victor." She tried to slide off his lap but his arm held her fast. "I'm not coming back. I'm going home."

"Home?" He arched a brow, gazing at her as if she had played a bad joke on him. "Why did I think you lived here, in New York?"

"I don't know." She tried to brush her hair into a semblance of order, looking around the room for the rest of her clothing. "The subject didn't come up between the massage table and the couch."

"Well hell," he drawled. "Where's home if not here?"

"Malibu."

"California?" There was a sound of exasperation in his voice.

"No, Tennessee." She laughed aloud when he kissed her behind her ear.

"We don't have to call it an evening, do we?" He tipped her chin up to kiss her soundly, trying to coax her into having more sex with him. "I'll get you to the airport on time."

"An offer I have to refuse." She slid off his lap. "I can't do that." She was searching for her shoes. "Raini probably has a search party out scouring the city for me now."

"She does have a way about her," he said, smoothing a strand of hair from her face.

She tempered her reply with a pat to his rear. "That's odd," she said. "Raini has a fairly low opinion of you too."

Victor thought over what he had said while straightening his tie. *Watch it, fella. There were some things you just didn't tell a woman, especially about her family.* While he watched her with longing, she peeked under the tables and the couch, still determined to locate her shoes. Unable to resist, he caught her in his arms, burying his face in her hair.

"I want you, Lauren." He lifted his hand to let her hair trail over his fingers. It felt like cool silk. "Stay with me a while longer."

"What's to keep you from getting on a plane?" She located her panties and pulled them on. "Ask your boss for some time off."

"That didn't sound too sincere, Lauren." He held her face in his hands, kissing her deeply, taking the time to taste her lips, their warmth and texture.

She opened her eyes, looking toward the door. "I hear footsteps outside. Someone's in the hallway." She groaned softly and hugged his waist. "I wish we had more time."

He made another attempt at convincing her to spend the night with him. "Let's find your shoes and have a drink before I take you home." He smiled at her, his mind tumbling over a barrage of ways to delay her departure.

"Victor, I'm used to being wheedled by my sister." She hugged his waist fiercely. "It hardly ever works."

"How cruel you are, Miss Rose." He ran his palm over her hips. "You won't reconsider?"

"Yes, but I can't." She stepped away from him, looking at the door. "Ready?"

"If you insist," he said, following after her. While they walked to the elevators, Victor ignored the open stares from the housekeeping crew. Lauren had his total attention. There was a serene expression on her face, and he would have given a king's ransom to know what was on her mind. Exhaling heavily, he retrieved her slippers and carried them to her.

"Your slippers, pussycat," he said, kneeling down to help her. He moved his hands up the calves of her legs and stood up slowly to gaze into her eyes. "I think I've found my Cinderella."

In the elevator, their passion flared once again. Lauren gave herself over to him completely. She clung to him, trying to bury herself in his white-hot strength. The point of climax was rushing toward her while he pressed her to the padded wall, teasing her nipples, igniting a firestorm with his hands. He held her tightly as she gave in to bliss, kissing her deeply until it was over.

"Stay with me, Lauren." He pulled the bodice of her gown up. "I want to sleep with you in my bed. I want to please you."

She kissed the warm skin of his neck, aching to say yes. "If you pleased me any more, I would die."

* * * *

Victor took the door key from Lauren's hand, turning it in the lock. He stopped her before she could open the door and touched her hair. Wanting to be close to him one last time, she put her arms around his waist, raising her face to him, trying to memorize his every feature. She thought she must be insane, leaving this man who absolutely gave her everything she had ever desired from a man. But that was sex, not love.

"You're incredible, Lauren." He took her hands, giving her a slow head to toe look. "Unforgettable."

"You'll forget me soon enough, Raven," she answered softly. "You still have Lucy Lacey."

"Don't tease a wounded animal." He pulled her close, inhaling the scent of CoCo that still clung to her warm skin.

"If I had time, I would ease that hurt." She struggled to fight off the growing feeling of sadness in her heart.

"Well." He released her, backing off a step. "Take care, Lauren."

She lifted her hand in farewell, watching him leave through an unexplained mist in her eyes. She scoffed at her earlier promise to give him something to remember. Instead, he had given her something she would never forget. Where was the elation of victory she had thought would teach him a lesson?

Standing alone in the quiet hallway, she had never felt so dispirited. She sighed against the quivering pain in her heart and gave the door of the elevator a last look before whispering, "Goodbye, Mister Wonderful."

Chapter Six

"Lauren." Who had the bloody gall to yank her out of the deepest slumber she had ever enjoyed? Lauren groaned and pulled a pillow over her head. Damn. There it was again.

"Lauren."

Recognition of the voice penetrated through her sleep drugged state. Adam rapped on her door repeatedly. "Lauren, it's about Raini."

The daze of sleep vanished and Lauren was out of bed in an instant, running to open the door to find Adam looking at her with worry etched on his face.

"What is it?" Lauren gripped his hand as he hurried her down the hall to the bedroom he shared with Raini.

"Her appendix." He let Lauren go to Raini's side. "I've called an ambulance and done everything possible to make her comfortable." He was checking Raini's pulse. "She wants you here."

Lauren had never seen her sister in so much pain and it frightened her. She clasped Raini's hand, afraid to let go. "Tell me what to do."

"Don't leave." Raini gasped in pain. "Stay with me."

"I won't leave you." Lauren was silently weeping. "I promise." She lost her bravado when Raini released her hand to clutch at her side, moaning loudly. She felt helpless and inadequate trying to sooth her sister, and the wail of an approaching ambulance siren magnified her fear.

Adam had gone to let the paramedics in. While the technicians worked, he issued orders. Lauren could see being a doctor didn't exempt him from worry. After Raini was bundled onto a gurney, Lauren ran to her bedroom to pull on a pair of Levi's and a T-shirt. She was going with her sister.

* * * *

Lauren paced the floor of the deserted waiting room, anxious for word on Raini's condition. She stopped anyone that looked like a doctor, desperate for information. She was assured by everyone that Raini was doing fine. Just knowing Adam was in the surgery room to observe the procedure kept her from going into a complete panic, but she was still scared. Surely he wouldn't hide a problem from her.

Huddled in the corner of a plastic-covered couch, she couldn't help thinking about her father. Hadn't they told her he was doing fine moments before he died? Her heart lurched with fear. What if they were wrong about Raini?

She couldn't sit idly by like a sheep in a pen. She abandoned the depressing room to stand vigil outside the surgery room doors. After what seemed to her to be a lifetime, the big doors swung open and Raini was wheeled out. A nurse moved Lauren aside when she tried to touch Raini.

"She's going to recovery," someone wearing a mask behind her said. "It will be awhile before she's taken to her room."

"She's so pale." Lauren wanted to touch her sister's ashen face. "What's really wrong with her?"

"Lauren." The mask came off, revealing Justin's face. "Everyone's a little pale after surgery. She's fine."

"Justin." Of all the people in the world she didn't want touching her sister, it was Doctor Justin Taylor. "Where's Adam?"

"Checking out the orders I left for Raini's care." He smiled at Lauren. "If you're worried about my skills, Adam stood by while I worked."

Lauren ignored her former fiancé's comment. The gurney was being wheeled down the hall and she quickly followed, trying to hold onto the fast moving cart. She wanted to yell at the nurses that refused to let her into the recovery room. The urge to yell at someone was trained on Justin when she saw he was still looking at her.

"She won't be able to talk with you for several hours." He tried to lead her away from the door. "Let me buy you a cup of coffee."

"No thanks." Lauren turned away from him, grateful to see Adam hustling down the long hallway toward them. "Adam. What's wrong?"

"Nothing," he said with a reassuring laugh. "You can see her after the nurses have taken her upstairs and settled her into bed." His arm went around her shoulders in an effort to comfort her. "Come into the doctor's lounge where you can relax."

His words eased Lauren's anxiety a small measure, but until she heard her sister speak, she would worry. Left alone in the small and cluttered lounge, she paced the floor, finally sitting down in a chair near the door to wait. She jumped in surprise when a tired looking intern came in to flop onto a couch. He promptly fell asleep.

She tiptoed out of the lounge; suddenly conscious she had worn her house slippers. It didn't matter. She wasn't leaving until she spoke with Raini. She had lost track of time, listening to the muted sounds coming from the nurse's station and the whisper of people walking by her in a rush. At last, Adam emerged from the recovery room to talk with her. Her heart began to beat again. He was all smiles.

"Raini is being taken to her room." He took her arm, leading her to the elevators. "She's already asking to see you."

"She darn well better," Lauren said gruffly, hugging Adam's waist.

Lauren was shocked by Raini's appearance. Her skin was pasty white and her lips were swollen. She wanted to cry with relief when Raini managed a weak smile and a gravelly hello. She didn't mind too much when the nurse issued orders.

"Don't stay long." The nurse that checked Raini's stats spoke quietly but firmly, and then smiled at Lauren. "We'll take care of her."

Lauren made up her mind she was staying with her sister and no grumpy nurse would run her off. She knelt by the bed to gaze at Raini, hoping she could at least feel her presence. While Adam studied Raini's charts, Lauren could see the worry had been erased from his face. He was back in his professional doctor mode.

"Is she in pain?" Lauren couldn't bear the thought of that.

"We'll do everything possible to keep that under control." Adam pointed to the chair near the bed. "Why don't you use the chair? You don't look very comfortable there."

"I won't be able to hear her if I sit way back there."

"Please." He grinned at her puckishness. "You're making me feel guilty."

"All right." She got to her feet, dragging the chair to a spot where she could see Rain's face. "Happy?"

"Not entirely." He leaned over to kiss his sleeping wife. "You should go home. Raini's fine."

"I'll go in the morning." She wasn't leaving.

"Okay." Adam gave up, seeming to accept the uselessness of belaboring the subject. "I prescribe a cup of hot tea and a warm blanket."

"Thanks Adam. You're the last of the good men."

* * * *

Two days later, Lauren and Raini were chatting and laughing as if nothing had happened. Lauren had given her sister a manicure, pedicure and was preparing an herbal facial for her.

"I don't know why we're doing this," Lauren said. "If ever a face didn't need mud, it's yours." She straightened the ribbon at the neckline of Raini's gown.

"You're sweet." Raini was glowing with good health and loving her sister's attention. "If I want to keep this skin, slap that goo on."

They both laughed, the joyous sound ringing through the sunny room that resembled a flower garden.

"Want to know what this reminds me of?" Lauren asked after smearing Raini's face with the cucumber mask. "Slumber parties and summer camp."

"It does bring back memories of the wonderful times we had together." Raini cocked her head to one side, looking at the thick goop on her face. "The times you sneaked my clothes out of my closet. How about the times I caught you reading my diary?"

"How else was I going to learn about men?" Lauren backed off to look over the mud on Raini's face. "Dad sure didn't give me much information."

"Speaking of men," Raini said. "Are you going to see Victor again? The two of you seemed to have a grand repartee."

Lauren knew that was Raini's subtle way of questioning her and decided to sidestep it with humor. "Just because he's the hottest thing in pants doesn't mean we're an item." Lauren grinned at her sister's green icing face. "We had a few drinks and a lot of conversation." Why had she made it sound as if her time with Victor had been a tea party? Why indeed? She didn't want to be reminded of the trophy girl thing.

"Well?" Raini touched her chin, testing the hardness of the mask. "Was it sizzle or fizzle?"

"Raini." Pretending to be horrified, Lauren clutched at her chest, but then grinned devilishly. "I refuse to answer that."

Heaven help her, Lauren thought. She went weak with yearning just thinking about how Victor had turned her into a Roman candle of desire. She wished Raini hadn't mentioned his name. It brought back that need as if it had only been hours since last being with him.

"I know you're not thinking about me, dear heart," Raini said. "But I'm so glad you're here with me at least in body." She dabbed a glob of the green concoction on Lauren's chin.

They were still giggling when Justin came into the room, followed by two nurses. Lauren immediately quieted, backing away from the bed.

"Good afternoon, ladies," he said with a flourish of white teeth and gold watch.

"Good afternoon, Justin." Raini poked Lauren, inclining her head in his direction.

She gave Raini a warning scowl and whispered a threat. "Stop it or you'll be wearing that mask until it flakes off." After scrubbing the glob of the goop off her own chin, she draped the cloth over Raini's face.

While Justin went about his routine of looking down Raini's throat and in her ears, Lauren pretended to be deeply absorbed in folding her sister's robe, but she watched every move he made. The nurses didn't escape her attention either. *Which one was he involved with at the moment? The perky redhead? Or the bleached blond with the bulbous breasts. Hell. He was trying to talk to her again.*

"We haven't had a chance to talk yet, Lauren." The professional smile on his lips had become personal.

"What?" Lauren pretended she hadn't been listening.

"Talk." He looked at his watch.

"Why on earth would we talk?"

Her answer seemed to amuse the blond nurse, but not the redhead. The silence in the room was deafening until Justin spoke up.

"No reason. Just a thought." He was writing on the chart the redhead had handed him. "Perhaps we'll have a moment before you take off for the Wild West again. I'll call you."

"I really wish you wouldn't." She didn't care if she embarrassed him in front of his nurses. In fact, she was grinning as she started out the door. "I'll be in the coffee shop, Raini."

She bypassed the coffee shop, turning off to look in the gift shop window. She was pleased with the way things had gone with Justin. No barbs traded, and best of all, no needy feelings of desire to let him walk on her again. Wariness was the only emotion he evoked in her.

Months ago, she might have been open to his apparent interest in her, but not now. She should thank him for letting her out of a terrible mistake in the making. Lifting her chin, she strolled into the small room; ready to do something she was expert at. Shopping.

She skirted the end caps filled with candy bars and went straight for the luxury-boxed candy displayed on glass shelves, selecting what she liked. Some wonderfully scented bath powder was added to the three boxes of chocolates before her gaze fell on a glorious display of cosmetics. She selected a wild red nail lacquer and fake nails to go with it. She could hardly wait to see Raini's reaction to the riotous colors.

Intending to fortify their supply of magazines, Lauren stopped to scan the shop's offerings. Looking over the top of the rack she almost laughed aloud. The find of a lifetime hung from a padded hanger just out of her reach. Grabbing several magazines, she hurried to claim the pink silk bed jacket.

She examined the pin tucking and tiny lace sewn in rows of perfection across the bodice. She knew the garment wasn't Raini's style, but that made no difference. Plus, the bit of fabric was just under two hundred dollars. A person would have to be nuts to buy the thing. She draped it over her other buys, admitting to herself she was a real sucker when it came to her sister.

She figured she had been gone long enough for Justin to finish up before she got back to Raini's room. Juggling all of her wonderful finds, she hurried to the checkout counter. "Will you hold these for me please?" Lauren patted her empty pockets. "I left my handbag upstairs."

The sales girl looked doubtful. "I'm not sure I'm allowed to do that."

Lauren pushed the items toward the young woman. "I'm going to the flower shop, then run up and get my bag." She glanced over her shoulder at whomever it was standing too near for her liking. "Surely you can take this off the market for five minutes."

A muffled male voice interrupted her conversation. "Of course she can't."

Wheeling around to confront the annoying person, Lauren was stopped by the barrier of an enormous and expensive floral arrangement of pink roses and white lilies. The tall troublemaker's face wasn't visible.

She would have her say at any rate. "Do you mind?" She gave the bouquet an indignant scowl before turning back to plead her case with the staring salesgirl. "Please. Just put my name on these things."

"But Miss." The clerk was showing stress on her thin features. "You have several hundred dollars in merchandise here and I was told not to hold items. People don't come back for them."

Lauren cast a look to heaven, clamping her jaw in determination. She glanced down quickly when she heard the click of plastic hitting the counter. "Of all the nerve." She brushed the credit card aside, looking over her shoulder again. "Please wait your turn."

"There must be a closeout sale today." The bower of blooms moved, shedding a few petals but still shielding the pest behind them. "Better use that card or she'll sell the stuff from under you."

Lauren turned completely around to face the man with the voice imprinted in her blood. "Victor?" She blushed, mortified he had caught her in the position of bartering. "I'm having a problem."

"I see that." He pushed the card toward the gawking sales girl.

Lauren reached for the card. "No. I can't let you do that." She looked down at his large hand covering hers, letting his voice surround her in a silken wrap of protection.

"We could stand here arguing about this or let the people behind us get to the counter."

Lauren's face grew pinker when she saw the line of impatient customers snaking from behind him to the doorway. "All right." She pointed to the card. "But don't you dare leave until I can repay you."

"I won't get out of your sight." He paid no attention to the final tally he signed for. Lauren had his complete attention. He laughed when she claimed the receipt. "That wasn't so hard, was it?"

"Just the hardest thing I've ever done." She grinned, still feeling embarrassed. "Thank you, Raven." She scooped up her purchases, leading the way out to the elevators.

While standing close enough to him to catch the scent of his cologne, she pretended to study the receipt in her hand. From beneath her lashes she gazed at his hands, remembering their strength. She was too warm, the memory of his hands waking her desire to be touched once more. She looked up to find him gazing at her with a smile of amusement.

"Lauren?"

"Yes." She answered almost dreamily.

"The elevator." He inclined his head toward the gaping doors.

"Oh ... yes." She stepped inside the car, instantly resenting the other passengers that kept her from being alone with him. She hated the intrusion, but her sensible voice suggested he must have been visiting a patient, not there expressly to save her butt. Curiosity ruled.

She touched a rosebud in the bouquet he held. "For someone special?"

"Very special." He smiled at her. "I like curious cats."

She locked her arms about her packages, returning his gaze of pure dare. "I believe I warned you about taking on a full grown cat before."

The crowd shifted to allow more passengers onto the elevator and Victor wound up standing in front of her. She couldn't restrain her impish nature. From beneath the packages, her hand slipped out to pat his solid rear. He turned his head to look at her, his wink bold as brass and witnessed by several gawking females.

"You have the advantage, Miss."

"And don't you forget it," she said. "Three hundred and four dollars and sixteen cents."

When they reached their floor, he was still laughing.

Lauren had been laughing too until a sobering thought hit her. He was there to visit Raini. She paused, looking at him with a jaundiced eye.

He shifted the weighty bouquet in his arms. "What's the trouble?" He winked at her. "This is the right floor, isn't it? Where your purse is?" He grinned at her.

She gave him a considering glance, biting back a barrage of personal questions. "You could have told me you were here to visit my sister."

"You didn't ask." He grinned at her, revealing more of his playful nature. "Of course I'm here to visit Raini."

"Of course," she answered quickly. "Her room is at the end of the hall." She waited until several nurses made their way past them, then bumped his hip with her own. "Don't plan on a lengthy visit. She needs her rest."

"Yes, dear." He caught her arm, drawing her close to his side. "You know, I get the idea you don't want me to pay a social call on Raini."

"Don't be ridiculous." She caught the tip of her tongue in her teeth. Damn. Snapping at him like a churlish hag. She softened her tone. "I'm happy you're so thoughtful."

"Well. Don't pat me on the back just yet. I was going to have these flowers sent up until I spotted you in the gift shop."

She was delighted and felt no shame at the way his comment made her feel. "In that case, visiting hours have been extended."

Raini looked shocked when they walked into her room together. "What a nice surprise." She quickly closed the romance book she had been reading and lay it face down on her nightstand. "My sister has a knack for brightening my days here."

Victor leaned over to place a peck on Raini's cheek. "I won't stay but a minute." He moved to stand at the foot of the bed, smiling down at her. "Lauren's already informed me visiting hours are limited."

Raini laughed softly. "Yes. She's managed to alienate most of our friends and half the staff here."

Moving around Victor to toss several bottles of nail polish onto the bed, Lauren joined the conversation. "He doesn't want to hear about my heavy handed method of keeping loiterers out of here."

Taking the arrangement from Victor, she made a new rule. "No more flowers for you lady. There's no space for them."

Victor coughed over a laugh. "You're in good hands, I see."

"The best," Raini said. "Of course she's going to stay with me until I regain my strength."

Lauren wrinkled her nose at her sister's remark. "Not a minute longer than necessary." She handed Raini a glass of water. "I'm gone the minute her complexion looses its green shade."

Sighing, Raini caught at Lauren's hand. "I'm going to be awfully weak for quite a while." She grinned impishly. "She won't leave me while I'm helpless."

* * * *

Victor chuckled, thinking Raini didn't know her sister at all. While the two women had a spirited exchange over Raini's failure to drink water, Victor took in the scene with new insight to Lauren's nurturing side.

Sure, he could become drunk on her sensuality, but he was awestruck with her sweet and somewhat bossy side. There were many facets to the woman turning to smile at him. It was a good time for him to leave them alone. He touched Lauren's arm, getting a nice surge of pleasure from the contact.

"I have to get going. Raini, you look wonderful."

"Thank you for dropping by, Victor." Raini touched her gowns frilly collar. "And for the lovely bouquet."

"My pleasure." He gave Lauren a wry grin when she turned to lead the way to the door. "Okay. I'm going."

"I'll walk you out." Lauren pulled him back when she remembered the scene in the gift shop. "Hold on a second." She found her purse, drawing out her checkbook, hurriedly scrawling out a check for what she owed him. "Okay. I'm ready to see you to the door, Victor." She held the check at her side until they were in the hallway. "Thank you for saving my life." She tucked the check into his jacket pocket.

He caught her hand, glancing around the hall as if they were doing something unsavory. "What if someone thinks you're paying me for my services?"

"They would say I wasn't paying you enough."

Her smile made his hearty thump crazily with all the memories it held.

He wanted to grab her, carry her off and make love to her until the next millennium. This exotic woman had played a dirty trick on him, showing up in his life again to make him want to whine for her attention like a baby.

Just being near her made him a little insane. Remembering the conversation she had with Raini, he smiled in anticipation of things to come.

"Did I hear you say it would be some time before you leave New York?"

"Yes, I'm staying until Raini and I have our big argument." She grinned broadly. "We always have at least one."

He laughed, astounded at the ease in which she revealed her personality. "Then we'll probably be seeing each other again?"

"Probably." She stood on her tiptoes to kiss his cheek. "That's all I'm allowed to do here."

He had been holding all his need for her in check but gave in to the longing that pushed him forward. "You know how damned much I want you so I won't bother playing the nice visitor saying good-bye."

"Umm," she purred. "I like the bad side of you."

With no more preliminaries, he pulled her close, burying his face in the curve of her throat, nipping playfully. He quieted her little laugh with a hungry kiss, hearing her sweet sigh instead. He lifted his head to whisper against her ear. "Tell me to get the hell out of here before I make a real scene."

Victor had seen the amused glances coming from a group of nurses, which reminded him of where he was.

"I'll see you off then," she said with a wide smile, delighting him when she took his hand. "You're making me forget about care giving and family responsibility." She leaned against him and whispered. "I want to go with you, wherever you're going." Then she laughed in her usual teasing way.

Damn. The elevator had arrived. Her laughter filled the quiet hallway when it became obvious he wasn't going to release her hand even after he was in the elevator.

"Don't ever change, Raven."

He held the door open with his foot, finally releasing her hand. "I'll never be the same." Someone jostled him, but he finished his comment. "Probably be a lot worse by the time we meet again."

"You couldn't possibly.... Could you?"

"You have a lot to learn about me."

Chapter Seven

Victor stood scanning the various groups of little girls that were chattering like nestlings. His gaze searched for golden curls and a bundle of nonstop energy. He picked her out of the most boisterous group. The swelling of pride and love in his heart nearly bowled him over. He'd heard of children crying while they were at summer camp, but Rachel always had a great time at camp and he was the one that felt like crying like a kid while she was away.

When he finally caught her attention, his daughter broke away from the group and ran toward him. He shook his head when he noticed the dirty band-aid on her knee, wondering what had happened to her. He liked the wildflowers in her hair that drooped tiredly over her ear. The spaces left by missing baby teeth gave her wide smile a comical sweetness.

He leaned down, arms wide to scoop up the joy of his life.

"There's my girl," he said, laughing under her dozen quick kisses. "I missed you, Princess."

"I missed you too, Daddy." Rachel clasped her arms about his neck, hugging with all her might. "What did you bring me?"

"Me. Isn't that enough?" He hugged her close and soaked in her innocent warmth.

She giggled. "Janie said I should ask." His phony glower pleased her.

"You're a precocious little thing," he teased.

She bobbed her head, smiling at him. "I know."

He kissed her cheek and set her on her feet. He would have to talk to her about the meaning of precocious. He didn't want her agreeing to anything unless she was certain of it's meaning.

"So what kept you busy for two weeks?" He waited for her to gather up her collection of flowers, shells and small rocks. "Are those for me?"

"Some of them. Maybe." She took the time to count the pebbles before dropping them into his pants pocket. "Don't lose any of those." She dusted her palms together, and then locked her small fingers about his.

Victor thought it was time to see if she had eased up on her selfish attitude. "Rachel. Since you're a grownup six-year old, you probably don't mind letting your friends play with your toys. Do you?"

"And you're thirty-six, Daddy."

"Yes, but what I want to talk about is sharing what you have with others." He glanced down in time to catch her dubious expression. "What's wrong?"

"My friends have brothers and sisters. They never get to keep anything for themselves."

"That's not so bad, honey." He swung her hand as they walked to car. "A selfish girl isn't a pretty girl."

"What's that mean?" She dug in his pants pocket, rattling the pebbles around.

"Pretty is as pretty does." He loved the look of feminine disapproval on her face.

"You're being silly, Daddy." She stopped walking and leaned over to peek under the bandage on her knee.

"Climbing trees again?" He wanted to baby her, but she would have none of it. Just the same, he checked the scrape for signs of infection. He grinned when she patted his head and described her mishap.

"No. I was running and my shoe was untied." She lifted her shoulders, spreading her dainty arms. End of explanation.

"I see." He patted the top of her blond head. "Let's go home and see what Anna has fixed for dinner." He gestured toward the group of little girls she had been talking with. "Want to say good-bye to your friends?"

"No. I'll see them at the golf tournament."

Victor helped her into the car, belting her into the seat. She waved at him as he walked in front of the car, and then hit the horn, laughing in glee when he jumped in surprise.

"That's one," he said with a chuckle and slid into the driver's seat.

"I love you, Daddy."

"I love you too, Rachel."

He glanced at his child from time to time as he drove toward home. Her lids had begun to droop and she yawned several times. He inhaled deeply, thinking what a treasure his daughter was. He was surprised when her eyes, which mirrored his, opened wide.

"What is it, honey?"

"Are you getting married, Daddy?"

He gripped the steering wheel and swallowed hard. This was no simple question and it needed immediate attention. He pulled to the side of the road and looked directly into her eyes.

"What a question. Where did that come from?"

"Janie's daddy is getting married. She said you would too."

"Janie's wrong." He took her small hand in his. "Look at me, Rachel. This is important. If that ever comes about, you would be the first one I would tell. Okay?"

She seemed reassured with his explanation and once they were back on the road, she was soon fast asleep. Victor didn't want her worrying about such monumental issues. If only she realized how the thought of remarrying chilled his blood, she would never concern herself about it again.

* * * *

For the next two weeks, Lauren spent every spare minute pampering her sister with loving attention. Raini was recuperating nicely, but proved to be a genius at using her sisterly wiles to keep her in New York. Giving into Raini's pleas for her to stay just a while longer, Lauren has taken charge of the number of visitors allowed in the apartment and if they stayed too long, she politely showed them the door.

While Raini slept, she worked on sketches of gowns for Swanson's fall line. Her employer had generously told her to take the time she needed. They struck a bargain that she would send work whenever she had something finished.

She worked furiously to meet the deadline and get the new sketches in the pattern makers hands. She felt as if she was meeting herself coming and going, but she could handle it. Taking care of Raini was her top priority at the moment.

During a rare moment of idleness, Lauren took time to look at the cards accompanying the flood of plants and extravagant bouquets that continued to arrive daily. One elegant arrangement of larkspur and camellia caught her interest. Its sheer beauty drew her in the beginning, and then the heavenly scent spoke to her. Her fingers caressed a creamy camellia, and then plucked the small card from its holder.

The message was brief and beautifully penned. But the signature was what held her attention. Victor had sent the extraordinary arrangement that spoke of intimate knowledge of what suited Raini. Yet another arrangement for her sister, and he hadn't so much as called her.

She was staggered by what she was feeling: a crushing desire to see Victor and yes, jealousy toward her sister. Not evil jealousy, but the kind one felt when a loved one gets something you want with your every fiber.

"Lauren."

Tossing the card into the depths of the flowers, she turned away and hurried to answer Raini's call. Even though she wanted to strangle her.

"You're determined to keep me in New York, aren't you?" Lauren sighed in exasperation, walking into Raini's bedroom.

"I admit it." Raini smiled happily. "I'd be lost without you."

"Well, one thing I can't believe, we haven't had an argument for weeks." Lauren shook her head in mock disbelief. "I think it's time for me to skedaddle back to Malibu before all hell breaks loose."

Raini looked up from the appointment book she had been writing in. She appeared aghast at Lauren's comment. "You can't leave on the Fourth of July weekend."

"And why is that?" Lauren handed Raini a vitamin and a glass of water.

"The picnic and the garden party." Raini ran her finger down the page, checking the list of things to do that she had carefully penned. "Please don't make me attend the father-daughter golf tourney alone."

"Lord." Lauren threw her hands up in resignation. "If I say yes, will you stop nagging me? I have to go home sometime."

"You're a good sister, Lauren."

"You can stop with the wheedling now, Raini. I said I would stay until the tournament." She caught sight of herself in Raini's dressing table mirror. "Why didn't you tell me I was such a mess? I need a style and a daylong facial. I can't be seen in this condition."

"You look wonderful." Raini opened her triple closet doors to look at its contents. "We've been cooped up in the apartment far too long. Let's spend the day at the spa."

The spa. An unexpected jolt of remembered pleasure flared in Lauren's blood and spiraled quickly to her lower extremities. A soft smile played over her lips. She would never think of a spa as a place to relax ever again.

"Secrets, Lauren?"

"I'll never tell." Lauren didn't want to share her thoughts at that moment.

"You don't have to," Raini sighed. "There's a new man in your life."

Chapter Eight

How fortuitous. Not that she hadn't hoped for this lovely opportunity that had just dropped into her lap. There he was. Victor, tall, dark and alone, coming out of the club's business office. She smiled while watching him replace his credit card in his wallet. Her senses were razor sharp by the time he had noticed her. His smile touching all the responsive places.

She held her ground and didn't rush toward him like she was dying to do. *Be still. Don't give him the idea you're here expressly to see him. Even though it's true. Sweet heaven, he's coming to you.*

He walked toward her with slow deliberation, his gaze never straying from where she stood. Close enough to touch her, he gave her a crooked smile.

"I couldn't be this lucky twice in my life." His warm gaze swept over her face and lingered on her lips. "You still knock my socks off."

His voice wrapped around her in streamers of intoxicating sweetness. She shook herself back to reality. "I'm glad to see you too, Raven." She couldn't help it if her voice had become a satin purr.

He took a long moment and let his sultry gaze slip over her. "If I didn't know better, I'd say butter wouldn't melt in your mouth, Miss Rose."

She clasped her hands behind her back and surveyed him with warming intensity. "Is that all you have to say, Raven?"

He reached behind her and caught her hand to move her away from the noisy group of children at the soda fountain.

"I haven't even started." He smiled lazily at her and brushed her cheek with his thumb. "I can't believe this angelic looking woman is the same one that seduced me into a boiling concoction of orgiastic agony."

Her earlobes tingled with shameless pleasure while he looked at her with raw desire in the depths of his blue eyes. His fingers on her wrist sent her into an orbit of delirium.

"Careful, Raven. You don't have a napkin to hide behind today." She knew her laugh was pure tease.

With the confidence of knowing her intimately, he put his arm around her waist and grinned down at her. "You look damned demure in that little dress."

Lauren's head spun when his chin brushed her temple, and his words seeped into her ears and stopped somewhere around her pelvic area.

"But we know better, don't we, baby?" He took a deep breath against her neck before he stepped back and glanced down at her feet. "You smell sexy as hell."

"I'm glad I decided to wear CoCo today. In all the secret places since you took so much pleasure in it." She wiggled her digits and enjoyed his wolfish grin.

"I'm surprised you're still here, Lauren." He wanted to know if she was thinking of staying in New York. "Have you decided to give up the beach house, sand and surf?"

"Not yet." She heard interest in his words and decided to see how interested he was. "Raini's been such a baby, I've hung around longer than I meant to."

"And how is she?" He smiled down at her as if she had just made the sun appear. "I'll have to thank her for the medical emergency that kept you here."

"She's completely recovered, and the flowers you sent were lovely. Both times." Lauren watched for changes in his expression while she spoke. "You seemed to know exactly what suited her."

"It's the same arrangement I send everyone." He caressed her waist. "Everyone but you, gorgeous."

She tapped her lower lip, and then breathed deeply. "And for me? Cat tails?"

"Hell, no." He reached for the clasp that held her hair only to be stopped by her look of warning. "For you, crimson roses and white orchids."

He took her hand, swinging it gently. "I was just wondering if your skin really feels like polished gold or was it something I dreamed up."

She let him lace her fingers through his, loving the strength of his hand. "Stop. You're going to make me blush." Her lashes dipped to conceal the joy that swamped over her.

"I don't recall you blushing, pussycat." He leaned nearer to look into her eyes. "You here with someone special?"

"Of course." She wanted to say she was definitely with someone special at that moment. "Are you?"

"Yeah." He looked a little disappointed. "Whose the lucky person with you?"

"You first." Lauren's legs were becoming rubbery as he tilted his head and gave her his devastatingly disarming smile.

"I'm here with a beautiful blond. She leads me a dog's life."

Lauren's fine brows lifted an indiscernible bit. Lord, she was actually damn jealous. It was hard to remember they weren't bound by anything but a hot session in the spa. After mentally lashing herself, she sucked it up and fell back into her former banter.

"I'm not buying that, Raven. Unless you just met her fifteen minutes ago."

"Believe me, it's true." He inhaled heavily for emphasis. "I'll introduce you to my keeper."

"I can't wait." Lauren didn't intend to stick around long enough for the introduction. She changed the subject. "I'm surprised you would come to the club today."

"Surprised. Why?" He was looking over her head at the noisy proceedings at the soda fountain.

"The place is overrun with children." The light scent of his aftershave made her think of the way it clung to her skin after they had made love.

"I'm not scared of kids. It's the adults you've got keep your guard up with." His forehead grazed hers when he leaned over to catch the scent of her hair.

Lauren enjoyed the slight roughness of his beard against her cheek as he raised his head. "Don't be shocked if I agree with you."

"I'm only shocked that you get sexier every time I see you." He drew her arm about his waist. "Do you know how damned bad I want to kiss you?"

"Don't hold back, Raven," she laughed. "Tell me how you really feel."

"I'd rather show you, baby," he murmured.

Lauren splayed her fingers over the warmth she could feel coming through his shirt and enjoyed the sound of pleasure he made in his throat. Here she was, working him and herself up into a foaming frenzy. What was it about the damned club that turned her into an absolute she-wolf?

She had never been so bold with a man and never with a relative stranger. She almost groaned in derision at her own thoughts. Stranger? That was a laugh. He knew her body on more intimate terms than she did. *Remember that dear, that's all you know about him as well. This isn't a prelude to a mortgage and two-car garage. It's all about sex.* She held back her clever retort when she noticed the slight scowl on his face.

He was looking over her head at someone across the room. She turned to see what had abruptly changed his flirtatious mood. The woman walking toward them was strictly champagne and mink. Nothing but the best Caviar quality. Feeling territorial, Lauren gripped Victor's arm. Damned if she was turning him over to the socialite making her move on him.

"Victor." The encroaching female cast a look of mild interest on Lauren. "I'm leaving now, darling. Explain to Rachel that I couldn't stay for the tournament." She showed her white teeth in a brief smile. "She'll understand. You always know what to say."

"Wait a minute, Jonelle. She won't understand. You've spent damned little time with her for weeks." He looked as if he were about to explode. In an attempt to keep the exchange between the two of them private, he lowered his voice. "And where are you off to now?"

"A thing I totally forgot about until this morning." Jonelle appeared eager to leave. "This appointment is crucial to me." She glanced at her watch. "I'll pick Rachel up in the morning. Be a dear one more time."

Victor appeared to be counting to ten. "Bridge game or pedicure?" His voice gave away a hint of his desire to shake Jonelle until her teeth rattled. "I'll try to smooth it over, but you are to pick her up by nine tomorrow morning. Please don't disappoint her."

Jonelle took time to look closely at Lauren, apparently accessing her worth. "I didn't get your name. Are you Rachel's nanny?"

"No, I'm after bigger game." Lauren decided she wouldn't back off, not for this person that talked down to her. "Will I be replacing you?"

Jonelle's green eyes narrowed as she returned Lauren's gaze. "She's young Victor, but able to handle herself." A smile of amusement softened her expression. "This could be interesting." She touched Victor's arm with familiarity. "Thank you, darling. I'll be there on time. Have fun at whatever you're up to." With an air of privilege, Jonelle walked away, showing no interest in Victor's parting comment.

"Nine o'clock, Jonelle."

He laughed when Lauren stepped in front of him like a small but determined shield. "That woman is too vain to describe, and I sometimes have trouble remembering she's my daughter's mother. But I make it a point to remain calm when it comes to Jonelle. I have to. For Rachel's sake."

Lauren watched the lines of irritation fade from Victor's face. He had been angry, the hard set of his jaw deepening the scar at the corner of his mouth. Now that he was smiling at her again, the cobalt blue of his eyes held only warmth and good humor.

"Where were we?" He lifted her hand to do a quick study of her fingers. "French manicure. Very sexy."

Lauren had to satisfy her curiosity. "Who was the iceberg that just blew us off?"

"A mistake."

"The ex-wife?"

"That's how she was listed in the divorce settlement."

"She's attractive."

"So is a cactus."

Lauren bit her lip. She didn't want to laugh at his comment. He wasn't trying to be amusing. It was time to speak of other things. "I like your outfit, Raven. Very country club." She tweaked the collar of his yellow polo shirt. "Perfect with those good fitting white pants."

"You're making fun of me, but that's okay." He stuck his hands in his pockets, giving her a crooked grin. "Rachel insisted we dress alike. Identity thing I guess."

"I keep hearing her name, Raven." Did she dare wander into his private domain, which Raini had warned her about? Of course. "When do I meet her?"

Victor turned Lauren around to face the soda fountain. "That would be her coming this way."

Lauren heard the ring of pride in his voice. She knew where his heart lay now, and it belonged to the beautiful little girl with a ponytail sitting askew at the side of her head.

He leaned down to catch the laughing child up in his arms. Lauren noticed the oversized Mickey Mouse watch on Rachel's arm as she hugged her father's neck. Before long, Rachel turned her attention to Lauren, smiling at her with the same openness that surely came from Victor.

"Rachel. Say hello to Lauren Rose."

"I'm pleased to make your aquarium." Rachel looked to her father for help. "Did I say it right, Daddy?"

He laughed, patting her back to reassure her. "You were perfect."

"Hello, Rachel." Touching Rachel's off kilter ponytail, Lauren noted the silky texture. She spoke to the delightful child on a woman-to-woman level. "I love your hair. Did you do that yourself?"

"No. Daddy fixed it." A merry giggle followed Rachel's

explanation before she rushed into her next comment. "I like your name. Want Daddy to fix your hair like mine?"

"I don't think it's long enough to make it look like yours." Lauren removed her hair clasp, letting her hair swing free. "How's that?"

"I like it." Rachel caught a handful of her own hair, looking thoughtful. "I want my hair like Lauren's. Can we cut it, Daddy?"

"I like Lauren's hair too, honey. But let's not start changing hairstyles just yet. Okay?"

"Okay." Rachel kissed his cheek, and then tried her hand at blackmail. "I won't cut my hair if I can have ice cream for lunch."

"No to both." Victor set her on her feet, holding onto her arm to keep her from scampering away. "What did I tell you about conniving?"

Rachel grinned up at her father, and then hugged his legs. "I love you, Daddy."

"I'll explain it again later." Victor looked at Lauren. The beautiful Miss Rose was thoroughly enjoying his attempt to corral one little girl.

Rachel gave out a tiny sigh of discontent and reached up to tug on Victor's shirt. "Can Lauren have lunch with us, Daddy? I like her."

"Does she want to have lunch with us?" He gave Lauren a wry grin. "Do you, Miss Rose?"

"I'd like that very much, Mister Raven." Lauren brushed a strand of hair from Rachel's forehead. "What time shall we dine?"

"We should be off the green in thirty minutes." Victor held onto his daughter's hand while extending a second invitation. "Would you care to watch Rachel tee off? She's becoming quite the golfer."

"I'd love to." Lauren watched Rachel as she scampered off toward the doorway. "She's wonderful, Raven."

He rested his hand on Lauren's waist as they followed the energetic little girl. "She's that all right." His gaze had taken on a definite adult intent. "By the way, I'm intrigued with your toe jewelry."

"I always wear it." Lauren looked at him from beneath her lashes, grinning impishly.

"That's strange," he murmured. "How the hell did I miss something so damned sexy?"

Lauren managed to walk beside him without stumbling over her own feet. But her smile told him she knew there was no way he could have missed seeing the smallest detail of her anatomy or it's adornments. He laughed with her when she couldn't hold back a soft chortle.

Victor was rocked by the powerful grip of the comfort zone he was sliding into. The scene was ideal, a perfect day, his child and a beautiful woman. It was too perfect, and way too comfortable. Getting cozy with a woman meant bonds to sever, and he wasn't eager to have demands made on him anytime soon. Slow down, his sensible voice warned. *But why?* Lauren wasn't any more ready to drop anchor in one port than he was. *Enjoy her fella. She's what you want. At least for now.*

Chapter Nine

Lauren's gaze kissed Victor as he walked off to join Rachel. Her pulse leaped when he turned to pinpoint her location in the crowd. Evidently bored with waiting, Rachael gripped his legs in a bear hug. With consummate patience, he leaned down to disengage her arms, then kissed the top of her head. Lauren saw a man of complex personality. He was always ready to shower affection and attention on women, yet he had shown he could also become angry. Her deep thoughts were interrupted when Raini touched her shoulder.

"The two of you look like teenagers on a first date."

"What?" Lauren knew her cheeks were flushed.

"Don't 'what' me." Raini tapped her sister's shoulder. "Oh yes. The toe scraping. A little touch here. The quick little stroke to the hair. Um huh."

Lauren reached out to grip her perceptive sister's elbow. "Stop it." Could she help it if she was grinning ear to ear? "It wasn't really that obvious, was it?"

Raini slipped her arm about Lauren's waist. "A blinking neon sign couldn't speak any clearer."

"He's expecting me to have lunch with them."

Raini's expression of shock was genuine. "Well. Consider yourself quite special."

"It's a fact." Lauren smoothed her hair with a playful gesture of self-importance. "I must have passed muster with Rachel."

"And then some I would guess." Raini lowered her voice, moving Lauren out of the path of a harried waiter. "I'm not going to belabor the point, but try to remember who he is."

"Frankly my dear, you're beating the subject to death." Lauren turned to study the man in question. "Raven and I know each other very well. We're members of the same club. You know the one-- Don't get serious about me."

"Point well taken." Raini's smile was apologetic. "I know you're perfectly capable of handling your own life. Mother hen you know."

"I understand," Lauren said. "You and Adam really need to have five or six kids to keep you busy."

"Yes, I think you're right." Raini narrowed her eyes while looking over the crowd. "As a matter of fact, we may just talk about that if I can keep him still long enough."

Lauren pointed to a group of men that had gathered under a huge oak tree. Her brother-in-law was in the middle of the crowd as usual. "There's your man." She spoke confidentially to her smiling sister. "He's probably more than willing to discuss the matter. Just remember to hide all the phones."

"I've already thought of that." Raini dusted at the skirt of her blue dress. "Excuse me, Lauren. I can't think of a better time to bring the subject up."

Lauren pondered the thought of Raini being a mother. Lord, hopefully the kid would be clever enough to enlist the aid of its softie father whenever Raini became too starchy. That's how she had survived her teen years if she remembered right. Going to her father had been the answer to most problems. Lauren clasped her hands behind her back, walking closer to the green. What would he say about this man? It didn't matter. Just as always, she would do what she felt was right for her.

Thirty minutes later, she was sitting with Victor and Rachel in the center of the club dining room. Lauren guessed they were the topic of many conversations if quickly averted glances and knowing smiles was any gauge of the onlooker's attitudes. When the waiter arrived to take their orders, Lauren smothered a laugh when Rachel tested her father's patience.

"No Daddy. I want to order for myself." Rachel pulled the menu from Victor's hand. She narrowed her heavily lashed eyes to peruse the menus offering. "Hamburger."

"Hamburger?" Victor scowled because of her choice. "You've been eating out too much. Why not chose something that requires a knife and fork?"

"Mommy always lets me have a hamburger."

"Is that breakfast or a midnight snack?" His expression had taken on a tightness that clearly said he wasn't happy.

"I'll have the same." Lauren ducked behind her menu to avoid being the recipient of Victor's grimace.

"Make it three hamburgers and three extra large glasses of milk." He shook his head when Rachel screwed her face up in a show of distaste.

Lauren met his gaze over her menu. He winked at her. Lord, she thought, the man had no idea how much she liked him at that moment. He was a marshmallow with a generous amount of crust. Poor man. She could see herself as a child in most of Rachel's antics. But Victor handled it all with tender firmness, managing to calm stormy seas like a pro. Real authority stepped in when Rachel tried to leave the table. There was a moment of silent warfare while father and daughter stared each other down for the final word. He won, and peace resumed.

When had a hamburger ever tasted so divine? Never as far as Lauren was concerned. Aside from an overturned glass of water, lunch moved along splendidly. She knew Victor wanted to speak of things other than Barbie dolls and Mickey Mouse. He smiled at her over Rachel's head while the little girl described in detail the script from a movie she owned. He got his chance to speak in adult terms when the children participating in the tournament were called away for group photos.

"She's a handful." He reached across the table to catch Lauren's hand. "Remind you of anyone?"

"If you're referring to me," Lauren said, "definitely, but I was much more demanding."

"I can believe that." He rubbed his thumb over her knuckles, smiling at her. "I'm glad you didn't go back to Malibu."

"I'm glad too." She squeezed his fingers. "I wouldn't have gotten to meet Rachel."

"I can see I'll have to separate the two of you and damned fast." He caressed her forearm, as if refreshing his memory on the silken texture of her skin.

"Raven?" Snapping her fingers close to his nose, Lauren laughed. "How was the view? You were drifting around somewhere in space there for a minute."

He covered his mental meanderings with a smile. "You really want to know? I was wondering how to ask you to spend a few days at my lake house."

"Would you be there?" She bestowed her most bewitching smile on him.

"You're trying to tell me something."

She took a rosebud from the vase on the table. "What do you want to hear?"

"Hell. I want to hear you sigh and tell me how damned wonderful I am." He was tense. "The need to be with you is killing me." His bravado sank a bit when she stopped smiling. "You have something to say?"

"I'm only here because of Raini, and she's wrung all of my vacation time out of me." Lauren almost felt anger toward her sister but squashed the selfish feeling. "I have two more days here and I go home. It's that or lose my job."

His brow knit into a slight scowl, but then he grinned at her. "Come work for me and you'll never have to punch the time clock."

"I never date the boss."

He smiled at her. "You're the most infuriating woman I've ever known, but Lord I can't be with you enough." His mood altered to nonchalance once more. "Well." He leaned back in his chair to study her for a moment. "Since the lake house is out, let's have one incredible date."

"A date?" She leaned over to draw the rose across his lips, trying to stay in her chair. Be calm, her quiet voice of decorum cautioned. "I haven't been asked for a date in so long, I'd forgotten how flattering it is."

"I have no intention of flattering you, Lauren. I just want to be with you."

"You make me feel awfully good, Raven."

He was quiet for a time, taking her hand to study the texture of her fingers that lay in his. "Let's stop the tit for tat, shall we?" He squeezed her fingers gently. "We don't have a lot of time, so I'll ask you again. Dinner and dancing. Tomorrow night. A real date. I'll even shave."

She liked what she saw in his incredible eyes. He was serious and had obviously given this some thought. "Okay."

He sat forward, nodding his head several times in apparent pleasure because of her uncomplicated answer. "Okay."

Their private moment ended in a flurry of clinging arms and one excited little voice. Rachel had returned. In a feminine gesture, she checked the status of her sideways ponytail as she talked.

"I tried to not smile." Rachel leaned comfortably against Lauren.

"Why didn't you smile?" Lauren asked. "You have wonderful dimples."

On cue, Rachel opened her mouth to reveal a gap where she had a missing tooth. "Lost it roughhousing, Daddy said."

"Don't worry about that," Lauren soothed. "You'll soon have a grown-up tooth in that space."

"Okay." Seemingly satisfied with her answer, Rachel draped herself across Lauren's lap.

* * * *

Victor caught himself becoming engaged in something he never did. Comparing his former wife to another woman. He knew it was a dangerous pastime, yet he couldn't help it. Lauren never held back when it came to sharing her thoughts, she wasn't stingy with her time and freely took part in new experiences. Being asked to have lunch with a six year old she didn't know would have sent Jonelle running and screaming in the opposite direction.

He thought of Lauren's gentle way with his rambunctious daughter. She hadn't shrunk from Rachel's dirty hands or the way she had mangled her beautiful dress. The woman was a natural with kids.

He shook his head to dislodge the homey scene painting itself in his brain. He was jostled from his mental meanderings by Rachel's giggle of delight. Lauren was showing her how to make a goofy-looking bird out of her napkin. Another good thing in Lauren's favor. She sure as hell was playful.

"I believe it's time for us to go home." Victor left his chair to pick his child up in his arms. "Until tomorrow evening, Lauren?"

"Until then," Lauren said. She was smiling, unaware that someone stood behind her chair. Victor wasn't leaving until she turned to look behind her and he was sure it was okay for him to leave.

Justin leaned over her shoulder, brushing her hair in a possessive manner. She leaned away from his touch.

"Lauren. It's good to see you out and about again."

He was obviously waiting for permission to sit down. It didn't come. After silently taking in the scene, he acknowledged Victor's presence. "Raven. Nice to see you."

"Taylor." Not being in a buddy relationship with Justin made it impossible for Victor to bluntly ask the younger man what the hell he wanted. He figured young Doctor Taylor wasn't twisting in the wind, waiting to talk with him. It was Lauren he wanted to speak to. Victor extended his hand to Justin.

The men shook hands, exchanging a few words before Justin seemed to realize he was intruding. He cast a last look in Lauren's direction, and then said his good-byes.

"Perhaps I'll see you again before you leave for California."

"That isn't likely," Lauren said with no sign of warmth.

Her brief reply drew an amused look from Victor. He sensed a repentant young man was stirring the ashes of a burned-out romance. He waited until the vanquished tucked tail and retreated.

"So that's Joe Blow." He shifted Rachel's sleeping weight up onto his shoulder. "You cut him pretty short."

Lauren dropped her napkin onto the table, getting up to stand by Victor. "Not for a long time." She brushed a blade of grass from

Rachel's hair. "I'll walk you out."

"Sure you want to risk it? You know. The association thing."

She laughed, understanding the meaning of his comment. He knew about his reputation and assumed she did. "I'll risk it all right." She smoothed her hair, and then lay her arm across his waist. "These people need something new to gossip about."

Lauren helped Victor secure Rachel in the backseat of his car, and then stepped back onto the brick walkway. Crossing her arms at her waist, she waited for him to turn around. He turned to catch her dreamy-eyed gaze, smiling warmly at her.

"Thanks for having lunch with us, Lauren." He stood as close as decently possible to her. "You made a real impression on Rachel."

"I like her too. She's honest." Lauren wanted to be kissed in the way he alone could do, but that would have to wait.

"Just one of her redeeming qualities." He slid his hand to Lauren's back, moving it up her ribcage. "Now. If we could do something about her problem with sharing."

"That will come, Raven. She's still a little girl." Lauren eased a step back. "Women have a hard time sharing what they care for."

"I see." He opened his door, watching Lauren walk toward the clubhouse. "Tomorrow. Eight o'clock?" He waited until she had nodded her head in acknowledgement and gone back inside the clubhouse.

He got into the drivers seat and shut the door quietly, not wanting to wake his sleeping princess. He was pulling away from the curb when someone rapped on the window to get his attention. He lowered the glass, surprised to see Justin looking in at him.

"Taylor? What's the trouble?"

"No trouble unless you don't take these expensive clubs home." Justin held up two putters.

"Thanks." Victor reached for his property. "I guess I forgot to keep track of them with Rachel being enough to handle." He was puzzled by Justin's reluctance to hand the clubs over.

"Say, Raven. Got a minute to talk?"

Victor glanced back at Rachel then at Justin. "Make it fast, Taylor. I don't like keeping Rachel out in the heat too long."

"I'll get right to the heart of the matter." Justin leaned further into the car. "I was surprised to see you having lunch with Lauren Rose."

"You think I'm too old for her?" Victor enjoyed antagonizing the obviously love stung young physician.

"She's only twenty-six. But that's not what I'm getting at."

"That young, huh?" Victor chuckled, amused by Justin's look of impatience.

"I would ask you to be careful in dealing with her. She's still easily hurt. Her father's death and...."

"Look. Taylor. I don't know what you're getting at and I'm not sure you are." Victor pulled the clubs from Justin's grip.

"It's complicated." Justin raked his hand over his mop of dark hair. "I'll put it this way. Don't ever tell her your corporation took over the Rose holdings. She believes the takeover was the cause of her father's death." He took a breath and hurried on. "She's quite bitter about the whole thing."

Victor wasn't about to go into finances with Justin, but what he had said gave him pause for thought. He dropped the clubs onto the floorboard. No use giving the young pup reason to think he had thrown a scare into the old man.

"Thanks for the advice, old boy." He grinned at Justin. "Is there something else she's bitter about?"

"That's all I have to say, Raven. Just thought you should know what you're up against and what could happen."

"Taylor, you're riled up way ahead of schedule." Victor let the window go up slowly. "It appeared to me she has a bigger axe to grind with you than she has with me." He smiled in spite of the knot of concern in his gut. "Thanks again."

Victor had known from the start that Leonard Rose had a daughter named Lauren. He had heard her name through conversations with the late Mister Rose and her sister Raini. Until he met her, Lauren had only been a name. That had all changed now. She was a warm, beautiful woman that he wanted. If her venom for the Raven Corporation ran as deeply as Taylor had implied, he would make damned sure she never put two and two together.

Chapter Ten

A date with Lauren. Victor laughed at himself and the unusual case of nerves that had plagued him since he'd asked her out. He knew he was anxious to be with her again, but this bordered on ridiculous. He'd lost track of the times he was forced to ask his secretary to repeat a question and caught her look of outrage when he totally forgot her name. He finally cut his workday short by several hours. On his way home, he stopped at the florist. Nothing but the best for Lauren would do. Set among the lush arrangement of scarlet roses and white Orchids was one cheeky cattail.

When eight o'clock finally dragged itself onto his watch, Victor stood outside Lauren's door. He waited for her to let him in and tried to hit upon the best way to give her the flowers. Hide them behind his back? No. Too corny. Grip them in both hands? No. Too nervous. Before he could decide on his method, the door opened.

"I like that," Lauren's greeting was soft as silk. "You're right on time."

Somehow he managed to get the flowers into Lauren's hands without her noticing his sweating palms. "Didn't want to be late."

"Did you take the stairs up here? You look warm." She smiled, moving back a step, waiting for him to come inside the apartment. "You probably didn't remember our date until the last second."

"Not true." Damned if he'd thought of anything else.

She tapped his cheek with the fragrant bouquet. "Did you forget something out there?" She gestured toward the empty hallway. "Come in."

Victor walked inside, taking a quick look around. This was the first time they'd been together without a crowd and all the noise that went with it. He watched her inspect her flowers. She was lovelier than the blossoms she held, splendid in a dress of sunshine yellow silk. Without thinking, he reached out to touch her waist.

"One of your creations?"

"Yes, it is." Holding her arms out, she did a slow turn for him. The dress revealed a good portion of her back, and the short skirt drifting softly about her thighs showed off her legs. "Do you like it?"

"Very much." His palm burned to touch her hair when he noticed the camellias nestled against the back of her head. "That's a nice touch," he said.

"Thank you for noticing." She checked the camellias with her hand, and then smiled at him. "You're not thinking of tinkering with them, are you?"

"Not yet." Why was he so damned nervous? He should be swaggering like a peacock, not feeling tongue tied and bashful. He tore his gaze from her long enough to glance around the apartment.

Lauren winked at him. "They're out for the evening."

"Who?" He grimaced, thinking she saw him as her life's worst date.

"Raini and Adam." She bit her lower lip and studied his face. "Is something wrong? Am I dressed all wrong for what you had planned?"

"On the contrary. Everything's great."

"You have a real habit of wandering off, Raven."

"That obvious?" He touched her chin with his thumb. "It won't happen again. I'm all yours."

She smiled. "You may regret those words." Noting his slightly raised brow, she laughed. "I'll take care of these and then we can leave."

The single cattail peeking audaciously from the midst of its extravagant companions seemed to delight Lauren. He was glad as hell he never forgot anything she said.

He could see her moving about, tending to her flowers, gathering up her handbag and keys. The woman was an absolute delight to look at, to be with. That little skirt hit her legs in just about the right place. Before he could think of a good reason to not become involved with Lauren, she was turning off lights.

"Ready?" She walked toward him, and then nodded toward the door.

He followed her out into the hall, catching the doorknob in a firm grip.

"Did I tell you how sexy you are?" He closed the door behind them, and then pushed the button for the elevator.

"Once or twice." Her voice had softened into a caress. "But you can tell me again."

"Many times before the night is through." He lifted her hand to kiss her fingertips. "Many, many times."

* * * *

Complete privacy was what Victor had in mind, and he congratulated himself for the decision to drive his car instead of relying on taxis. He wanted nothing to interfere with his few precious hours with Lauren. So far, so good, he thought as they walked into the restaurant he'd chosen. As expected, Lauren drew more than her share of appreciative looks. He understood their feeling of being hit by lightning. When they were seated, he breathed easier, now that she was within arms reach and looking at him with those mysterious dark eyes.

"I know you don't imbibe a great deal, Lauren, but would you care for a cocktail before dinner?"

"White wine would be fine." Lauren felt as if she had chugged a quart of the stuff already. Her senses whirled merrily. It occurred to her that this was her first official date in a year. And what an event to end her fast with. Victor was a magnificent man.

The instant Victor glanced up, a waiter approached their table to take their order. Lauren ordered first, and then listened to Victor's voice as he told the waiter what he wanted. She could live with that sound forever.

He quirked an eyebrow at her. "Now who's wandering?" He gave her face careful scrutiny. "I don't mind if you wander. As long as you keep looking at me that way."

"Pleasant thoughts, I assure you." She lifted her shoulders, tilting her head from side to side. "Do I have something in my teeth?" She started to pull her compact from her bag.

"There's nothing in your teeth. I just can't help myself." He had to tell her how he felt about her. "I don't think I'll ever get used to your beauty."

She leaned toward him. "Give it a while, Raven. Hang around long enough and you'll be running for your life."

He shook his head. "Are you trying to scare me off? It won't work." *Listen to yourself man; you're up to your knees in quicksand.*

"Don't say you weren't warned," she said, working her brows in question. "Is there something you need to warn me about?"

Of course there was plenty he needed to warn her about. *How about the fact she would hate him if he told her about the things he'd done, not knowing she'd be hurt by his actions.* But he had an idea this lady would cut him no slack and at the moment, and he didn't want to take the risk. The fact he couldn't be totally honest with her bothered him immensely. He changed the route of conversation.

"I think you'll like the club we're going to after dinner."

Lauren leaned closer to him. "How did you know I liked to dance?"

"Lucky guess." He liked the sparkle in her mysterious dark eyes; wishing he was the only one that caused that spectacular light show. Her lips were moving. *Wake up man, she's talking to you.*

"Raven, do you know how rare you are? A man that likes to dance."

"The experience was forced on me by my mother." He grinned as he spoke. "It was either take lessons or quit the hockey team."

"I was supposed to take ballet." Lauren laughed, remembering her years of training in the fine art of dance. "My father would've been damned upset if he'd known I used the money to learn how to belly dance."

Victor watched her expression as she related her secret to him. He doubted her father would've been too upset with his remarkably beautiful daughter. He gestured lightly toward her. "I'm sure there's more to that story."

"You're the first person I've told that, Raven." His look of amusement seemed to please her. "You know, I am having no problem at all telling you the dirty little secrets of my life. Are you harboring sinister secrets from me?" She laughed happily. "Probably, but that's your business. I know all that's necessary. And I think we need to take our elbows off the table now. Our dinner is here."

"Wonderful," he said. "I'm famished." He wasn't exaggerating. Just being with Lauren whetted his appetite to taste the wealth of pleasure she brought to the table.

"Me too." Lauren licked her lips in expectation as she picked up her silver. "I waited all day for this."

Victor watched Lauren cut her steak into bite-sized portions and butter her dinner roll. No pushing push her food around the plate or pretending she wasn't hungry. She didn't pretend or fake anything. He derived as much pleasure from observing her chew as she did from the food she ate. By the time she'd polished off her filet mignon and asparagus, he was dying to kiss the mouth she dabbed at with her napkin.

"Raven." She gestured toward his plate. "Do you really like those things?"

He gave the oysters on his plate a quick glance, and then smiled at her. "Guilty." His grin broadened. "A man of my years you know."

Lauren couldn't hold her tongue, something she found impossible around this man. "You never have to worry about your performance, Raven."

"That's quite a compliment coming from the most passionate

women I've known."

He couldn't help it if he looked at her in a way that would have melted an iceberg. Lauren apparently basked in the warmth, slipping her bare toes along his leg. Conversation was sparse after that, interrupted by passersby stopping to say hello to Victor.

"Does everyone in New York know you, Raven?" she asked.

He caught her hand. "They think they do. Care for dessert?"

"Not on your life. I want to be able to dance." She dropped her napkin onto the table, smiling at the man that stirred her carefully hidden emotions. "Were you teasing about dancing?"

"Completely serious," he said. "Let's go, beautiful."

* * * *

The club he took her to was designed for adult enjoyment. No strobe lights or spinning glass balls here. The interior was patterned after a forties Hollywood bistro. Lighting was low and mellow, illuminating white cloth covered tables and a large, gleaming dance floor.

Lauren felt the Latin rhythm course through her body before they were seated. She couldn't control the shiver of delight that riffled over her when Victor caressed her bare arm.

"Cold?" He leaned over to hear her answer.

"No. Excited." She glanced at the couples filling the dance floor. "The music does that to me."

"I think this is our dance, beautiful." He stood up, holding his hand out to her. "Rumba, sexy lady?"

"Can't wait," she said, taking his hand to follow him to the dance floor.

He twirled her about several times, and then caught her about the waist. "Hang on, baby. This may be a bumpy ride."

She laughed in delight, putting herself into his capable hands. "Go ahead Raven, thrill me."

As far as Lauren was concerned, they were the only people in the place. *Tonight you have wings on your feet and a devilishly handsome man holding you in his arms. What more could you want?* The quickening in her body answered her question. The rumba was only an appetizer, followed by the samba and her favorite, the tango. She gloried in his touch, letting her body mould against his as the tempo changed to something more intimate. He lifted her arms around his neck and kissed the corner of her mouth.

"I was beginning to wonder."

"About what?" she asked. His voice toyed with her sensitive earlobes.

"If I was going to get the chance to be close to you tonight."

"Is that all you wondered about?" She skillfully sent a message meant to assure him of success, boldly pressing her hips to his.

"Not by half and you know it," he said. "If you felt any better, I'd have to hide under the tablecloth again."

Laurens flashed him a wicked grin. "Want to go neck in the parking garage?"

He tilted his head back, laughing at her gutsy suggestion. She was smiling up at him with such sweet honesty, his heart threatened to do flip-flops. *How could he not be attracted to her? Lauren, Lauren. He knew it would be hard as hell to say good-bye to her.*

"Raven." She pressed her cheek to his chest, sniffing his good scent that whispered of moonlight and sea blown heather. "You didn't like my idea?"

"Crazy about it, but you're way too sexy for that." He placed his hand at the back of her head. "My couch is much more comfortable."

"I'm sure it is, but haven't you forgotten something?"

"I haven't forgotten anything about you, baby."

She touched his hair, scowling a little. "You have a child at home."

"Rachel's spending the night with Annie and four of Annie's granddaughters." He pressed a kiss to her temple. "Care to have a look at that couch now?"

"Don't you have a bed?"

"I was working up to that."

"Good man." Putting her arms around his waist, she slid her hand down to pat his rear. "Race you to the car."

Lauren swept her handbag off their table as Victor led her toward the exit. He held onto her hand as they ran through the dimly illuminated garage, the stares from curious passersby not dampening their enthusiasm. Inside his car, Lauren slid across the seat to lean against him.

"I had a wonderful time tonight, Raven." She touched his jaw, slowly tracing the shape. "You get four stars."

"I'll ask for a revised rating later," he said. "The evening isn't over. Is it?"

"It's just begun."

Chapter Eleven

Lauren stood impatiently while Victor took what seemed an incredible amount of time, switching on lights, closing drapes. She locked her hands behind her back and looked expectantly at him. What was wrong with the man?

"Raven." She tossed her handbag at him, stepping out of her shoes at the same time. "Let me help."

"Almost finished." He smiled at her before pressing the mute button on the answering machine.

"Is that a good idea?" It was none of her business, but she had already crossed the line. "With Rachel being at Annie's?"

"You're a worrywart." He inclined his head in the direction of his bedroom. "There's a cell phone on the nightstand with a number only Annie knows. So far."

She grinned at him, thinking he was the closest thing to perfect she had ever known. And here you are, feeling warm and fuzzy about a man that has made it clear that he will not be taken. *Snap out of it. You're not going to be taken either. This is going to be a romp in ultimate pleasure meant to be savored for as long as it lasts.*

He strode toward her, stripping off his tie. "Now, Miss Rose. What's your pleasure?"

She stretched her arms out to her sides, closing her eyes. "Whatever you're serving, Raven." She licked her lips. "I want it all."

He caught her up high on his chest making her gasp in surprise. When she opened her eyes, he looked at her with unguarded desire. She couldn't wait another second, covering his mouth in a soft, lingering kiss. She wreathed her arms about his neck in declared possessiveness. Sweeping urgency sang through her, whispering to her. *A tender kiss isn't enough. Show him what you want, starting with the buttons of his shirt.*

While her fingers release the pearl buttons, he nuzzled her neck. "I like the way you do that," he murmured. "You have beautiful hands."

She rubbed her palm over his warm skin. "You have a beautiful chest." Catching his hand to carry it to her hip, she whispered coaxing directions. "There's a zipper at the back of my dress."

"Already on it." He caught the tab in his fingers, pausing to smile at her. "What are you wearing under this piece of imagination?"

"Maybe nothing," she teased.

"I think you just issued a challenge." He lowered the zipper several inches, and then raised it again. "I really shouldn't. Christmas is several months off."

She hooked her fingers in his belt. "Well. I always sneak peeks at my gifts." She worked on his belt buckle.

He grinned down at her. "Open yours first. I want to savor mine."

"Go ahead," she huffed, pulling his belt free. "Suffer. I don't intend to waste a minute of this party." She didn't hesitate in pushing his slacks down, smiling with satisfaction as they fell about his ankles.

Victor's calm demeanor was evaporating. She was driving him over the brink, messing with his plan to disrobe her in a leisurely fashion. He eyed her with a teasing grin. "Finished yet?"

Quick as a blink, her hands were in the waistband of his shorts, skinning them off his hips to his ankles. When she knelt to remove his shoes, he stopped her. "Uh uh. Leave that to me." His shoes were soon mixed with Lauren's in a heap by the entry door.

He stood naked and aroused for her inspection, eager to peel the clothes from her body, but letting her take time in deciding if he were a fit partner for her royal self. It was the longest few seconds he'd ever endured while she slid her palms over his belly and curled her fingers in the coarse hair above his erection. Obviously satisfied with his contributions to the evening, she placed her arms about his waist, splaying her cool fingers over his tense rear.

Pulling her close, Victor was awed anew with the solid but delicate woman in his arms. That little sound she made would haunt him forever. Sighs of sweet longing that seemed to spill over her lips like wild honey. Gathering her as close as possible, he knew he was the hungry bee that couldn't leave her without taking his fill. *Taste her mouth, the sweetness of her tongue and lips. Taste her slowly. Don't rush her like a wall of flame.* He covered her mouth in a kiss of intense persuasion, holding her firm in his embrace when she trembled. Slipping his hands to her shoulders, he freed her zipper and let the delicate gown drift slowly to the floor.

He moved back a half step to look at her, reeling with desire and anticipation. Perfection was a puny word to describe Lauren. Clad in nothing but ivory silk panties, she took his breath away. Her skin was polished and scented, begging for his caress. How could he have missed the way her small nipples jutted upwards from her high round breasts? Careless man, tonight you'll miss nothing.

Sensing her warm gaze, Victor cupped her chin in his fingers to kiss the corner of her mouth. "Well now," he murmured. "I know for certain I got the better in this gift exchange." His hands moved to her waist to pull her close.

She slid her hand over his rear and then down his thigh, smiling at him with challenge in her eyes. "How do you know? You haven't seen it all yet."

He tilted his head back, his grin wolfish. "Oh, I intend to see it all. Right now."

She laughed and turned away to scamper behind a couch where she stood daring him to pursue her.

He vaulted over the back of the sofa and caught her up in his arms. "I love fox and hound, but I would rather finish unwrapping my goodies."

"Hurry," she whispered. "I think they're melting."

He helped her wrap her legs about his waist, kissing her until she was breathless as he walked a few steps. Her arms clung to his shoulders and clasped him as tightly as she could. She understood his groan of eagerness to dip into the well of pleasure that waited.

She murmured her approval when he dropped to the floor with her. His weight was heavy and delicious as they sank into the depths of the lush carpet. It didn't matter where they were. She just wanted to be with him. When she heard him chuckle, she dug her fingers into his hair, gripping tightly.

"This is no time for fun, mister."

"Yes it is, pussycat." His eyes twinkled with mirth. "It just hit me that we're only a few steps from my bed." He got to his feet, grinning broadly down at her while she perused his lean body.

"Raven. I think you're wrong about our trade." She propped herself on one elbow to stroke her hand over his calf. "You're a hot item."

"Stop pandering to my worst side," he teased. "Come with me, baby."

He took her hand and pulled her up, letting her lean against him. A glorious fire blazed up when their bodies came in full contact. He leapt into the blazing inferno swirling about them, letting it devour all his insignificant plans. Lifting her up in his arms, he carried her toward his room and the call of the wild.

He paused momentarily at the threshold, hoping there were no surprises hidden in corners to blow up this night of pleasure. Before setting her on her feet, he kissed the corners of her mouth. He eyed the panties she still wore and wanted to rip them off.

"Your pleasure is my happiness, beautiful." He nearly choked on his randy thoughts while cupping her breasts in his palms. "What can I do to make you purr?"

Covering his hands with hers, Lauren pressed closer to him and moved her hips against his in a seductive manner. "I think you know what to do." She closed her eyes while he slid her panties from her hips and down her legs, gasping at the touch of his palm brushing her stomach. "Oh yes, you do know what to do."

Being swept up against his chest didn't surprise her, only convinced her she'd never had sex before Victor came into her life. In his arms, she realized she was the keeper of something extraordinarily powerful. Shy? Not for a second. She let herself bloom under his touch. His whispered words said she was spectacular in his eyes, desirable and all he wanted.

Feeling like a drifting feather, Lauren opened her eyes to stare into his gaze of stormy blue she was learning to care for. She lay still beneath his study, smiling at his obvious fascination with her feet. "Go ahead. You know you want to touch it."

He laughed softly, shaking his head. "I have to find out." He leaned over to examine her toes. "I'll be damned."

"I wore it just for your enjoyment." Lauren wiggled her toes, the dainty toe ring glinting in the lamplight.

He moved to the bottom of the bed and took her feet in his hands, gently squeezing. "I've never seen feet so delicious looking or so damned sensual. I have to taste them just like every part of you." Lifting her left foot, he took her toes in his mouth and sucked as if they were a delicacy.

Lauren wriggled in a rush of erotic pleasure. "Raven. You're a tomcat." Bending her leg, she reached down to tangle her fingers deep into his hair. "I'm purring, but I want to yowl."

Her body was alive with new sensations beneath his touch. Everything that was his became hers, causing great celebration in her heart. A thousand years might pass yet she would never lose the sound of his voice, the texture of his hair. The sheets of silk, the very air that moved through the room was hers to hold forever. She drew in a breath that delivered the fragrance of his skin to her tongue and she licked her lips to savor the essence. Overcome with the rapture of her emotions, the sob of elation she had held back passed over her lips with velvet softness.

Instantly he was on his knees and drew her up to straddle his thighs. She liked that, facing him while he touched her. The deep growl in his throat gave her a sense of power when she took his erection in her hand, pleasuring him until he closed his fingers over her hand. Could this really be happening to her? This soaring feeling of flight, giving herself completely and being lifted on the wings of indescribable pleasure.

"You're getting me there too fast, baby." He touched her face, looking at her with a hint of a grin. "Do you have something in mind?"

"I'm ready," she whispered. "Let me do it this time."

"Anything you want." Locking his arms about her waist, he smiled at her attempt to join with him. "I like your idea, kitten."

"I'm so glad you do, Raven." She wriggled forward until the tip of his sex slid into the heated oven she had waiting for him. She glanced up to smile wantonly at him. "I'll get better at this."

"Lauren, it can't get better than this." His hands cupped her bottom in an effort to help her without intrusion. She was making it damned difficult to hold back the explosion building in his body. "I'd be real happy to help you there."

"I know you would, but this time is mine." She was eager to try new things she had never experienced before Victor. He banished the last of her inhibitions with his touch and whispered words of encouragement.

She loved the feel of him against her skin, the weight of him in her hand and the male sounds of pleasure he made while she explored his body. Gripping his shoulders, she eased forward, biting her lip in sheer delight. *What have you found here*, her sirens voice laughed seductively. *Pleasure almost too much to bear, but you can't stop.* She shuddered in the aftermath of a shimmering wave of ecstasy.

In Victor's eyes, she saw her image, the wildly erotic savage she had become. Magically, there were braids in her hair and vivid paint on her cheeks, branding her as huntress claiming her prey.

Lamplight glanced off her golden warrior's body like the glow from leaping flames in a night sky. He was bringing her ecstasy, clasping her against his powerful body, encouraging her to join him. Beneath her hands, she felt his muscles tense in anticipation of the coming earthquake. With her deliberate forward motion his body quickened, filling her with his heat and driving need.

Complete abandon took her in its powerful wings, pushing her to new heights of pleasure, whispering of the rapture to come. They fell back together, hearts pounding as one. In control of the moment, Lauren pressed her palms to his chest, holding him captive beneath her surging body.

Caught up in a storm of bursting heat and runaway passion, she dropped onto his chest to cry out in fulfillment. Victor rolled her onto her back and drove into her, plunging into the scarlet fire that lapped around their bodies, seizing the hot flame to find release from his torture.

Gasping for breath, he eased Lauren down to earth. Kissing her deeply, slowly to tell her she was incredible. He gazed down at her in amazement. She was the powerful one, the one in command, leading him by his libido. Above the roar in his ears, he barely caught her sultry comment.

"I think you had better feed me a snack, Raven if we're going to do this all night."

He chuckled. "Thank God I had those oysters." He groaned, rolling to his side with her.

"Not tired, are you?" She touched the intriguing scar on his cheek. "Is that a battle scar?"

He laughed, catching her hand to kiss her palm. "College hockey. Somebody high-sticked me."

She gently touched the scar. "The dirty goon," she crooned. "Did it hurt?"

"Hurt like hell." Catching her chin in his fingers, he smiled at her. "You have incredible skin. Not a scar or freckle anywhere on your body. Didn't you play when you were a kid?"

"Just lucky, I guess." She raked the damp hair from his forehead. "I was a full-fledged tomboy. Raini was terribly ashamed of me at times."

He stroked her shoulder, grinning as he thought over her comment. "I can't see you as a tomboy. You're just full of life. Maybe Raini is a little too reserved to appreciate your take on life."

Lauren propped on an elbow to look at him. "You seem to know a great deal about my sister's personality."

He busied himself with her hair.

She rubbed his flat belly. "How well do you know Raini?"

Instead of answering her question, he rolled her over onto her back and smoothed her brow with his thumb. "Hmmm. I think I see one freckle."

"That's no answer, Raven." She caught his hand stop his evasive motion.

"Raini's a lovely woman, but I like her sister best." He gave her a crooked grin. "How's that?"

"It'll do for now," she said, pulling him down to lie against her breasts. "You just keep saying the right things, you devil."

He sat up to look at her, wanting to end the game of twenty questions. Discussing Raini would lead to her father. He didn't have a clue what the right thing to say was. He swung his legs off the bed, taking her hands to draw her up with him.

"Now let's see if you always say the right thing." He gazed into her eyes, grinning a little. "Don't you like my first name? I do have one you know."

She tilted her head to one side, smiling warmly up at him. "Yes, I know you do and it's a beautiful name." She reached up to touch his hair. "But you're so wonderfully dark and big. I just can't call you anything else. Raven's much sexier."

He caught her chin in his fingers, and then kissed her softly. "That's fair. Say my name again and I'll show you just how bold I can be."

"You've already shown me, and I'm well satisfied."

"Enough compliments." He went to a stack chest, pulling out two pair of lounge pants and a couple of T-shirts. "I believe you said something about a snack."

She held her hand out, accepting the clothing. "I believe I did," she said, laughing as she held the things up to check their size. "If I keep eating like a horse, I'll be in this size really soon."

"You would be sexy no matter what you weigh." He dropped a kiss on her nose.

"Flattery will get you everywhere." She hugged the things to her breasts. "Now. What are we having?"

"The best omelet in New York." He grinned when he noticed the extra rosiness on her cheeks and chin. Whisker burn. He would shave again for her sake. "That okay with you?"

"That's some snack," she said. "But I'll probably need it." Her smile was like a pixie's that had recently gotten away with something incredibly bad.

"Take your time, baby." He rubbed his chin, waiting until she closed the door to his bathroom before going to the guest bath for a quick shave. A strange flutter played over his gut. Not painful, just a flutter. He was happy. Alone with the woman he couldn't stop thinking about. He felt exceptionally lucky.

Making her an omelet was a thing of pleasure. Not too spicy, not too many onions and don't burn it for God's sake. He stopped cracking eggs into a bowl when she stepped into the kitchen. She had taken the time to cuff the pants up and knot the shirt at her waist. Damn. She was sensational.

"My pajamas never looked like that before." He handed her a

slice of green pepper. "Of course it's the sweet little body wearing them."

She leaned against the counter to watch him. "You know, Raven. You're an awfully large man." Her gaze moved slowly over his lean frame. "But I'm not complaining."

"Good. Can't have my woman dissatisfied."

His woman. Lauren liked the sound of those words. But that was all they were--words he used as casually as whisking eggs in a bowl. *What did you expect? Casual is what you need, not an undying declaration of devotion. Don't get involved in something that won't last. Just keep a lid on your emotions, and he can't hurt you.*

Victor stopped what he was doing and gazed at her with a half smile. "Quiet again?"

She reached out to touch his back, rubbing the solid warmth. "I'm simply awed by your culinary skills. Among other things." Her hand slipped to his rear.

He laid the whisk down and pulled her close. "And I'm completely mesmerized by you."

She sighed with contentment, touching his chin. "You sly devil. You shaved for me."

The need for food was replaced with a deeper hunger, intense and urgent. His kiss relit the flame that demanded quenching. One kiss was never enough between them, never totally satisfied the yearning. This would require time.

Following the wall of fire to its ultimate end, Victor released the knot in her shirt. "You taste so damned good," he growled. "I could do this all night."

She clung to him, weak with the ache to be with him again. Her words were a soft caress. "This will be the first time I've wanted to do this all night."

His smile was wicked. "Lord, I am a lucky man."

Chapter Twelve

Lauren wasn't confused by her surroundings when she looked about the room through half-closed eyes. The scent of heather and warm moss beckoned her to stay in Victor's king-sized bed. It hadn't been long ago that she fell asleep from sheer, blissful exhaustion. She stretched leisurely, smiling when she recalled how they had broken every record in the book and probably set new ones.

Her dreamy thoughts ended with a jolt of reality. What time was it? Where were her clothes? Why was it so quiet? Raven. Where was he? Rolling off the bed, she grabbed the shirt he'd tossed over the back of a chair. Lack of sleep made her head swim as she walked out of the bedroom. She followed the aroma of freshly brewed coffee, the clink of china leading her toward the kitchen. At the threshold, she pulled up short, unsure who was in the kitchen. The image of a robust woman named Rosie popped into her mind. She peeked around the doorway. Relief flooded through her to find a pair of dark blue eyes observing her with warm welcome in their depths.

"Hello, beautiful," Victor said, giving her a slow, admiring once over.

Her hair was in a tumbled, mindless knot and her eyes and lips were swollen, but he made her feel beautiful. Trying to smooth her hair with her hands, she grinned at him. "I don't always look this good in the morning." Her smile was a little crooked. This was a first for her; a morning after with a man who'd had kept her awake all night. She knew with a bit of coaxing that she would hop back into his bed and spend the day there with him.

He set his cup on the counter, pulling her into the nest between his legs. What a beautiful woman she was. Even more so after they had spent the night in erotic pleasure seeking. He knew he was becoming thoroughly infatuated with Lauren Rose. It had to end. But not yet. He held her face in his hands to kiss her lips, taking his fill before Eden vanished.

Lauren looked at him in question, touching the knot of his tie. "A suit and tie?" She took a sip of his coffee. "Is this a new way of making love?" She had tried to sound amused, but she recognized the change of wardrobe meant he was resuming his normal routine. "Let me run home and get my trench coat and red heels."

He caught her close, nuzzling her neck. "I'd love to play any game with you, baby, but I have to go make a few bucks today." He inhaled the scent of her hair. "Why don't you sleep in this morning, then let me take you to lunch around one or so?"

Lauren grimaced. "You're going to work? Lord. Seems like I have forgotten that little detail." She raked her hair with both hands in mild frustration. "If I don't get my rear back home soon, I won't have a job to go back to."

He heard what she'd said but couldn't let go of his idea of having her around. "Okay. I admit it. I'm trying to make you forget that job for my own selfish reasons." His grin was mischievous. "Now. How about our lunch?"

She hugged his neck, nibbling his earlobe until he made his familiar sound of surrender. "If I hadn't promised Raini I would help with her latest charity project, I would take you up on lunch." She patted his thigh, pulling back a little.

Inhaling deeply, Victor let her go. The woman had made up her mind to leave, and he would sound like a jerk if he said any more. "I'll drive you home, baby."

She shook her head, giving him a bewitching grin. "I don't think so, Raven. She's not going to be happy with me, and I don't want you to hear my answers to her grilling."

Victor reran her comment in his mind. He doubted she was overly concerned with her sister's questioning. Lauren was her own woman and answered to no one. He felt a bit of unbidden pleasure at the thought. "Okay. If you insist on leaving me, I'll call downstairs and have the doorman order your taxi."

She gave him an arch look, carrying his hand to cup her breast. "You didn't ask for it, but I'm leaving my Malibu phone number." She looked thoughtful for a moment. "You can call whenever you have time or the inclination."

A sip of his coffee and she hurried off to his bedroom. Turning his cup around in its saucer, he felt the squeeze of uncertainty in his gut. *Did she want him to call her at home? Or was she just being Lauren? Hell. It hadn't sounded like she was going to be grabbing the phone on the first ring in anticipation hoping it would be him.* Disappoint threatened to smother him. Somehow he hadn't expected to feel so empty at her departure. If he were smart, he would leave before she did. But he wasn't feeling especially intelligent at the moment. The muffled sounds coming from his bedroom meant she was hurriedly gathering her things, preparing to take up her life again without a hitch. *Wasn't that what he wanted? To be her lover for a while, then move on to someone new? Hell. He didn't know what he wanted.* Then, she was back looking like a dew-kissed daisy, showing no sign of their exuberant lovemaking. It was damned clear she wasn't worried about him or his bleeding ego.

"Raven." She stood waiting, gripping her evening bag in both hands. "Aren't you going to walk me out?"

"Of course." He picked up his keys and wallet. "I'm right behind you."

Outside in the bright sunlight, Victor waited with Lauren until her taxi arrived. He couldn't think of clever things to say or shake off the feeling of dread at her coming departure. He couldn't help looking into her eyes for some clue that she wasn't really going to abandon him for some job thousands of miles away. She was no help, smiling a little when the hack pulled up.

He knew it was a mistake, but he had to touch her one last time before she got into that damned cab. She looked startled when he caught her against him and kissed her with hot abandon, leaning her over his arm in a grand flourish. Her arms hung limp at her sides while he took his fill. Slowly lifting his head, he gave her a crooked smile. "So you don't forget me, Lauren."

"I could never do that," she whispered. "Never."

And then she was gone, turning to look back at him through the taxi's rear window. He didn't know how long he stood in the sweltering heat, gazing off in the direction of Lauren's departure.

The doorman tapped him on the shoulder to get his attention. "Everything all right, Mister Raven?"

Victor smiled wryly. Sure, everything was all right. He just didn't know how he was supposed to live with the emptiness that consumed him. He wanted to complain loudly, but the doorman wouldn't understand if he said the lady had gotten away with his heart. Instead, he handed the doorman a tip. "Everything's dandy. Just dandy."

* * * *

Lauren fully expected to hear the security alarm sound off when she stepped into the entry hall. She took her shoes off and glanced around. Well, she thought, the coast seems to be clear. You just might evade Mother Raini. She took three steps when she heard Raini's footsteps coming down the hall. Give it up. She was waiting for you. When her sister approached her, Lauren shrugged her shoulders and smiled.

"Hi." She dropped her shoes and handbag onto a hall table. "It was so quiet, I thought you might be sleeping."

"Hi yourself. You're just in time to help me close boxes." Raini was holding several articles of clothing.

"I told you I'd help you. Why didn't you wait?" Lauren sagged under the weight of guilt. She'd let her sister down.

"I didn't do much." Raini smiled in a satisfied manner. "I'm afraid they're not very neatly packed."

"I know you too well to believe that." Those damned boxes were probably gift-wrapped.

"Want coffee?" Raini held a sweater up, examining it closely. "I made a coffeecake."

Lauren relaxed. Here was an opening to discuss something besides her slipping in like a cat burglar. "Yum. I can hardly wait." She dreaded eating the cake, privy to her sister's way of ruining the simplest recipe. "I'll bet it's wonderful."

Raini hugged Lauren, then kissed her cheek. "Adam left most of his. He said he wasn't hungry." She smiled wistfully. "He may be right about hiring a cook."

"He's just trying to be a good husband." Lauren figured she should help Adam out by agreeing with him. "I'll have some of that cake as soon as I change."

Lauren grabbed a pair of walking shorts and a T-shirt from her closet, and then got into the shower. Lifting her arms, she inhaled the last of Victor's scent before it washed away forever. The depression she'd been fighting came home with full force.

Bracing her hands on the cool tile wall, she closed her eyes, gritting her teeth to stem the desire to bawl. *Stop it. Stop it. He's too complicated for you--too much everything. You're not ready for anything more than a fling. You're on the rebound. That's crap. You're a fool. You care for him.* She was physically weak after letting her heart hear the truth.

Twenty minutes later, she went back to the kitchen and sat on a stool at the counter, eyeing the cake Raini had made. She sampled a small piece, forcing herself to chew and swallow.

Raini wore an expectant expression. "How is it?"

Reaching for a second bite, Lauren said the kindest thing she could think of. "You've been practicing."

"It's out of a box," Raini admitted with a grin.

"Box?" Lauren's brows lifted. "All those preservatives?"

"A few won't hurt you." Raini leaned against the counter to study her sister. "What did you have for dinner?"

"Dinner?" Lauren didn't want to discuss her evening with Victor.

"Didn't he feed you?"

Lauren swallowed hard, ignoring the question. "Yep. This is really good."

"I take it he didn't." Raini straightened her back, crossing her arms at her waist.

Lauren wiped her fingers on one of Raini's fancy napkins. "For Pete's sake. Why don't you just come out and ask me?"

"You're being awfully touchy, Lauren."

"And you're being nosey." Lauren wasn't going to volunteer any information.

Raini exhaled noisily. "Not nosey. Concerned."

"About what?"

"Your safety and happiness."

"Raini, I'm old enough to spend the night with a man." Lauren let her words flow out of frustration and weariness of being dictated to. "He fed me sinfully fattening things and we didn't worry about preservatives. Later, he took me to a waterfront dive where we did dirty dancing. After that, we went to his low rent flat and had hot, sweaty sex--all night long."

Raini's face paled except for the bright splotches of color on her cheeks. "That's more than I needed to know."

Lauren grimaced, hating the nasty way she had spoken to her sister. "You don't need to know anything about it, Raini. Why do you keep butting in?"

Raini reached for the napkin Lauren had wadded up in her hand. "I'm only thinking of you."

"That's not an answer." Lauren swiped the napkin out of Raini's reach. "Don't tell me you and Adam didn't spend a few nights together before that big hullabaloo wedding of yours. I found your birth control pills."

Raini opened her mouth to speak, but laughed instead. "I don't suppose you took any of them?"

Getting to her feet, Lauren went to her sister and hugged her tightly. "I had my own you silly thing. Now, let's get to those boxes."

On the way to the den, Raini explained that the work was almost finished. "See. Just several to close."

Lauren started to tape one of the boxes shut, but stopped when she noticed an evening gown she'd made for Raini laying among the clothing being given away.

"What's this?" she asked. Picking the beautiful gown up in two fingers, she gave her sister an accusing glare.

"It's not my style. I..." Raini stuttered after being caught in the unforgivable act of discarding her sister's gift.

"It's the best thing you own." Lauren tossed the gown back into the box. She didn't really care what Raini did with the gown. She just needed to get away from her. She tried to escape to the living room.

"You had several calls this morning." Raini followed close on her heels. "One from Swanson's."

"Can't wait for me to get back to work. I'll call them in a minute." Lauren gazed at Raini, waiting to hear whom the other call had been from.

"The others were from Justin."

Lauren covered her mouth with her hand, holding back a torrent of vile comments describing her feelings about Justin. She swallowed her anger and smiled at Raini. "As you told me, that's more than I wanted to know."

"Maybe you should reconsider mending old relationships, Lauren."

Lauren practically guffawed and threw her hands up in resignation. "I see where this is going." She walked toward her bedroom, turning at the door to look at Raini. "You expect me to reconcile with Justin? After the beating I took from him? What if I said I don't love him, never did love him."

"I can't believe that. After all the time you two spent together, the wedding plans."

Lauren didn't want to hear any more and plunged into the business of shocking her naive sister. "I always faked orgasm with Justin you know. A reconciliation isn't going to happen."

Raini crimped her lips. "What do you expect to gain from your liaison with Victor?"

"Raven isn't a liaison. He's not ashamed to be seen with me." Lauren leaned against the doorframe. "He makes me happy. Why do you resent the fact I'm seeing a real man for the first time in my life?"

Raini hesitated, and then spoke wearily. "I want you to be happy, but you're probably in for an enormous letdown. Right now you're new and exciting to him. But if he sticks to his normal routine, he'll simply end it and you'll be wondering why. He's left more than one woman with an aching heart."

Lauren felt the sting of hurt. "What if he falls in love with me?"

She smiled at her stunned sister. "Could happen, you know."

She walked to the bed in her room and plopped down, grimacing when she thought over her sleazy comments to Raini. She felt low and was consumed with loneliness. You want to be with Victor. She scoffed at her overpowering yearning. You've gotten yourself into a real pickle, walking off a pier, you idiot. Better start swimming because Victor's no lifeguard.

Raini peeked around the door. "You still upset with me?"

Lauren blinked back the start of tears. "Sure I am, but I don't know what I'd do without you."

Raini walked to where Lauren sat and touched her hair. "I don't know when it happened, but somewhere along the way you became a beautiful woman. It makes me feel a little lonely. What happened to the little terror that used to do such rotten things to me?"

Lauren laughed, tossing a pillow at her sister. "Oh, she's still around."

That evening while they had dinner, Lauren had a hard time paying attention to the small talk going on. Her thoughts were with Victor. What was he doing? No, don't go there. You'd probably be hurt if you knew. She did know there was emptiness in her that refused to go away.

Adam tapped Lauren's hand to get her attention. "You're not eating. You're either not feeling well or you're in love." He laughed at his own humor.

"Neither, Mister Know-it-all," she said. "I was trying to figure out how to squeeze all the things I've bought into two suitcases."

"You're a woman," he said. "You'll figure it out."

"I suppose I will." She placed her hand over her desert dish when Adam tried to spoon more Jell-o into it. "I'm going to the cemetery in the morning to put flowers on Dad's grave. Then I'm out of here and out of your hair."

"We were hoping you would decide to stay in New York permanently." Adam refilled her wine glass. "We miss you when your gone, Lauren."

Raini set her glass down, adding her bit of encouragement. "It's something to think about, Lauren. There are dozens of design houses here that would hire you now that you have some working experience."

"I left here because I couldn't get a job on my own merit. Frankly, I am really happy in Malibu." She sighed wistfully. "I do miss being able to see you two whenever I want. But I'm staying where I am for a while."

While he stirred his coffee, Adam smiled at Lauren. "You always know what you want and never sway from your ideals." He leaned back in his chair to gaze at her. "That's why I was so thunderstruck to hear you were seeing Victor Raven."

Lauren bristled at his comment. "Oh. And what bothers you about that?" Damn. Another person telling her how to live her life.

"It doesn't bother me, Lauren. On the contrary, Victor's a friend and a fine man." Adam gave her a crooked grin. "It came as a shock simply because..."

"Adam." Quick as lightening, Raini's hand flashed out to grip Adam's wrist. "She doesn't need your counseling."

Lauren narrowed her eyes, leaning forward to stare into Adam's eyes. "Let the man speak," she said flatly. "I'm missing something here."

Adam looked at Raini, then at Lauren, his brow furrowing a little. "It surprised me, that's all."

Sighing, Lauren lay her spoon on her plate. "You're all surprised that an adult male finds me attractive." She smiled at her brother-in-law. "It's okay. You can't help it if you still see me as Justin's victim."

"Lauren, I apologize if I seemed to be intruding in your personal life." Adam stood up to hug her shoulders. "Victor's particularly lucky to have met you."

Lauren grinned at him. "Stop trying to get on my good side." She knew Adam would never say or do anything to hurt her.

Raini reached out to move the Jell-o that had begun to melt into red soup. "Let's have our coffee in the living room." She stood up and tapped Lauren on the cheek. "I think you'll find a job here. Your designs speak for themselves."

"Is that why you were tossing the gown I made for you?"

"I've discarded better ones."

"In your dreams." Lauren got up to follow her sister into the living room. "You wouldn't know fashion if it was hung from your nose."

Adam walked in to take his favorite chair. He dropped the newspaper he had been holding, raising his hands up in a plea for peace. "Can we please have no more quarreling?"

Raini corrected her husband. "We're not quarreling--we're talking."

Plopping down on the sofa, Lauren touched Raini's leg with her foot. "You were saying--about the gown?"

"I said it was lovely. When are you making another one for me?"

"The day you admit you have no taste."

Chapter Thirteen

Lauren heard a car door being slammed shut. She paid little attention and kept her head down, giving the person time to leave the area.

She didn't want company and busied herself puttering with the flowers she had brought to her father's burial plot. While she waited, she dipped her hand into her pocket, drawing out a smooth stone of jasper. She stood up to place it on the headstone, gasping in surprise when she saw a man standing several feet away.

"Justin."

"Lauren." He smiled at her. "Raini told me you were out here."

"Did she?" Lauren's tone of voice was bland.

He stood looking at the stone she had added to the others on the monument. "Yeah. I've been meaning to come out here for a while."

Her resentment flared. "Why, for Pete's sake? It's nothing to you."

"Lauren. I care." He tried to touch her hand. "We were close once."

"Not close enough, apparently." She dusted her palms together. "What do you really want?"

He looked at the toes of his shoes. "You're never going to forgive me, are you?"

"You're trying to make me say all the ugly things I had stored up for months." She eyed him with icy reproach. "Stop wasting your time. Don't you understand? You no longer matter."

Justin gazed at her with a hint of a smile. "It's not a waste of time to renew old romances."

She bit her tongue. The loathsome character assumed she wanted him and was playing hard to get. "You wouldn't have the foggiest idea what romance is. We certainly didn't have one."

She took several steps toward her car that was parked at the curb. "If you'll excuse me, Doctor Taylor, I have to be somewhere."

He reached for her arm. "Lauren ... wait. A minute longer, please. You know I want you and I made a bad choice."

"That's too bad, Justin. I feel nothing but contempt for you." She turned her shoulder to avoid his touch, walking a few steps away from him. "I'm leaving. Will you step aside?"

He frowned darkly at her. "You're willing to throw away all we had? It's your pride, isn't it?"

She gazed at him with disbelief. "Right now I'm the happiest woman in the world. I was spared the grief of marrying you." She shook her head, brushing by him to get to her car.

"It's Victor Raven, isn't it?" His face contorted into a sneer. "Don't be a damned fool, Lauren. He's using you. There are things you should know about him. Things you won't like."

Lauren opened the car door and tossed her handbag onto the seat. How ironic. He was ignoring the fact he had been unfaithful and unspeakably cruel. Now he blamed Victor for her refusal to resume their tepid affair. She wanted to slug him. She got into the car, slamming the door. When he leaned on the fender, she grimaced with disgust.

"Move your carcass, Justin. I wouldn't want to squash you like a bug." The urge to scare him was powerful.

He stayed where he was. "Get out and talk to me."

She turned the key in the ignition, revving the engine several times. She was a little disappointed when he moved out of harms way.

"You'll come crawling back to me one day, Lauren." He yelled after her as she pulled away from the curb. "And I damned well won't have you."

She hit the brakes, backing up to where he stood and calmly met his angry gaze. "My only regret is that it took three years for you to tell me that."

She drove away, glancing back in the rear view mirror. There was nothing Justin could say to alter her feelings for Victor.

* * * *

It wasn't going well. Those everyday little things that were normally done without much thought were becoming difficult to remember and carry out. Victor leaned back in his chair propping his feet on his desk. His eyes were closed, but he wasn't sleeping. He was trying to collect his thoughts.

He knew the source of his memory lapses and sudden indifference to his daily routine. She was in California and damned well not forgetting to read mail or get a haircut. It had been seven weeks since he had seen her and that damned emptiness in the pit of his stomach couldn't be filled.

He stood up, sauntered to the window and stared out at the endless sea of buildings spreading out below him. He turned his head and looked at the calendar on his desk. It was October. He dreaded the coming winter. He looked out the window again and braced his palm on the sill. He needed a new diversion. Going out to meet someone new didn't hold the attraction it once had. In fact, none at all. Rubbing his chin, he thought of his little black book. Then he snorted in derision. *You can't find your little black book.*

He heard a phone ringing in the outer office. The sound reminded him of Lauren's card. He knew the number by heart having looked at it countless times. He laughed at himself, picturing the once pristine card that now was frayed from excessive handling. *Why didn't he call her? The answer became more blurred by the day. Ties. Don't be ridiculous. She isn't interested in an exclusive relationship with you. Admit it. You're afraid she isn't interested in seeing you. But you miss her. Call her.*

His secretary opened the door, her voice shattering the silence in the room.

"Mrs. Raven is waiting to see you."

He glanced over his shoulder shrugging. "Why not? The day's gone to hell anyway."

"Yes sir." She left as quietly as she had arrived.

He turned around to see Jonelle walk into his office in her usual commanding way. The scent of her perfume and jangle of layered gold bracelets announced her arrival. She glanced about the room in what he thought was a predatory way. Flop. There went her suitcase-style handbag on top of the irreplaceable documents on his desk. She reached into the depths of her bag, pulling out a pack of cigarettes.

"Don't light that in here," he said. "There's a smoking area outside the building." He glowered at the cigarette that was poised near her lips. "I thought you'd given that up."

She shrugged. "You're certainly in a rare mood, Victor." She smiled at him before dropping the cigarette into the wastebasket beside his desk. "Don't frown so. I don't do this around Rachel."

He gave her a brief smile of annoyance, the corners of his mouth lifting slightly. He felt the urge to snarl, but tamped the desire down. "What brings you here?" he asked, figuring there was only one answer to his question. Money.

"School clothing for Rachel." She brushed at the sleeve of her red jacket.

He rested his hands on his hips, gazing at her speculatively. "Jonelle. She wears a uniform to school."

"She also wears shoes, socks, undergarments and a coat. Do you want her to look like a ragamuffin?"

"Of course not." He went to his desk and took out a checkbook. "How much?"

"I'm redecorating her room as well." Jonelle searched in her handbag until she found a gold cased tube of lipstick. She took her time applying a fresh layer of scarlet to her full lips. After checking her appearance in a mini mirror attached to the case, she pulled a tissue from the cavernous depths of her purse. "That takes money."

He had observed her ritual with little interest, remembering Jonelle had always put her appearance before all else, including money. "And your account is at ground zero. I'm making this a nice round number." He filled in the blank spaces on the check and ripped it off the pad and placed it in her hand.

She glanced at the check. "This will help," she said. "While the decorators are working, I'll have to miss my weekend with Rachel."

"Of course." He smiled wryly. "Is there something else, Jonelle?"

"I have to ask. What's wrong with you?"

"Wrong? Absolutely nothing."

"Hmm. That explains your non-combative attitude," She dropped the check into her handbag.

"You know I could never do battle with you, Jonelle."

"I'm not speaking of myself, dear." She gave him a speculative smile. "I think you've finally met someone who has tamed the tiger into a kitten."

"Excuse me," he said. "I wasn't listening."

Jonelle tapped her cheek, cocking her head to one side. "You always could do that. Shut me out at will." She looked closely at him. "You're a fabulous looking man, Victor. I'm not surprised you have a young innocent baying at your heels."

With calm deliberation, Victor replaced the cap on his pen and dropped it onto his desk. How was he to answer that leading comment? The rumor mill must be grinding again. No answer was best he decided. Talk about Jonelle. It was her favorite subject.

"So what's the new décor going to be this time?" He got up, pointedly walking to the door. "Rachel's deep into Barbie things now."

"All right. I'm leaving, darling." She waited for him to open the door for her. "We've decided on chintz,"

"I'm sure," he said drolly.

She placed her hand on the door before he could open it. "There's a birthday party to plan and..."

"I know. You'll be needing further monetary assistance."

She patted his cheek and let him open the door. "You're so perceptive, dear." She strolled out of his office, apparently content with her latest windfall.

"Jonelle." He followed her to the reception area. "What are your plans for the holidays?"

"Don't tell me you want to spend them with me." She smiled at him, obviously pleased with his look of disgust.

"I'm speaking about our allotted time with Rachel." He wondered how much of an argument she would put up when he made his suggestion. "It's my Thanksgiving with her and since she'd be out of school for several weeks--I thought you might be willing to let her spend all of the Christmas vacation with me."

"Victor." Her expression was one of pure amusement. "And you wonder where Rachel gets her ability to connive? She spent last Christmas with you and Thanksgiving." Jonelle arranged her scarf about her throat. "Looks like you will be spending the holidays alone this year. That is, unless you want to go to with us to my parent's home in Connecticut."

"Thank you, but no." He grinned at the mental image her words had evoked in his mind. If nothing had changed, and he was positive it hadn't, her parents would see to it he understood the depth of their dislike for him. After all, in their eyes he was the downfall of their baby girl, the monster that had impregnated her and demanded she have other children. That was their twisted version of the sorry match between him and Jonelle. "I'd have to take a food taster to survive."

"They hate you, darling, but not quite enough to murder you." She glanced around the plush reception area and then smiled at him. "Who--I mean, what will keep you busy over the long, bleak holidays?"

"I'll stay occupied."

"I'm sure of that. Where can I reach you if the need arises?"

"The west coast."

"The west coast?" Jonelle arched her brows. "Blond or brunette?"

"Business. Pleasure if I sew up the deal that's in progress there."

She tsked, shaking her head. "Why Victor. You're getting positively dull. You mustn't disappoint the ladies."

He gave her a half smile. "The only one I don't want to disappoint is Rachel."

Jonelle gazed at him with interest. "I can't believe it has finally happened."

He'd always found her fondness for drama aggravating. He was more interested in getting his desk cleared than her snippet of gossip. "You can speak your mind, Jonelle. We're not trying to please each other."

"All right." She leaned toward him, practically whispering. "I believe you are in love for the first time."

He didn't allow the shock to register on his face. In love, he grimaced inwardly. No damned way. That profound statement coming from the woman who saw being in love as a weakness made him stiffen his spine. No use letting her make more of this conversation than necessary.

"You know you were my first love, Jonelle."

She smiled knowingly at him. "Yes dear, but certainly not your last." She was still smiling when she finally left.

When he was alone, Victor went back to his desk and sat down. His fingers tapped the pull of a drawer several times before he opened it. He reached inside and drew out the treasure it held. One expensive silver hair clasp. He turned the bit of feminine finery over in his fingers, enjoying the way sunlight struck a fiery reflection off it. He smiled wryly, closing his fingers around the cool metal.

He groaned aloud. "Maybe I'm not in love, but Lauren, I think I'm a damned fool over you."

Chapter Fourteen

Lauren bunched her shoulders together and leaned over the drawing board in her cubicle. She folded the memo that had been in her work area when she arrived that morning. Just the company's way to reinforce the electronic mail they had sent everyone at the studio, announcing that six weeks from that day, there would be no more Swanson's.

She glanced around the informally run studio. Several of the young designers stood huddled in a private conversation. She didn't have to hear their words to know they were talking about losing their jobs. Lauren felt sorry for the young woman that wept. She personally wouldn't be hurt financially like some of the others, just emotionally wounded. When she had first heard the rumor of the closing, she had felt like howling. But her resilient nature wouldn't allow her the luxury of self-pity.

The young women broke off their chitchat when Avery Swanson strolled through the main door way. He wasn't smiling as he stopped to speak to them before approaching her work area. Intuition alerted Lauren the big moment had arrived for the official announcement about the closing.

"Good morning, Avery." She swallowed hard, trying to sound cheerful.

"Morning, Lauren." He glanced at the doodles on her sketchpad and smiled wryly. "Nice work."

She darted a glance at the nonsensical scribbles on her sketchpad and grinned sheepishly. "I was just putting the finishing touches on some things." She wasn't a skillful liar and couldn't look straight at him. "Did you want to see me about the last sketches I gave you?"

"The sketches were great. We'll talk about them later." He rubbed the back of his neck. "I'm asking everyone to come into the conference room for a quick meeting."

Her heart beat out of sync several times. "Right now?" Her sensible voice chimed in warning her to get a grip. *If you feel like crying, have the grace to wait until you're alone.*

"Now, if you don't mind." He turned and walked toward the conference room.

Lauren picked up her coffee cup and followed him. The room was filling fast. She found an empty chair and sat beside the newest member of the staff. The brunette smiled at her, and then went back to fiddling with her hair.

"Okay, everyone. Listen up." Avery sat on the edge of the huge table, looking around at the faces of his employees. "You've all seen the letter I posted on the bulletin board and have each gotten your own copy." He hesitated while looking at the faces of the silent group.

Like her coworkers, Lauren sat forward. She set her cup down, wiping at the splash of coffee that dribbled down the side.

"Because of you, the real success of this studio, we have an enviable reputation and it hasn't been missed by an outside corporation. The offer they've made on the firm is one I can't pass up, especially now that my wife wants to go back to England to be with her gravely ill mother."

An immediate buzz erupted. Buyout. Selling. To Lauren that meant unemployment.

She sat back in her chair barely hearing the mix of voices whirling about her head. Avery was saying something about the offer coming at a good time and how his employees had always made him proud. This is real irony, she thought. You left home to find work and now, you'll probably be going back there to find work. Maybe you could be someone's secretary.

She grimaced slightly. Her typing skills alone would get her canned. Glancing at Avery, she realized he was a great boss that understood creative blocks and the need to have some space to yourself. She hadn't really appreciated him enough until now. He held his hands up, obviously wanting to add to his announcement.

"Now, I know you're all thinking negative thoughts right now, but just calm down." He glanced at the notes in his hand and swallowed hard. "I've sent out word about our closing and we've already gotten good feedback on new positions for all of you." He held a large sheet of paper up to emphasize his meaning. "The buyer wants to keep most of the current program we have going, add it to their own line. A shot in the butt for them if you will." He chuckled.

"That really sounds promising, Avery, but I design for the beach combers and surfers." The comment from a young designer was followed by mutters of agreement. A second comment startled Lauren into giving her complete attention to what was being said.

"I'm from California. The east coast isn't for me."

The east coast. The very place she had run from seemed her only choice now. Her heart thudded in distress at the thought of going through the disappointing search again.

He rolled up the papers that he held, adding a last comment. "I know you've all gotten email notification from the head office, but I want to make sure you get all the information you need. I've posted all the particulars on the bulletin board. It should answer any questions you may have. If any of you have problems of a personal nature, come to my office and we'll talk." He looked at his watch. "I want to add my thanks to all of you for the fantastic things you've done here. You're the best."

He took a deep breath before smiling at the somber group. "Okay people. For the next six weeks, we're still Swanson's. If you want your designs in the final showing, you'll have to hustle. But let's have some fun while we're still here."

Lauren didn't have anything to say. She didn't like feeling separated from the security and real purpose this job had given her. Where was she going to find another job? She was an unknown entity and considered a huge risk by the old design houses. The entrenched designers jealously guarded the door against interlopers like her. Her eyes blinked as her survival voice tickled her brain. You're damned well not going to be the one pinning patterns on cloth in some factory.

She stayed in her chair, not taking part in the melee that surged around Avery. She waited until the room emptied before seeking him out for a private word.

She gestured toward the crumpled notes he carried. "That must have been rough."

He gave her a tired smile. "Toughest thing I've ever done." He glanced around at the people that were slowly going back to their work areas. "I hope you all understand my reason for accepting the buyout offer."

She touched his arm. "I'm sure everyone does." She exhaled softly and found the proper words to express her self. "I've enjoyed working here, Avery. Thanks for giving me a chance."

He grinned at her. "Just a stepping stone for you, Lauren." He quickly fell back into a business mode. "If you want to make alterations on what you've done, make them as soon as possible."

"Alterations?" Her mind was racing with the seemingly millions of details that would need to be sewn up. "Are you saying the spring showing is still scheduled?"

"Like I said, this is still Swanson's." He gestured toward the showroom door. "Give it your best shot, Lauren. The biggest names in fashion buying will be here for our last show."

"I know and that scares me." She bit her lip forgetting it was a habit she was trying to break. "I've waited for this for years, and now I'm not sure I'm ready."

"This could be the break you need, Lauren. Give real consideration to a job in New York if this firm offers it. Okay?"

She almost winced, remembering the conciliatory jobs she had been offered. But he was showing concern and she responded with a smile. "Of course I will."

That evening, on her way home, she thought about stopping at a fast food place for a burger and large fries. She decided against it, remembering the food in her fridge going to waste. When she pulled into the driveway of her house, she was struck by the idea she would probably have to give up her little sanctuary.

Her routine never varied. The first thing she did when she went into the house was sort through the mail. Bills, magazines and something in a fancy envelope from Raini. What was she expecting, a long hot love letter from Victor? Yes, damn it, she was. He had her address.

She decided to stop beating herself up, remembering she had been the one who had laughed gleefully in the face of common sense. No commitment for her. No man would chisel a place in her life again. Sagging under the weight of disappointment, she tossed the mail onto the kitchen counter.

After checking out the contents of the refrigerator, she went to the window and opened it wide. The surf lapping up on the beach held her attention for a while, the sound of the waves always easing her tension. She sometimes strolled along the beach watching the seagulls, but not this evening. The mood wasn't right. Maybe she'd grill something. Too much trouble and she had lost her appetite. She wound up throwing some lettuce into a bowl and sloshing some dressing on top of it.

Needing some noise in the quiet house, she turned on the television. She grabbed the remote, going through the full run of channels until she came to one of those fluffy entertainment shows. Forking a bite of lettuce into her mouth, she watched the parade of beautiful people that were caught on film at a New York fundraiser of some kind. She was only interested in the fashions the women were wearing until the camera panned to a spectacular couple that had been cornered for a few words.

It wasn't the beautiful redhead Lauren stared at. Pulling her feet up to sit in a crouched position on the couch, she stared at the television screen. Raven. Exactly as she remembered him, completely in his element, his damned hand plastered on that--woman's naked back. Well, not exactly plastered but in an awfully friendly way. He appeared to be having a grand old time if his easy smile and casual stance spoke for his mood. Damn. He wasn't sitting home, eating bland food. He sure wasn't turning down dates or wearing sackcloth and ashes.

She threw the remote to the end of the couch, fighting the urge to scream bloody murder. The man who had once made her feel like the queen of Sheba had just downsized her to Orphan Annie. Damn. She went to the fridge and pulled out her stash of Ho-Ho's and ate three of the sweet treats while composing a half dozen résumé's. While she was at it, she penned a long letter to Raini, telling her she might be coming home to stay if things didn't work out in California. She didn't mention the pain of defeat or the ache in her heart. After all, she had brought it on herself.

In the following weeks, Lauren kept busy finalizing the endless details of getting things ready for the last showing. She had managed to not think about Victor more than once every half hour. She knew it was a good thing no one expected her to create anything at that time. She didn't have a thought in her head anyone else would be interested in.

Yes, she did have one and it was all consuming and maddening. No matter where she was or what the subject might be, that damned film clip featuring Victor as the star haunted her. He was dating. She was traumatized and lonely. How had this happened to her? She wasn't supposed to be longing for anyone. Not that she had given anyone else a chance. All the men she knew had stopped asking her out because of her repeated turndowns.

Opening the daily mail didn't lighten her mood either. The resumes she had prepared and sent out resulted in four job offers, all of them from firms in New York. All of them from friends of her father's. None of them had any thing to do with designing.

* * * *

Lauren was nervous, hurrying from one model to the other, checking for stray bits of thread or an incomplete zip up. This show was her one shot at getting her work recognized. What was taking so long? Waiting for the show to begin added to her case of jitters. She gripped a clipboard in her hands to hide their shaking. At last the flattering spotlights bloomed on the runway and the crowd noise became a hushed murmur. Disco music blared from hidden speakers. For the first time, the music failed to make her want to dance.

She leaned against the runway wall for support, pressing her palm to her forehead. Over the music she heard her unusually quiet woman's voice began to nag. *Snap out of it dearie. Look out there. Those people sitting in the bobbing spotlights hold your future in their hands. Straighten your spine and paste a smile on your numb lips.*

Dragging in a gulp of air, Lauren moved out into the aisle. She didn't want to hear their comments. But she had to see what their facial expressions revealed. Moving to an advantageous spot out of the lights, she gave the crowd a quick scan. Avery had been right. She recognized dozens of faces as world known clothiers. Damn. She couldn't read anything into their expressions. They weren't paying attention to what was being shown or was she being paranoid. Damn. One of her gowns was coming up next and she wanted to yell at them to be quiet.

Cold dread squeezed her heart but she moved into the pit with the buyers. If nothing else, she would be able to say she had been part of the fashion world for a while. She looked up to see a brunette strutting down the runway in a quilted lounge outfit she had dreamed up. She didn't remember it being listed to show. The aqua and white outfit was gorgeous and the crowd seemed to be taking note. She was grateful the model knew to twirl in the ankle length duster to show off its lavish floral lining.

Her heart pumped furiously when a single blue spotlight highlighted her masterpiece. An ivory skinned model with flaxen hair stood in regal beauty for a moment, and then moved slowly down the runway looking properly bored. The gown was exquisite, made of sensual black crepe to hug a woman's breasts and hips. The draped skirt fell in soft folds to the floor in a midnight black pool.

Lauren couldn't watch any longer. She was either going to faint or be ill. She was in a quandary of emotions, thinking she heard applause for her work and whispered comments about the designer. Calm down, calm down. She tried to think clearly but now she was experiencing something new. Hallucinations. Of course she was dreaming, but the man standing at the back of the hall was a dead ringer for ... Raven. Her heart hammered in joyful thuds. It really is him. What's he doing here? It doesn't matter why, you idiot. Her heart took joyful flight.

The urge to run to him was powerful, but she didn't lose control. She shivered with excitement. Was he looking at her or was she simply too overwhelmed with spiraling emotions to think clearly.

Her heart beat in her throat when his stormy blue gaze settled on her. He seemed startled to see her. His expression had altered from surprise to warm recognition. She touched her throat feeling her racing pulse beneath her fingers. *Hang the cool reserve woman. Go to the well and drink your fill.*

Answering her urgent woman's voice, she took several steps. She stumbled over someone's feet. A friendly hand caught her elbow, steadying her. She heard someone urgently calling her name. "Lauren."

"Lauren. Your black crepe is being brought back for a curtain call. Look."

"What?" Lauren swayed slightly, consumed with excitement and panic. "What do they want?" she asked, blindly looking at the hands reaching down to her from the runway.

She heard applause and the calls for her to step into the spotlight. She looked toward the back of the room, wanting desperately to be with Victor. The dozen different scents of perfume made her ill. No, it was her charged nerves and raging heartbeat. Several of the models walked her to the stage and left her alone to stand in the brilliant light. She laughed aloud when her arms were filled with a bouquet of red roses. For the first time in her life, she was speechless while the buyers, models and designers crowded around to congratulate her. She swiped at the tears of happiness that blurred her vision, thinking she wasn't going to survive the intensity of the moment.

The clamor around Lauren forced her to acknowledge that there were other people on earth, that she had to forget the magic that stood just out of reach at the back of the showroom. The houselights were being turned on and she breathed deeply, assured Victor was still there, smiling at her, waiting for her. Reluctantly, she turned away from him to accept several more bouquets and to revel in the pure joy of the night.

At the back of the viewing area, Victor had reasonably recovered from the shock of seeing Lauren. He had all but swallowed his tongue when he had first seen her standing at the front of the room in her short skirt and signature three-inch heels. It didn't take an Einstein to put the puzzle together. Sure, he knew she worked in California, but what were the chances she was with Swanson's? He mentally slapped his forehead in frustration, wishing there was a deep hole he could crawl into.

She was going to hate him. He'd just erased her job. Until that moment, he hadn't given much thought to the employees of the firms he bought. He was a numbers man, not a human relations guy. Well, hell. That had all done a u-turn in a split second.

His thoughts jumped past that night and what was going to transpire. Now what, Raven? You could tell her why you're here, and while you're at it, the way things happened with her father. He groaned deep in his chest just thinking about the hurt that would be in her eyes. He couldn't do it.

The desire to leave like a skulking rat flitted through his brain. Male rationale took over and adrenaline pumped through his body. You're the guy who makes things happen. You can fix this if you use your head. He caught a waiter's attention and took a martini from his tray. After his second swallow, he knew exactly what he had to do. It would be simple and clean. A call to his secretary and a letter from the parent company and Lauren would have a position in New York. Clean or not, he still felt the knot of nagging guilt in his belly. He spotted Avery in the crowd. He walked with a determined stride to stand beside the current owner of Swanson's.

"Good crowd here, Swanson." What did he care about the crowd? He wanted to talk about Lauren. "I didn't know Lauren Rose designed for you."

"She's going places and damned fast." Avery glanced at Victor before turning his attention back to the runway. "You acquainted with her?"

"Yes, I am." Victor accepted a fresh drink and took a healthy swallow. "She wasn't expecting me to be here tonight." He grimaced and decided not to expand his lie. "Look. She doesn't know I'm the reason Swanson's is folding. I'd appreciate you not mentioning that. I'd rather she heard it from me."

Avery stared at Victor for a moment before speaking bluntly. "I'll keep it to myself if that's what you want."

Feeling like a back alley chiseler, Victor tried to appease Avery's curiosity. "I want her to be part of the new operation in New York. I know she has talent and will fit in nicely with the company's plans to expand."

"But you don't want her to know anything else?" Avery shook his head. "Like I said, I'll keep my mouth shut."

"I'd appreciate that, Swanson." Victor took a deep breath and hoped he had covered all the bases. He was still a mass of jangled nerves. "How soon is this over?"

"In a few minutes." Avery extended his hand to Victor. "Nice talking to you again, Raven. I'll see you at the final signing tomorrow."

Left to his own devices, Victor didn't like being isolated from Lauren. He strode closer to the wall of people pouring accolades of praise over her head. After what seemed like an eternity, she looked his way with a soft-as-silk smile on her lips. He felt the same explosion of wonder that had rocked his senses the first time he saw her. When she leveled her chocolate-brown gaze on him, he realized he was captured like a hare in a satin-lined snare. Like one of her serfs, he stood waiting for her to acknowledge his presence.

He planted his feet securely to the floor, waiting for Lauren to decide the moment was right to allow him entry into her space. She was a star, gleaming with moonlight in her dark hair and dewdrops on her cherry lips. Lord. She was a splendid woman and he felt desperation in his soul just to touch her. A sniggle of worry crept into his mind. What if she was involved and didn't want to see him?

Intense male pride fired his libido. You aren't going to let the unknown stop you. Step up and take your rightful place.

He almost laughed aloud because of his macho thoughts. Tread carefully, mister. You didn't exactly make your feelings known to her. Steel yourself for the most painful rejection of your life. His stomach did a couple of funny jumps when she finally tore herself away from the crowd and walked toward him. She was smiling and her eyes glowed with a tender light.

She shifted the huge bouquet of roses in her arms and held her hand out to him.

"Raven." Her voice broke on that note. "You came for my show."

She was dazzling in her white poet's shirt, but her slender hands seemed to quaver on his arm. He couldn't be sure, but she looked faint.

"I wouldn't have missed it," he said and chuckled as he leaned over to kiss her cheek. "Congratulations, baby. You're the darling of the fashion world tonight."

"How thoughtful of you." She touched every point of his face with her marvelous gaze, moistening her cherry lips before going on. "Now, what are you really doing here of all the places you could be?"

He stopped just short of scuffing his toe on the carpet like some bashful kid about to tell a lie. "I'm here on business. California, I mean." The heaviness of guilt weighed like a ton of bricks on his chest while he gazed into her eyes. "A friend is here, attending the show.

"I see," she said, still smiling up at him.

He grabbed for anything to pull himself out of boiling water. "I'm a guest and in case you're wondering, I didn't crash the party."

To his great relief, she laughed, the honeyed sound pouring over him like a soft spring rain. He could breath normally again and let himself enjoy the way she affected him without physical contact. That wasn't going to last long if she persisted in brushing against him and touching his hand. When she turned to lay her roses on a table, he felt the flare of desire sizzle up his inner thighs and spin crazily in his crotch. He was feeling like a roasting rabbit while giving careful scrutiny to her legs and backside.

"Will you be here long, Raven?" She straightened and turned to look at him. She seemed hesitant. "Maybe I could take you and your friend out for dinner." She glanced around at the thinning crowd. "Which is your friend?"

Victor felt the familiar squeeze of being put on the spot. "Oh, him. He had to leave. I'll catch up with him later." He told her the complete truth in one soft sentence. "But I'm still here. I couldn't leave without seeing you first."

For one blissful moment, their gaze met in the splendor of sweet reunion. Lauren ducked her head, dragging in a breath of air to stem the flow of tears threatening to spill down her cheeks. Why didn't her feet touch the floor any longer? She needed something solid to cling to. Reason spoke gently through the fog of her thinking. *Calm down, dear. He's not proposing, just being polite.* The one way to find out if he really wanted to see her was to give him the chance to escape. Try to be adult. Her smile grew in proportion as she looked into the eyes of the man she knew she loved.

"I'll just go and get my handbag from my desk. It will be just you and me then." Her gaze moved over his face like a loving kiss. "Will you wait for me?"

"Will I wait for you?" He covered his quaking emotions with humor. "Nothing can move me out of this building short of nitro."

She scooped the roses up from the table, laughing at his comment. He had described perfectly how tense she was. Nitro would be a soft poof compared to what would happen if he so much as touched her. Before he could see the mess of nerves she was, Lauren walked briskly away to get her things from the back room.

While Victor waited for Lauren, he strolled about the showroom, watching the place empty out. Most of the lights had been turned off and his footsteps echoed in the silent room. He walked to the doorway she'd used to go out and looked down the empty hallway. Where was she? He was beginning to feel a little foolish. The woman had turned him into a shop towel. Was this his cue to take a hike? A soft noise behind him caught Victor's attention. When he turned around, he saw Lauren's smiling face.

"I was getting worried," he said with a crooked grin. She may have thought he was teasing but he had been serious as hell.

"You needn't have been." Lauren drew his arm about her waist as they walked into the dimly lit entryway. "I would have found you."

Her soft teasing words spun through his blood like bubbling hot taffy. He was actually dizzy, almost swaying into Lauren when she drew his arm about her waist. He had no idea where she was taking him, but he was willing to let her lead him like an eager puppy.

Before they reached the exit doors, the lights were completely snuffed. Lauren's soft exclamation of surprise was his cue to catch her in his protective embrace.

He nuzzled her ear and kissed her neck. "I want you to know I wasn't leaving here without you, baby."

Held tightly in his arms, Lauren tossed aside her reserve. She didn't want to distance herself from Victor. Pressing to him, she gave herself up to his urgent kiss, sighing in its rapture. A shudder of pleasure rocked the world about her when he braced her against the wall to deepen his kiss. Sweet fire licked about her body when he cupped her breasts and gently held their swelling weight in his hands.

At that moment, Victor couldn't remember anything about yesterday, yet he remembered everything right down to the finest detail of Lauren's body. The way her lips plumped beneath his, the way her dark lashes fluttered in the bloom of her rising passion. He heard her soft whimper of ecstasy and plunged deeper into the surging pool of desire pulling him out to sea. His mouth covered hers hungrily and he held her fast when she slumped against him. He lifted his head, listening to her soft gasps.

"I'm so damned glad I found you, baby."

She clung to him and lifted her arms about his neck, kissing his face repeatedly. "I think you'd better come home with me, Raven." Her hands slid down to cup his firm buttocks. "You might get lost."

His voice was husky with emotion. "Don't you know? You can't lose me."

Chapter Fifteen

Victor followed Lauren, trailing closely enough to ensure another car couldn't separate them. The drive took only twenty minutes, but it seemed like three days to him. When she pulled off the highway and into a secluded driveway, he parked behind her car. He couldn't see a great deal of the house, but he could see it was Lauren's. Neat, warm and inviting.

Things happened fast after that. He was vaguely aware of the slamming of car doors and the crunch of dry leaves beneath his shoes as he walked double time toward her. She was in his arms, kissing him, igniting the long simmering fire in his veins, feverishly guiding him to her front door. He took the key from her trembling hand, willing the damned door to open while he worked the key into the lock. It swung open and she backed through the doorway, pulling him along with her.

They came together quickly, paying no heed to a basket of flowers that had been tipped in their quest for the sweet pleasure of being one again. In the darkness, she sought his strength and warmth to sustain her. Her voice whirred about in the fragrant room, filling the emptiness with delightful promise.

"Come with me, Victor." She stepped out of her shoes and took his hand to lead him into her bedroom with its downy bed and silk sheets.

"Anywhere," he promised, wondering where she was leading him with the comfort of a conventional setting a step away.

She led him through a door and out into the enclosed patio just outside her bedroom. Going back into his arms, she pressed close to him, shuddering a little when a breeze swept over them.

"Let's make love out here, Raven." She touched the top button of his shirt. "I'm feeling wicked tonight."

Her direct way with words caused his heart to pummel his ribs. She had flipped the switch and his sex drive was at magnum force. He would have done anything she asked. Wicked, she had said. She was a sorceress, claiming his will to function independently of her. He gladly gave himself over to her, letting her take his passion to the limits. In the silvered glow of moonlight, he saw the teasing smile on her ripe lips as she removed his clothes and dropped them in a smoldering heap at his feet.

He caught her close, quaking as their bodies touched. "Wicked, wicked woman," he groaned against her lips. "Where's the hemlock?" His fingers worked to open the blouse she wore and then dispatched it to join his clothing piled on the cool flagstone beneath their feet.

Her laugh was mysteriously dusky. "Hemlock?" Her fingers played in the coarse hair about his erect sex. "It's the nectar of Shangri La I'm offering."

His skill at removing her clothing was punctuated by the wolfish grin on his lips. "And I know where it's hidden," he said, kneeling down to draw her hips against his face.

He inhaled deeply and became besotted with the essence of her silken skin. His tongue lapped at the sweet wine taste of her and he gorged his hungry soul with her fragrance, probing her softness until he felt her fingers lock in his hair and the quaking of her legs. He held her fast until the quivering of her thighs ceased and her fingers touched his face.

"Raven," she whispered shakily.

He stood up, lifted her in his arms to carry her to the glider that was piled high with pillows, and lay her down on it's soft expanse. He went into her open arms and covered her with his body. She took his erection in her hand, guiding him to her sweet heat. Being one with Lauren was euphoric for Victor, his laurel wreath and prize for surviving all the weeks of hungry waiting.

He heard her command above the roar of the surf.

"Fill me to my heart, Raven."

He drove into her until she cried out in bliss, the sound rushing through his blood like hot brandy. He was aching and heavy with the need of release, but Lauren's satisfaction came first.

"Again, baby?" he asked. The cords of his neck stood out in his effort to restrain himself.

"No," she whispered against his mouth. "I want to feel you spill inside me."

Her legs gripped his hips, taking him in as deeply as possible, before she clasped him to her breasts. His powerful need was unleashed and he rode the dizzying rush of exultation, slowly spinning back to reality.

They lay wrapped in each other's arms letting the steady sound of the surf lull them into a dreamlike cocoon. Victor reveled in the time for lingering kisses and their whispered words of praise for one another's incredible lovemaking.

He lay on his side and traced the curve of her hip with his fingertip. "Lauren?" he asked with a grin. "How many people do you suppose are watching us make love?"

She laughed against his mouth and pulled him closer. "Getting inhibited, Raven?"

"Not me," he growled and nipped at her bottom lip. "I just don't want another man seeing what I'm looking at right now."

Her laugh was sultry. "That's what the six foot walls and rose bushes are for." She patted his rear. "But I wouldn't do this during the day. Out here, I mean."

He thought about his words. It had been years since he'd said anything close to sounding possessive to a woman. The need to claim her for himself was strong, battering at his will to remain single. What he'd felt for her from moment one was changing into something new and gut wrenching for him. He had practically gone up in flames the first time he'd seen her, blazing hot with the desire to make love to her. Oh yeah, that was still there, but the selfish drive to satisfy his lust had become a lingering, unquenchable need for her that would burn in his soul forever.

Groaning with contentment, he wrapped her in his embrace, relishing her sweet warmth. His voice was husky with rising desire when he spoke to her. "I'm glad you made that clear, baby." He teased her nipple, feeling it harden under his palm. "I think we could really let go if we had a little more privacy."

She sighed, trailing her fingertips over the strong line of his nose and jaw. "So, you're not a bad boy through and through?"

"Yes," he said and playfully gnawed at her shoulder. "Bad to the bone."

She laughed and pushed him onto his back to straddle his legs. "I'm so glad to hear that. You're too much fun the way you are."

She raised her arms up in a languid stretch, rocking against him slowly while taking deep breaths of the cool night air. He stroked the smooth curves of her hips, smiling at her lack of inhibition. His impulse to pull her down to lie against his chest was strong, yet he forced himself to let her work her magic on him. His thoughts began to weave mental imagery of having her with him twenty-four-seven. Was that what he really wanted? Hell, yes. When she dropped her arms to her sides and looked down at him, he smiled lazily at her.

"What were you thinking, Raven?" She toyed with his nipples. "Something wicked, I hope."

He caught her hands and took them to his lips, kissing each

knuckle. "I was just wondering how much trouble it would be to get you into one of my suitcases."

She laughed merrily, going into his arms. "That's a new one, but we can try it."

His voice grew serious. "We could have this all the time if you were living in New York."

Had he said the wrong thing? She was silent and her hands went still on his chest. Damn. He'd wanted his words to put the glow of anticipation in her lovely eyes. Where were the tiny vibrations of excitement in her slender body? What the hell was going on in that creative mind of hers?

"What are you thinking, baby?" He wasn't sure he wanted to know. "Didn't sound that bad to me."

She moved off him to prop herself against a pillow. "You're just feeling a post-coital glow, Raven." She held out her hand to catch the rose petals that a gust of wind showered on them. "I'll be in New York for the holidays."

He caught her hand, trying to get his meaning through to her. "I mean now, Lauren." He didn't pick and chose his words. "Chuck California and come back to New York with me. I'll help you pack."

"You know of course, that after a few weeks of me as a steady diet, you'd be buying a one-way ticket to send me back where you found me."

He exhaled heavily, trying to digest what had just passed between them. He'd made a fool of himself again with this maddening woman. He'd probably sounded too pushy, too possessive. She liked her independence. Plus, there was the little matter of all his past sins against her, real or imaginary. He should clear the air between them. Be honest or be quiet? He would ease off and let things fall into place. Right now, he didn't want to risk being kicked out of heaven.

Hanging his leg off the glider, he set the swing into motion and contented himself with holding her close. He smiled wryly in the shadowed darkness. Lauren would be coming back to him. She would come back of her own free will and then he could tell her how much he cared for her. Her soft voice wandered into his dreaming.

She touched his lips with a tender kiss and climbed over him to get off the glider. "Let's go fix dinner."

He couldn't remember the last meal he'd eaten. Now that he was with Lauren, that mundane act seemed unnecessary. He stood up and stretched broadly, smiling down at her.

"Good idea, " he said. "What exotic delicacies are we putting together?"

She drew his arm about her waist and walked him toward the house. "Pizza." She paused, gesturing toward the trail of clothing scattered over the patio. "Want to put those back on?"

He swung her up in his arms, grinning wolfishly at her. "Later."

"What about the pizza?"

"Later. Much later."

After another earthshaking round of lovemaking and a shower together, Lauren went to the kitchen. She knotted the sash of her robe loosely about her waist, trying to sort out her tumbling thoughts. What was wrong with her? He had said almost everything she had wanted to hear. Almost. It had been just enough to tease her heart into a joyful fairytale of pleasantries, but she wouldn't settle for being his constant plaything when the mood struck him. It would be obvious to a halfwit that he loved having sex with her. He just wasn't in love with her.

Her hands shook while she put the pizza together. She felt clumsy and close to tears until she saw him walk through the door carrying several pieces of luggage. *How can you stand here like a weepy ninny while that gorgeous and* virile *man is moving into your bedroom?*

Her heart filled to the bursting point with happiness. There would be no more pity parties. Her man was here and she would enjoy him, pamper him and make love with him as long as fortune allowed her.

While Lauren was in the kitchen, Victor stowed his luggage in her bedroom. The four poster bed was out of sync with the Chinese chests and rugs, but it was Lauren. An array of combs, brushes and bottles on her dresser caught his eye. He uncapped a bottle of perfume and sniffed the delectable fragrance.

"What are you doing?" Lauren stood in the doorway, smiling softly at him.

He put the bottle down, grinning at her. "Just trying to see what potion you're using on me."

She took several steps into the room, pointing to the bed. "Did you test the mattress?"

"Not without you."

He did know the right things to say, she thought while looking around the room. She liked seeing him in her home. His things mixing with hers. Lord, she was crazy about the man.

When he held his arms out, she went to him, to the happiness he offered. When he lifted her off her feet, she put herself in his control, forgetting all the stern talks she'd had with herself about trusting too much. Raven was different. He made no promises, told her no lies. She knew it wouldn't be forever. Right now, she would savor every second with him and expect nothing more.

* * * *

Lauren couldn't have wished for anything more perfect than their time together. She breathed deeply of the delicious aromas of freshly brewed coffee and hot cinnamon rolls that wafted through the house. They had made breakfast together and crawled back into bed to enjoy it. The bedroom door was open, letting in the sounds of sparrows quarreling over the building rights to a nesting site. Well, she had her little nest here with Victor.

She yawned and stretched before turning her head to look at Victor. Perfect, she thought with sigh of contentment.

A copy of the Sunday New York Times was spread over the bed, making comforting crackling sounds each time they moved beneath the quilt. She smiled, congratulating herself for not letting her subscription to the paper run out. Her gaze lingered on his strong profile until he looked at her with a grin. She couldn't resist interrupting him.

"Raven."

"What? Want more sex?" He lifted a brow and grinned at her.

"I'll let you know when I do." She tugged on the section of paper he was reading. "You have the part I want," she complained playfully.

"Since when did you read the sports section?" He patted her stomach. "I believe you're just greedy."

"You know I am." She rubbed the warm ridge that lay between his thighs and went back to the entertainment section.

Looking trough the celebrity filled page brought back the memory of seeing Victor in that damned film clip. She burned with curiosity to quiz him about the redhead. But how to do it tactfully? What the heck. She wasn't known for mincing words. She sighed and rattled her paper several times to get his attention. Her smile was sugary when he finally looked at her.

"I saw you on television the other night. An art gallery I think."

"Umm. Yeah." He smiled and lowered the paper to his chest. "How was I?"

"Damned friendly with that redhead locked onto your arm." Oops. That had probably been a mistake, letting her jealousy work her tongue.

He propped up on his elbow to grin at her. "If memory serves me correctly, that redhead was Madelyn Witherton, married to a close friend and administrator of the charity foundation throwing the bash at the gallery."

Lauren met his steady gaze and determined he was telling the truth. Well lady. You certainly stepped in it again, making an ass of yourself. But not enough to show you are embarrassed. She leaned over to kiss his mouth and went back to her paper as casually as possible and tried to ignore his chuckle.

Ask him something all men love to talk about you idiot. "Raven. What do you do?" She wasn't looking directly at him but she could see he was rubbing his jaw. "That bad, huh?"

He grinned and nodded. "You could say that. I buy things people no longer want."

"Antiques?"

"Sometimes."

"I love antiques. Maybe you have something I would be interested in."

He tried to go back to his paper. "These antiques are machinery. You know, tool and dye. And some old buildings. Nothing pretty enough for you." He gave her a sideways glance.

"My father owned a major pharmaceutical business."

"And I'll bet he ran it damned well."

"Do you have one of those in your portfolio?"

"Yes." He turned to the next page of his paper before meeting her steady gaze. "Someday I want to show you my portfolio and let you pick the company you want to manage."

"I could handle it." Her eyes twinkled with pleasure. She loved talking with Victor. She rubbed her stomach to ease the ache of love that trembled there. She didn't question him further. She'd found the society section.

The last page offered something worthy of serious conversation. There was no mistaking the identity of the sleek blond pictured in the midst of a crowd of beautiful people. Lauren couldn't hold back her questions. Why should she? She'd already sounded like an obsessed mistress.

"Would you be interested if told you there's a very nice picture of your ex-wife in the society section?"

"Do you want me to be?"

"Definitely not." She checked his profile for a reaction to her question.

He was taking a long time to fold his paper, not looking at her and not saying anything. Why couldn't she keep her mouth shut? He was probably going to tell her to do just that if he ever looked her way again. He sat up and leaned against the pillows and gave her his full attention.

"Lauren. It's time we talked about ourselves." He kept his hands away from her. "What do you want to know?"

"Were you very much in love with her?"

"No, we were having an affair and became careless. The result was our beautiful daughter."

That was it? He sure was spare with his account of the situation. She wanted to know more.

"As crazy as you are about children, I'm surprised you don't have several more."

He rubbed his jaw and hooked an arm about her shoulders. "I wanted more children and when I suggested we enlarge our family, she suggested I move out. After that we began to argue loud and often. So, we agreed to end it, before Rachel became traumatized."

The words he used didn't hide the regret in his voice. She kissed his hand that curled about her shoulder. "I'm sorry, Raven."

He smiled at her and raked the paper off the bed. "So am I." He pulled her down to lie against his chest. "What happened between you and Taylor?"

She swallowed hard, not eager to talk about her own humiliation. She shrugged a little before opening up her secrets closet. "Nothing much to tell. He tired of the situation and wanted to date other women."

There was a lengthy quiet in the room before Victor spoke again.

"He's a damned fool." He touched the tip of her nose, pulling her closer to him.

She caught his hand to lace her fingers through his. "His timing was cruel. Three days after my father's funeral." Victor's arms tightened about her. She'd never been so protectively hugged. "It doesn't matter anymore."

"You were very close to your father, weren't you?"

She nodded and sighed. "I thought the sun rose only because of him."

A quiet healing warmth nestled around them while she tried to picture him as a child.

"I'll bet you were your mother's little darling."

He drew her arm about his neck. "When I was four years old, my birth mother left me on the doorstep of my adoptive parents."

"I'm so sorry, Raven."

"Don't be, baby. She did me the greatest favor of my life. My parents were wonderful people."

"That makes me feel much better."

He stroked her hair and touched her cheek as if he were handling angel's wings. "Want to hear about the house I plan to build in Connecticut?"

She leaned back to smile at him, her curiosity running wild. "A house? Of course I do." She nestled close to him, loving the way his arms held her securely. "Describe it to me."

He made a sweeping gesture with his hand. "Picture this. Ten acres of park with a rambling ranch style bungalow smack in the middle."

She had been watching his hands draw descriptive pictures in the air. "That doesn't look like a bungalow to me."

He chuckled and held his hands further apart. "Okay. It's going to be about forty-five hundred square feet. Lots of yard and a pool. Maybe a tennis court and of course a stable."

She smiled dreamily at him. "Go on. I can see it all now."

"Well, I really want this for Rachel. An apartment is no place for a girl to stretch out." He lifted his arms over his head in a leisurely stretch and grinned at her. "And what can I do to make you happy?"

She threw the quilt off the bed and posed provocatively. "Let's make love and then go for a walk on the beach."

He sat up and caressed her thigh. "I have a better idea. Let's make love."

She held her arms out to him. "Come here you," she enticed softly. "Make me too tired to get out of bed."

Later, when they were too spent to do more than hold each other, Victor brought them back to earth when he looked at his watch.

"That late already?" He groaned and sat up. "Want to shower with me?"

"What's going on, Raven?" She wrapped her arms about his waist.

"I completely forgot the appointment I have in an hour." He covered her hands with his and pressed her palms to his belly. "Will you be here when I get back?"

"Would you be disappointed if I wasn't?" she teased.

"Me upset?" He caught her up in his arms and hugged her tight. "I'd sit on your doorstep, howling in misery until you showed up."

"Sure. I'd expect that." She released her hold on him. "Go ahead. Get the water just right for me. I have to find some underwear."

He got out of bed, giving her a lingering gaze while she dangled her legs over the side of the bed. "That's odd," he said. "I don't recall you wearing undergarments."

She stretched and smiled impishly at him while getting to her feet. "You mean I don't wear them while you're around." She smacked his rear as she walked past him.

He observed her for a minute, grinning when she leaned over to rummage in the bottom drawer of a stack chest.

"One more kiss before I go?"

She stopped what she was doing and went back into his arms. His kiss was a cocktail of rare erotic drugs that bubbled through her body, leaving her breathless and wanting. Standing on tiptoes, she clung to his neck, shivering in delight when he pulled her hips to his. He was erect and eager to share his passion with her.

"Umm," she murmured against his mouth. "I'll find my clothes later.

* * * *

After Victor kissed her good-bye, Lauren leaned against the door smiling a little because he was going to be late for that important appointment. She watched his car until it was out of sight and closed the door. Looking around the living room, she was shocked by the well lived in appearance of the place. She straightened the magazines and replaced the throw pillows on the couch. After she had the kitchen spanking clean, she went into the bedroom to put fresh linen on the bed and arrange the pillows the way he liked them.

She lovingly folded the clothing he'd hastily dropped on top of his luggage. Lifting the flap of the largest bag, she checked out the contents. There were wonderfully tailored shirts, neatly rolled pairs of socks and a shaving kit bearing his initials. She ran her finger over the gold embossed lettering and wondered what the middle initial stood for. She started to close the case, but something about those bold letters reminded her of the letter she'd found in her father's papers. She felt a rush of anger. Why? It was pure coincidence that Victor's initials were so similar to the never to be forgotten C.R. She was disgusting herself with such morbid thinking and left the room. Besides, he probably wouldn't appreciate her fondling his undergarments while he was gone.

To help fill the empty space his absence had caused, Lauren made a jumbo fruit salad and prepared a couple of game hens to roast. The idea was to keep him from overeating and lessoning his desire to play with her. She had what she wanted, at least for a while. He was there, staying in her house. The lovemaking was if anything far exceeding her expectations. *But remember this is temporary so don't get too confident and for Pete's sake don't get possessive. Enjoy him, girl. While it lasts.*

The postman came and her heart beat pitifully in her chest when the hoped for job offer didn't arrive. She didn't want to feel anything but joy while Victor was with her. She felt like a jealous shrew each time she looked at the clock, counting the hours he'd been gone. Deciding to do something constructive, she put the game hens in the oven and grabbed her sketchpad to flesh out the ideas that had lay dormant in her brain after seeing Victor again.

After wasting half a pad of paper, she lay aside the idea of getting anything accomplished. There was one thing on her mind and he had been gone an awfully long time. Maybe he wasn't coming back that night. Nothing said he had to. Stop it before you meet him at the door with a rolling pin. The titter of her bitchy woman's voice danced on her earlobe. You're jealous, and you think he's with another woman. She swiped at her ear and went to the window to stare out at the driveway for several minutes.

Enough. She called a halt to gazing out the window, like a cat waiting for someone to come home and open the tuna. She was no cat; she was a tiger lying in wait for her mate. She went out to the patio to relax her tightly coiled nerves. The gentle motion of the glider was calming, and she began to enjoy the beauty of the waves sweeping the shoreline.

The calm ended as soon as the delicious aroma of roasting game hen drifted to her through the open kitchen window. It reminded her of how long Victor had been gone. The slight furrow of concern on her forehead vanished when she heard Victor's car pull into the driveway. Her mood instantly jumped from gloom and fog into a field of wildflowers and butterflies. When he came around the corner, she got up from the glider to meet him half way.

"Hello, Gorgeous," he said and reached for her. "Sorry that took so long, but you know how those things go."

She didn't know anything except she loved him with all her being. "You're here now." She hugged his waist, trying to calm her racing pulse. "Hungry?"

"For you." His smile was teasing, but his voice was smooth as fine cognac. "What do you suggest?"

She draped her arms about his neck and smiled up at him. "I'll take care of your appetite first, then feed you."

* * * *

Coffee on the patio with her man was icing on the cake as far as Lauren was concerned. She gazed at Victor over the rim of her cup; she was still flushed and weak with surrender after the awesome sex they'd had an hour earlier. A slight smile played over her lips. What a switch this was. Unlike her, he wasn't thinking sex. He sat across from her, working out of his briefcase, making money on paper and looking irresistible.

She leaned back in her chair and watched him shuffle documents. He compressed his lips and the scar at the corner of his mouth became more pronounced. She wanted to kiss that scar tenderly. She sighed and stayed where she was, and enjoyed the fragrant blizzard of rose petals a gust of wind had freed to shower over them.

Catching one petal in her hand, she studied its velvet texture. The pristine white reminded her of the coming holidays. By Thanksgiving, it would probably be snowing in New York. Touching the petal to her nose, she began to think seriously of what her plan of action would be in the coming weeks. With no prospects of employment in California, it was inevitable she would be heading back to New York. And why not? She'd gone back and hadn't died of shame or heartbreak.

Her mouth softened into a gentle smile when she looked at Victor. If she hadn't gone back, she wouldn't have met him. Maybe it was time she returned to her roots. She harrumphed under her breath. Roots, my aching back. You're only thinking of how fast you can get back in his bed.

Oh, yeah. You're getting too secure of your place in his life. Can you spell temporary? Forcing herself to look at her situation realistically, she experienced pain akin to remorse in her soul and pressed her arms tightly against her stomach. Her moment of despair was interrupted when his cell phone rang.

When he got up to walk a few feet away, she slipped the rose petal between her lips, tasting the perfumed essence, observing his various gestures while he talked. Damn, she liked the way his slacks fit over his rear and the way his hair caught sunlight in its ebony depths. When he ended his call, she pretended to be reading the book she'd left on the patio a week earlier. She looked up and smiled at him when he sat down beside her.

"Rachel," he explained with a chuckle.

She sat up straighter. "I hope there's nothing wrong."

He patted her hand that had reached out to lay on his. "She's fine. Just reporting on her dental progress."

Lauren laughed, remembering Rachel's sweet smile. "Little girls worry about their appearance."

He shook his head and chuckled. "Would you believe she doesn't care if her new teeth come in or not? Seems a certain young man in her class admires her smile."

Lauren sat quietly, sensing a change in his demeanor. His thoughts were on another part of his life and she had to keep her emotions tightly wrapped. He was closing his briefcase and she saw that as a warning of pending loneliness. When he looked up, she was staring at him.

"You're looking awfully good today, baby." He exhaled heavily and glanced around the patio. "I wonder if you have any idea how much I don't want to leave you in the morning?"

Her heart beat so wildly she could hardly speak. "That soon?" she managed to squeak out. "I had hoped you might stay longer."

Why had she made that whining comment? He's looking at you and what do you see in his eyes? Uneasiness, resentment? When he chose to leave was his business and she had no right to assume anything.

"I meant we didn't do much sight seeing." She lay her book down and brushed her hair from her cheek.

He gave her a crooked smile. "I'd like nothing better, but I got the feeling Rosie needs a break from my little angel."

She touched his ear with the rose petal, not realizing she had sighed. "Okay. I won't whine anymore."

He leaned over to kiss her lips and gazed into her eyes. "Don't do that, baby."

"Do what?"

"Make that little sound that drives me crazy, the one I can hear for days after we say good-bye."

He was looking at her in the way that always turned her into a woman possessed, the color of his eyes so intense she could see forever in their depths. Not now, she thought. Don't make this any harder than it must be.

She sat up and put her arms around his neck, breathing in his scent of sea washed heather and sun warmed moss. Straightening her face, she looked at him and tried to speak normally.

"Need help packing?" Tears stung her lids, but she wouldn't ruin their last hours together. Before he could answer, she stood up and took his hands in hers to coax him out of his chair.

He tipped her face up to tease her lips with his tongue and kissed her hungrily. She clung to his strong body, trying to capture the feel of him so completely she would never be without him. He caught her face in his hands when he spoke to her.

"I don't know if you'll like this idea of mine, but the first two weeks of December will be nonstop traveling for me. After that, it's our time." He leaned his head to one side to meet her steady gaze. "That is, if you're coming to New York for the holidays."

Her hands were trembling and it was useless to attempt a cavalier attitude while her body was practically levitating. He wanted her to come home.

"That would be perfect, Raven."

"So, it's a date?"

"One you'll never forget."

He drew her close and nuzzled her hair. "Santa might have some new tricks in his bag."

She laughed and fought valiantly against tears of joy threatening to stream down her cheeks.

"And he knows I'm the gal that loves surprises."

Chapter Sixteen

Had it only been two weeks? Lauren ached to see Victor and couldn't fill the void of his absence no matter how hectic her schedule. How many times had she run to the mailbox, hoping for that letter of acceptance from someone ... anyone? Each time she spoke with Victor on the phone, he buoyed her spirits with his think positive attitude and best of all, his telling her how much he wanted to be with her. But the moment the calls ended, she wanted to cry like a baby. But she wouldn't allow herself that luxury.

She felt as if she had put the horse before the cart again. The real estate agent who had looked at her house had called and gleefully announced she had an eager buyer for her house. That was all well and good, but she didn't feel like playing the part of a gypsy with nothing settled and nothing to call her own. Uncertainty made her nervous and fearful. She chided herself regularly for the drastic change in her personality.

Just like most mornings, this one was starting the same way. She decided it was impossible for her to face another day of writing resumes and waiting for the postman. *Don't sit in the house, woman. Do something constructive.* Okay, she thought. This is good, sitting on the patio with a huge mug of coffee.

She lay on the glider and listened to the wind whisper around her. Her eyes were closing when the sound of the postman's truck invaded the quiet.

She gripped the handle of the coffee mug. Should she run to the mailbox, or play the game of nonchalance? You're far from not caring, lady. You're just waiting for the letter carrier to get out of sight so you can run like a bloodhound to get your mail. The man had begun to look at her with deep curiosity and some concern after she'd practically yanked the mail from his hands several times.

Squeezing her eyes shut, she lay back and took in deep breaths. She needed fortification and this was her way of preparing for more disappointing news.

Her resolve to be calm went down the drain, and she got to her feet and sprinted around the house and straight to the mailbox. The box overflowed with all the usual ads and magazines.

Her heart fell to her feet when she recognized the large folder that held a portfolio of her choice designs. She wouldn't bother opening it because it represented failure. Nestled among the bills and personal letters was one business size envelope that stood out from the rest. Another sorry letter, she thought.

She had an armload to carry into the house and gave the grocery ads a dreary glance while depositing everything unceremoniously onto the kitchen counter. She had plenty of time to read another rejection letter and see what the power company had charged her this month.

The utility bill was tossed aside when her gaze was drawn back to the rich looking white envelope with its fancy printed return address. Christopher Creations. She didn't recall contacting any firm with that name. Probably a magazine offer.

"Well, what message of dejection do you bring?" she mumbled and tore the flap open. Before she could unfold the letter, the phone rang.

In no mood to hear a telemarketer's spiel, she decided not to answer. She changed her mind instantly when she heard the voice that caressed her ears with its masculine baritone.

"Lauren."

"Raven."

She carried the phone into her room and crawled onto the bed. She listened to his voice while nestling into the pillows he had slept on.

"You haven't said much, baby. What's wrong?"

She pulled a quilt up over her legs and sighed before answering him. "Lots of things are happening, but nothing I want."

"Want to talk about it?"

Her voice bore none of its usual playfulness.

"Nothing's going right. Unless you call someone trying to push you out of your house a good thing."

He was quiet far longer than she wanted him to be.

"Raven. Are you still there?"

"Right here, baby. Tell me about the house."

She idly tapped the unread letter on the nightstand. "I made the mistake of having a realtor look at my house. Now, someone wants it so badly, she calls with a new and bigger offer from them every day."

He chuckled. "Somehow I don't see that as a problem." A second later, he seemed to be more sympathetic. "What else is bothering you? I'll try to fix it."

She made a kissing sound against the mouthpiece while working the letter open. "Thank you for offering, but I'll have to...."

She was speechless for a half second while the first few lines of the letter registered in her brain. She clamped her hand over her mouth to stifle her scream of joy.

"They want me," she gasped. "I've been offered a real job with a design studio." She laughed and hugged the pillow he had rested his head on.

He laughed. "Whoever they are must be smart as hell."

She held the letter above her head and purred into the mouthpiece. "Aren't you curious where that studio is?"

"You know I am."

"New York." She let out a gleeful whoop of happiness.

"And you're not the least bit excited. I can tell." He laughed with her.

She rolled across the bed, clasping his pillow to her breasts. Her riotous emotions couldn't be held in.

"I can hardly breath I'm so excited." She got to her feet and jumped up and down on the bed. "They want me to begin work the first of the year. That's perfect I tell you. Perfect."

"Lauren. What are you doing?" he asked through a laugh.

"Having fun." She plopped down onto her back with a happy chortle. "Just think, Raven. I'll be home for Christmas."

She slid off the bed to lay on the floor. "I hate to miss Thanksgiving with Raini, but I just have too much to finish up here before I can leave. Isn't it wonderful?"

Victor broke into her euphoria that flowed through the phone lines. "What's the first thing you want to do when you get home?"

"Make love. With you of course." She sat up. "My Lord. I'll have to find an apartment as soon as I get home. Raini and I can't live under the same roof for very long."

He exhaled audibly. "Well, looks like we'll have to postpone the lovemaking. You're going to be awfully busy."

"Raven. You had better be kidding." She tapped the mouthpiece several times for emphasis.

"I was teasing you, Lauren."

She heard his deep laugh and decided to test him. "Okay. Now say something lewd so I'll know you are anxious to see me."

"Uh huh. I'm saving all the good stuff for the moment we're alone."

"See that you do." Her mind was racing with all the things she had stored up to tell him, but there was so much and she didn't know where to begin.

He ended the brief silence. "Lauren. I'm saving it all for you. I...."

She caressed the receiver with her fingertips and waited for the words that would send her into orbit. "Raven?"

"Just hurry home, baby."

Not exactly what she'd wanted to hear, but close. "I'm on my way."

* * * *

The next three weeks were a blur of signing papers and selling her furniture to people who streamed through her home. When the realtor asked if the canopy bed was for sale, Lauren had curled her fingers about one of the post in a protective manner.

Of course the bed wasn't for sale. How would she put a price on something so filled with precious memories? The bed would be shipped to New York and put in storage. While she finished packing her personal items for shipment to Raini's apartment, Lauren wondered briefly about the man that had purchased her home. Lucky man, she thought. She hated to leave the beautiful seaside nest but her eagerness to be back in New York swept away any feelings of regret.

One more week and her feet would be on her native soil. She could hardly contain herself when the thought of being with Victor would consume her soul like ambrosia of indescribable pleasure.

The day before she was to leave her home for the last time, Lauren faced the possibility of Raini still being in the mindset of running her life. Well, she decided, what Raini doesn't know won't hurt her. But if the subject were brought up, there would be no hedging or avoiding the topic. She would be with Victor as long as he wanted her.

That night, there was a long phone call from her sister, and they made elaborate plans for Christmas and all the festivities that went with the holiday.

After the call ended, Lauren was bursting with love for the whole of creation. She was the luckiest woman in the world, and above everything else, Victor Raven took precedence in her life.

At midnight, she walked to the beach and stared out at the water, still awed by its beauty. She picked up a tiny pink shell and tossed it into the foamy surf. "I love you, Raven. God, how I love you."

* * * *

Being met at the airport by her sister and brother-in-law hadn't been the homecoming scene Lauren had dreamed of for her return to New York. But she understood Victor's work had required him to be in another state and he couldn't be there. That gave her more time to dream up ways to drive him crazy with desire when she finally did get her hands on him.

Staying with Raini was quickly losing its charm. It seemed to Lauren the woman had become pickier, if that were possible. After four days, Lauren mumbled fervent and frequent prayers for an apartment of her own.

That wasn't going to be easy. Apartments weren't plentiful in New York. Maybe she was being too selective. Her requirements were simple. Not too far from her job and in a nice building. After several weeks of calling rental agencies and declining places to live, she was a nervous wreck.

After a particularly disappointing day of searching, she looked at the section of paper where she had circled and crossed out ads for apartments. This wasn't what she had expected at all. On top of being a boarder at Raini's, she was meeting her new employer the following Monday. The thought made her worry that along with everything else, he might have changed his mind and would relegate her to the switchboard. In an uncontrollable show of disgust, she tossed the paper up in the air. It was falling around her head like confetti when the phone began to chime out its ridiculous melody of La Boehm.

She answered it to stop the music. From the corner of her eye, she could see Raini peeking around the doorway. Lauren couldn't help but laugh at her snoopy sister's antics after she hung the phone up.

"Feel like looking at another place?" Lauren looked at her watch. "That was a realtor and he says he has exactly what I specified in my application at his office."

"It's getting late and I don't know what your rush is." Raini came into the living room and sat down.

"Come on, Raini." Pulling her sister to her feet, Lauren laughed. "You're as anxious for me to find my own place as I am."

"You know that's not true. I love you."

"Yeah, I know and I love you, but I can't stand living with you." Lauren walked to the hall closet and pulled out their coats and hats. "Come along, sis. My new home awaits."

"I'm not anxious for you to leave, but this will be the sixth one you've looked at this week."

Lauren grimaced and belted her coat about her waist. "If this one isn't it, I'm buying a place."

"Pardon me for asking, dear, but what exactly was wrong with the last one you looked at?" Raini handed Lauren a pair of mittens.

"The view. I don't particularly want to open my bedroom window and hit my head against the wall of the building next door."

Raini nodded in agreement. "It was pretty bleak."

"Alcatraz has more curb appeal."

They were still laughing when the taxi the doorman hailed for them pulled up in front of the building. Lauren squeezed Raini's arm in her excitement.

"This one simply has to be the one. I have a good feeling about it."

When they got to the address the agent had given Lauren, she gazed up at the second story windows. She liked the neat gray brick structure. The small park across the street was a definite plus. A gust of icy wind reminded her that winter was setting in.

"I'd forgotten how wonderful New York could be." She buried her nose in her muffler. "Don't you love it, Raini?"

"Thank God for winter cruises. I just hope nothing crops up to ruin our next one." Raini pulled her scarf up to cover her ears. "Where is that realtor? I'm getting frostbite."

"That must be him sprinting toward us." Lauren inclined her head in the direction of a portly gentleman who lumbered toward them. "That noise you heard was the sound barrier being broken." She giggled into her muffler.

"Control yourself, Lauren." Attempting to stifle her own giggle, Raini grabbed Lauren's arm. "Stop it. You don't like living with me. Remember? You want this apartment?"

"Only if he comes with it." Lauren glanced at the man again before meeting her sister's wide-eyed stare. "Nothing to say? You're jealous."

Raini leaned against Lauren, laughing helplessly. The two women traded light slaps of sisterly discipline that they both knew had never worked before and certainly wouldn't now.

"Excuse me ladies."

The man who had caused their fit of giggles broke up their laugh fest and gazed at them with a puzzled expression.

"Miss Rose?" He looked from Raini to Lauren. "I'm meeting Miss Rose to show her the apartment at this address." When he smiled, his cheeks looked like two red apples.

Lauren arched her brows and smiled at him. "I'm Miss Rose."

"Fine. Fine." He jangled an enormous ring of keys and led the way to the front steps of the building. "Shall we?" After opening the heavy glass front door and turned to look back at the women. "I'm Bruce Arnold by the way."

Once they were inside the buildings spacious entry hall, he took the flight of stairs to the second floor with amazing agility. The women followed him.

Lauren's earlier good feelings about the place intensified. There was a sense of calm and a clean fragrance in the air. While Bruce unlocked the apartment door, she made conversation. Or was she rambling like an idiot?

"I'm anxious to see the place Mister Arnold. After our phone conversation, it sounds too good to be true." She wanted to rip the keys from his hand.

"It's a steal for the price we're asking, but you have been given very high recommendations."

It must have been the letter of reference Raini whipped up. "And the price is still what you quoted over the phone?"

"Yes. The fee hasn't changed." Bruce stood aside when the gleaming mahogany door swung open.

The scent of beeswax wafted out to greet Lauren when she stepped inside the living room. She knew her grin was ear to ear and reached out to grip Raini's arm to express her delight.

Honey oak woodwork and ceiling to floor windows were a definite selling point with her. She examined the large pocket doors that separated the dining room from the huge living room. She tried to conceal her happiness when she toured the living room that had vaulted ceilings and a sea green marble fireplace. The master bedroom boasted a triple walk-in closet and storage drawers in one wall. She checked out the bathroom and bit her thumb to hold back a shriek of delight. It was huge and outfitted with a pink marble sunken tub. She couldn't believe her good luck. Before she ran to sign the lease, she went to the window and pulled the drape aside. She grinned. No wall to bump her head on. She was home.

"I'll take it," she said after viewing the sparkling clean chrome and tile kitchen.

"Good decision, Miss Rose. We've had dozens of inquiries about this particular rental." The realtor opened his briefcase and produced a ten-page lease agreement. "I took the liberty of bringing the lease so you could claim the place immediately."

Lauren beamed while she scanned the rules and regulations. She signed in all the indicated places while in her mind she had already hung pictures on the walls.

When all the papers were signed, Lauren gladly wrote out a check that made the place hers for the next year.

"You can take possession anytime now, Miss Rose," the realtor said and stuffed her check into his overflowing briefcase. "Here is your set of keys and a copy of your lease." He walked to the door and called back over his shoulder. "Enjoy your new home."

The moment they were alone, Lauren jumped up and down with happiness. The place wasn't as fancy or half as large as Raini's, but she didn't care. She felt extremely lucky to have gotten such a marvelous place. She caught Raini's hands in hers, swinging them to and fro.

"Let's go out for lunch to celebrate and then get some Christmas shopping done."

"Sounds good to me," Raini said with a grin. "I can show you exactly what I want."

Lauren looked around her new home and then made a suggestion. "We can also look at furniture while we're out."

"What happened to the house full you had in Malibu?"

"Sold it all but the bed."

Raini rolled her eyes in apparent resignation. "I'm sure there's a long story that goes along with that statement, but I don't think this is the time to share it."

While she locked the door behind them, Lauren grinned mischievously at her sister.

"I was thinking how wonderfully things are turning out for me. Just think. I have a real job in the town I love and a fantastic place to live."

Raini nodded her head in agreement. "You really have had a lovely run of good luck lately."

"Yeah and just think ... I didn't have to sleep with anyone to get it."

Chapter Seventeen

Lauren knew she was home by the throngs of people who jostled her on all sides, all with one thing on their minds. Shopping. She loved the beautifully decorated shop windows that were filled with wonderful things to buy. And it had begun to snow.

"Let's go in here," she urged Raini. "One stop shopping."

"This isn't a good idea." Raini held back. "Look at the horde trying to get inside the place."

Lauren grabbed Raini's hand and tugged her toward the entrance of the department store. "Come on. I'll lead the way."

With her less assertive sister in tow, Lauren forged a path through the crowd and entered the store with a triumphant grin.

"I learned that in California." She laughed at Raini's look of dismay. "Ready to shop?"

"Ready." Taking time to smooth her chignon, Raini voiced her surprise. "I can't believe someone your size can be such a bully."

Lauren ignored the comment. She was eager to buy gifts, not waste time discussing her lack of manners. "Come help me find something nice for Adam and I don't mean cologne. Let's fight our way to the men's department."

"Speaking of men, have you heard from Victor," Raini asked the question with no hint of disapproval.

"Who?" Lauren remembered her vow to hash that subject over with Raini, but not here in a crowd of thousands. "I think I see something I want."

"You are so sly, Lauren." Holding her sister's arm to stop her from moving away, Raini laughed. "But not so much that I can't still see that little guilty glaze in your big brown eyes."

Removing Raini's hand from her arm with deliberate politeness, Lauren grimaced in mounting irritation. "And you still nag, nag, nag." Might as well throw her a new curve ball, Lauren decided. "Which way to the children's department?"

Raini's jaw dropped slightly and her daisy blue eyes were almost perfectly round.

"Are you trying to tell me something, Lauren?"

"No. I'm not pregnant. I'll meet you over by the cosmetics arena in fifteen minutes and don't leave. I want to keep you in sight."

Lauren smiled when she walked away from her curious sister. Doing things like that to Raini had been a lifetime source of fun. Her mood struck a somber note and she touched her stomach. She wanted a baby, several in fact, and she wanted them with Victor. What would he think about the idea? She would ask him the next time he was limp with exhaustion and in the mood to plant the seed.

The children's department was easy enough to find. Racks of frilly holiday dresses stood out under pink spotlights trained on them. Lauren examined several of the extravagant frocks while searching for what she wanted.

Among the mountains of gaily-colored scarves, gloves, hair barrettes and hats, she found a treasure trove of fancy gift items for little girls. She picked up a tester bottle of perfume and sprayed a little on her wrist. The scent was soft and delicate, a perfect brew of apple blossom and orange flowers. Remembering Rachel's fascination with her fingernails, she added a dainty manicure set to her purchases. She settled her bill and went in search of Raini.

She didn't have to look far. Raini stood at a nearby cosmetics counter. After making eye contact with her sister, Lauren motioned toward a display table. When a super charged young woman bumped into her, Lauren shrugged and began to check out the fine leather gloves spread over the table that had stopped her fall. She selected a pair for Adam.

Shopping this way is insane, she grumbled to herself. One thing at a time and no one to help you. Her growing irritation vanished when her gaze leveled on a tall, dark-haired man wearing a forest green leather jacket. His broad back was turned to her, but she knew him. Her heart pounded when she noticed the little blond girl that leaned casually against him.

"Raven." She had tried to shout, but could only manage a whisper. She tried to move forward but couldn't. Her damn legs were frozen. *Try harder*, her woman's voice coached. *Move it*, came an order from her newfound friend, inner strength. Gripping the gloves in her hand, she moved into the swirling crowd that separated them. Tears of frustration glistened in her eyes when it seemed she would be carried away by the surging tide of people. Fear of losing him was beaten back when he turned around and looked at her.

"Raven." The world had been thrown into slow motion until reason's voice hissed in her ear. Hurry, he's fighting to reach you and his arms are opening to hold you.

She saw the opening he'd made for her and ran to him, choking back the sob in her throat when he pulled her close to his big, strong body. His lips sought hers in a heady kiss that sent her reeling.

He lifted his head to gaze into her eyes with a smile that spoke of secret and delicious desires. She covered his face with quick kisses and didn't care that people stared their way.

An insistent tugging on her sleeve caught her attention and made her remember Rachel watched the scene. With a laugh, she leaned down to hug Victor's daughter and kissed her cheek.

"I can't believe how much you've grown, Rachel. And you've gotten even prettier."

Lauren drank in the rush of happy laughter and greetings that flowed between the three of them. She held her world of love close to her heart and delighted in Rachel's show of affection and Victor's wonderful smile. She put one arm around his waist and hugged Rachel with the other.

"I couldn't have wished for a nicer surprise." Looking from one to the other, Lauren let sweet rapture take her heart. "My two favorite people."

Raini touched her shoulder and whispered in her ear, "I think this answers my question."

Lauren knew her cheeks were flushed with an unbearable barrage of happiness. She spoke in a rush. "Look who I've found." She immediately turned her attention back to Victor. "I didn't know you were back in New York."

He leaned over to kiss Raini's cheek but didn't remove his hand from Lauren's waist. "Hello, Raini. As I was about to tell Lauren, I got back late last night, but that didn't stop Rachel from waking me up at the crack of dawn to go shopping." He playfully tugged on Rachel's knit hat.

After straightening her headgear, Rachel handed the shopping bag she carried to her father and leaned against him. "Um hum. That is for my mommy. Now we're going skating and then we're having hamburgers."

Victor grinned at Lauren at the mention of hamburgers. "Rachel's going to Connecticut with her mother. Christmas with her grandparents."

Lauren gave quick study to his expression. He seemed perturbed by what he'd said. She realized that somewhere along the way, she had erased Jonelle from the picture. Idiot. She'll always be in the picture. But right now, he's looking at you as if you're a star in his universe. She grew weak with bubbling love under his dark sapphire gaze. *Pick up the reins to your destiny*, her internal voice whispered.

"Raven. That means you'll be having Christmas dinner with us." She glanced at her sister. "We do have room for Raven, don't we?"

"Of course we do." Raini shifted the packages in her arms. "We'd love to have you."

He sent a beaming smile in Lauren's direction. "I'm not much of a cook, but what can I bring?"

"Just yourself," Lauren said emphatically. "And I'll expect you early."

For a long moment, Lauren became lost in Victor's warm gaze and forgot everything else until Rachel chimed into the conversation.

"Daddy. I'm hungry now." She gripped his arm while she talked to him. "Lauren can come with us. Okay?"

Was it that obvious even to a child she had laid claim on him? Lauren tore her gaze from Victor to speak to his daughter. "I'm so happy you thought of me, Rachel, but I'm sure your daddy would like to spend today alone with you."

Rachel patted her father's back and agreed with Lauren. "Uh huh. We have lots of stuff to do." She let go of Victor's arm to reach up to hug Lauren's neck. "Will you come to our house when I get back from grandmamma's?"

"The minute you get back." Lauren kissed the pink velvet cheek Rachel turned for a kiss. For heavens sake, don't cry you ninny. She's not your little girl. Don't think you have too large a place in her life. And yes, you want that desperately.

Raini stepped in to end the brief silence that had closed over the little group. "Have a wonderful Christmas, Rachel." She paused long enough to accept the quick farewell kiss Victor placed on her cheek. "Enjoy your lunch and skating."

In the flurry of good-byes and hugs, Lauren averted her gaze from Victor's mouth. This could be awkward, but they never parted without a lingering kiss. Would he break with tradition because his daughter and Raini watched? When he stepped forward and drew her close, Lauren shook to her toes with emotion. True to his habit, his lips settled firmly on hers with sweet possession. When he lifted his head, he smiled at her.

"Lauren?"

"Yes, Raven."

"I'll call tomorrow."

"Yes, Raven."

Lauren regained her senses when Victor led Rachel away. The

little girl looked back at her and waved, the impish grin on her sweet face, priceless. Lauren waved and released the asinine giggle that was never far away when she was deliriously happy.

"Good Lord." Grasping Lauren's arm, Raini laughed. "How long has that been going on?"

"I can't remember when it wasn't." Lauren's heart thumped pleasantly, echoed by her soft sigh.

Raini took charge, prying the gloves from Lauren's hands and found a counter to pay for them. She took her sister's arm and moved her toward an exit.

"I think you need a cup of tea, my dear."

"Um hm. That sounds nice."

Lauren followed Raini into the posh tearoom adjoining the department store. When they were seated, she was suddenly consumed with the desire to talk.

"Do you realize how much I have to do, Raini?" She rummaged in her handbag and pulled out an address book and pen. "Darn. I've left my cell phone somewhere. Do you have yours or do I have to use the public? I have to call the storage company."

"Why?"

"To have them deliver my bed to the apartment."

"Your bed?" Raini's brows shot up to her hairline.

"I have other things too," Lauren blurted out, then grinned broadly. "You know ... towels, bathmats and of course, sheets."

"I think I have the picture." Raini took a sip of her tea. "You are going to consult a decorator, aren't you?"

The thought of someone else decorating her home irked Lauren. But she knew time would be limited once she began working again.

Raini handed her a cell phone, eyeing her as she punched in numbers.

"Calling a decorator?"

"Storage company."

"So much more important."

"Of course."

* * * *

The next day, Lauren met Victor at her apartment. She knew he wasn't really interested in her decorating ideas, but he listened patiently while she rattled off the names of fabrics and colors. She stopped being Miss Homemaker when he caught her in a hard embrace. He let her know he was in need, fondling her breasts and kissing her senseless. She tried to stall him because she didn't want to be interrupted in the middle of something wonderful by the deliverymen.

"Well. What do you think?"

"Oh hell, what do I know about stuff like that?"

"You're no help, Mister Raven."

"I'm not trying to help you, Miss Rose. I'm trying to figure out where we can make love."

She narrowed her eyes with a feigned smile of sympathy. "Can you wait until the bed gets here?"

"It's been a hell of a long time," he murmured and nipped her neck.

"What do you normally do when you get like this?"

"Play handball."

He pressed his hips to hers to emphasize his meaning. Her blood ran hot and fast, erasing everything else from her mind. "How does the kitchen counter sound to you?"

"Perfect."

"This will have to be a quickie."

"Perfect."

He lifted her up in his arms and carried her to the kitchen, stopping at the first counter that presented its self. He set her on the counter top and began to release the buttons of her blouse.

"Raven. Take my panties off." She trembled with anticipation when he touched her bare thighs. Lifting her butt, she helped him slip the pink silk off her hips and down her legs.

He groaned and pulled her forward again until their bodies touched. "This counter has never had it so good," he murmured against her lips.

Pressing her fingers to his erection, she smiled seductively at him. "My, my, Raven. You're like steel." With great care, she unzipped his slacks and dipped inside his shorts for her treasure. A dusky laugh bubbled from her lips when his erection jumped forward into her hand.

He tilted his head and gave her a knowing grin. "And you're ready to cause a meltdown."

His kiss that had begun slowly and sweetly whipped up a whirlwind of fiery need in her. She locked her arms around his neck and happily free fell into Xanadu. His tongue teased and probed until she knew fainting wasn't out of the question. Lord. She heard bells in her excitement. Bells? She groaned and tore her mouth away from his.

"The doorbell, Raven." She felt like crying in her frustration. "The men with my furniture." His dazed expression mirrored hers. She jabbed a finger toward the living room. "They're ringing the doorbell."

He buried his face in the pulsing curve of her neck and sucked hard until she laughed. She patted his rear and tried to soothe his raging libido.

"I'll hurry them on their way."

"I'll get the whip to make damned sure they do just that."

He helped her off the counter and handed her the panties.

She spared the bit of pink silk a brief glance. "I don't have time for these." She tossed them under the sink.

Victor's continuing expression of agony added to her determination to hurry the men out of the apartment. She walked to the living room, smoothing her skirt and hair before opening the door.

She let the men inside the apartment and issued direct, concise directions to them. While she checked on their progress, she could see Victor making mock threatening gestures aimed at the burly men he blamed for his current misery.

While the men assembled the cherry wood poster bed, Lauren looked back at Victor and shook her finger at him. Lounging against the doorframe, he gave her a wolfish grin and touched his belt buckle. She winked at him before running her hands over her hips and up her ribcage to graze her aching breasts. When he touched his fly, she laughed and shook her head.

Satisfied that the deliverymen were working quickly, she looked through the stacks of crates and boxes. She found one that had linen written across the side. Turning to find Victor smiling at her, she snapped her fingers and pointed to the large container.

He chuckled and sauntered across the room to smile into her eyes. "I know you're not wearing any knickers and it's making me hard as granite."

"I'm pretty anxious to see your underpants too."

"Want me to stop with the sex words and make the bed?"

"That's right." She touched his lips with her fingertips and whispered, "I'll hurry these guys out of here. We don't have to have sheets."

"Lauren. I'll find the sheets." He caressed her butt and then went to work opening the hefty container.

At last the men were gone and she locked the door and hurried back to the bedroom, kicking off her shoes and holding back a yell of anticipation. Her heart swelled with love to see Victor scrambling around throwing sheets and a quilt over the bed. He looked up with a wry grin.

"Will that be okay?"

"It's more than okay, Raven." She crawled onto the bed and put her arms around his neck. "Now. Where were we?"

"Right about here," he said and slid his hand under her blouse.

He looked slightly apologetic when buttons popped off the dainty top, but didn't slow up in the removal of her clothing. While he slipped off her bra, she unbuckled his belt and unzipped his slacks. They fell to the floor making a soft clicking sound. Pushing his shirt aside, she pressed her lips to his belly and inhaled the clean scent of his skin.

Wanting more, she worked his shorts off his butt and kissed the hard flesh of his stomach, teasing him with a lick of her tongue. His muscles tensed under her hands and she had to taste more of him.

In a flash, she lay back to roll her skirt off and tossed it into the air. Licking her lips, she watched him shed the last bit of clothing he wore. Feeling like a hungry cat, she got onto her knees and hugged his waist before he could lay down.

"Don't move Raven." She met his intense gaze with a witchy smile.

He closed his eyes, caressing her hair and then let out a loud groan when she gripped him firmly in her hand.

"You're still my tomcat, Raven."

His second moan was louder, creating new desire in her to know everything about him. She nuzzled the coarse hair surrounding his ridged member, lapping out her tongue taste the weighty flesh that rose up from the dense forest of hair. She liked the feel of it and touched the tip of his member with her lips. Taking him into her mouth, she explored the smooth flesh with her tongue. His groan encouraged her to go further, to take him deeper into her mouth. She felt his hips lurch forward and his hands catch her face.

"Enough, woman," he said in a husky voice. "I can only stand so much." He laid her back on the bed and leaned to kiss her stomach before working his way up her inner thighs to nuzzle her quivering heat.

The strength drained from her body while his tongue teased and probed her quivering warmth. Digging her fingers into his hair, she held his face close until the agony became too much to bear. A tiny nip of his teeth and a hard suckle of his lips made her cry out to him.

"Raven ... together."

He lay her back on the bed and went into the spread of her legs, sliding into her with the urgency borne of a long deprivation.

Arching her back to take him into her soul, she clung to her love, giving herself completely. The sheer joy of being in his arms and being joined with him was too much to withstand. Tears streamed down her cheeks with the power of her climax, the power of love.

Rolled up together in the quilt, a soft quiet of contentment fell over them. Lauren hadn't completely recovered from her emotional ride when he spoke to her.

"I've never known you to cry before." He tipped her chin up to smile at her. "Personally, I wanted to yell like Tarzan."

She smacked his cheek playfully and laughed. "For your information, you did."

"Why did you cry?"

"Being a man, you wouldn't understand."

He sat up to bunch his pillow under his head. "Try me."

"Okay." She sighed softly. "Because I love ... being with you so much that it becomes too much to hold inside." Was he understanding her words or even listening? His brows lifted as she related her deepest emotions to him.

"Was that so hard to tell me?" He pulled her across his chest and gazed intently into her eyes. "Listen to this pussycat. The reason I want to yell like Tarzan is because I feel the same things about you."

Her lips parted as if she would speak. He pressed his thumb to her mouth. "Wait. I'm saying this before I lose my nerve. This is a first for me, wanting to be with just one woman twenty-four hours a day and feeling like a dead man until the next time I see you."

"So, Raven." She worked her body into position to lie on him, rerunning his words over in her spiraling thoughts. *Don't cry again. He obviously isn't comfortable with tears.* "What are you saying?"

"I'm saying life is hell when I can't be with you."

She couldn't help the soft smile that widened into a grin. "You really mean that, don't you?"

He kissed her hard and held her close to his heart. "I'm so much in love with you, Lauren, that I feel you in my blood." He cocked his head to one side and raised one brow. "And you, Miss Rose. Don't you have something to tell me?"

She lay her head down on his chest and breathed deeply to stem the fresh flood of tears stinging her lids. What could she say in answer to his statement without sounding possessive or expectant of forever with him.

"You know of course that I'll expect to hear that on a regular basis." She raised up to gaze into his eyes and her grin had reappeared. "So, just exactly when did you realize you were nutty about me?"

"It took just one look, Lauren." His strong hands moved her off him and onto the bed. "I'm still waiting baby."

She moistened her lips and swiped at the single tear welling in the corner of her eye. Getting onto her knees, she pressed close to his body and ignored the break in her voice.

"I'm not complete without you, Raven. I can't wait to be with you and I feel like crying when you leave me." Her hand trembled against his cheek. "I fell in love with you the night we met."

He laughed and hugged her tightly while kissing her cheeks repeatedly. "Hey, I think we're going steady."

"Want to wear my toe ring?" She smiled and let happiness evict the little sliver of doubt that pierced her heart.

"In my nose if that's what you want."

"Just tell me you love me. That's all I want."

"I love you, Lauren. Now and forever."

"Now and forever," she whispered. Her life was full, now and forever.

Chapter Eighteen

Lauren looked the part of the consummate professional woman, taking the elevator up to the sixth floor of the Christopher Building. She caught a glimpse of her reflection in the mirror at the back of the crowded elevator. Appearances were important to these agencies, and she didn't want to give the boss any reason to doubt her ability to fit in.

She had worn a fitted black jacket over a matching short skirt. A twinge of self-doubt hit her. Maybe she should put her coat on. Was there too much leg showing above the classic black pumps on her cold feet? Well, honey. Too late to worry about that now. The elevator doors are opening and you have no place to go but into the office of Steve Alton.

The firm was quite a change from the Swanson's with its mahogany furniture and expensive window treatments. Her heels sank into the sand colored carpeting with each step she took across the floor. She straightened her posture and walked into the beautiful reception area.

"Miss Rose." A sophisticated woman seated at a country French desk greeted her. "I'm Helen Dole, Mister Alton's personal secretary. Come with me, please. Mister Alton is expecting you."

"I'm so early. I mean, are you sure?" Stop the prattling. You're not acting like an adult. "I mean, that's wonderful. That he could see me so soon."

Helen moved across the carpeted floor with enviable grace while Lauren prayed she wouldn't break off a heel in the deep plush. How was she supposed to appear cosmopolitan while high stepping like a goose? Stop it. You've come too far to blow it now.

Helen turned to look back at Lauren. "You're his only appointment today because of the holidays. The staff is always given a generous vacation at this time." She waited for Lauren to reach the door and smiled at her. "Mister Alton is anxious to meet you."

Lauren's brows lifted imperceptibly, but she didn't question her preferential treatment. Just enjoy it, woman. Lord knows you've been getting more than your share lately.

Without knocking on the formidable looking door that bore Steve

Alton's name, Helen turned the brass doorknob and pushed it open. Sitting at a gleaming teak desk was a giant of a man in a dark blue Armani suit. He was as fair as Victor was dark and his eyes twinkled when he smiled at her. He stood and held his hand out.

"Come in Miss Rose." He moved around to the front of the desk and pulled out a chair for her. "Thank you for agreeing to come in today. I know you are busy settling in and getting your shopping done."

Had she heard him correctly? "It's no trouble at all, Mister Alton." She shook his hand, glad his grip was non-injurious and sat down. "Please. Call me Lauren."

He nodded in agreement. "Around here, everyone calls me Steve." He went back to his chair and sat down to look at the papers on his desk. "Lauren. After seeing your work, we feel fortunate to have you with us."

Was she dreaming? He wasn't aware of the dozens of turndowns by other design houses. She straightened her shoulders and smiled with swelling confidence.

"I'm pleased you like my work. Finding a place with a name house in New York is almost impossible. I'm the fortunate one."

He thumbed through the pages of the folder before commenting. "Your work speaks for its self. We've gotten glowing referrals from everyone that knows you."

Lauren wondered whom the referrals had come from. A twinge of suspicion grew in her mind. "Were you a friend of my father's? Samuel Rose."

He leaned back in his chair and shook his head. "I'm sure I would remember him. You say that as if he's passed on."

"He's been gone for some time." She took a shaky breath; confident he hadn't hired her for any reason other than her ability to design clothing.

He closed the folder and set it aside. "We've been wanting to work in a new line for some time, the revival of glamour. And you have the eye for it."

She struggled to remain calm and not say something foolish. "I have several collections to show you." She stood when he did. "Do you have definite ideas or sketches for me to follow?"

He came around the desk and took her arm. "I don't believe in getting in our designers' hair. You'll have all the creative room you need."

"I appreciate that. More than you know." Was he kidding? The man's words thrilled her to death. "Would it be possible to see my work area?"

"That's what I like. A designer eager to create." He opened the door and walked her out into the reception area. "After you see your office, Miss Dole will have some forms for you to fill out. The usual personnel questions."

Was there a goofy grin on her face? Probably. The tour he took her on was like walking in a dream. What she had expected to be a cubicle with bad lighting was a spacious room with windows and ergonomically corrects chairs. There were three drawing tables and open closets along one wall to hang her creations. At one end of the room was a coffee nook, supplied with everything to keep the fancy pot going constantly.

She had to be the luckiest woman in the world and couldn't wait to share her happiness with Victor.

* * * *

What the hell had he gotten himself into? Victor could think of a dozen reasons why he shouldn't be having Christmas dinner with Lauren and her family. What if someone brought up the subject of his buying out Samuel Rose? And the other little thing with Raini? It hardly mattered that their relationship had fizzled like a wet firecracker. Lauren probably wouldn't see his romance with her sister as nothing. He was wise enough to know women never wanted to be second to their sisters. He hadn't lied to her, just hadn't told her about it. Damn. Why hadn't he been upfront with her? That's a laugh, you sneaky bastard. You were afraid of missing out on a minute of being with her. You never once considered you would fall in love with her.

He yanked his tie loose. He wasn't going. *Yes, you are, you damned fool. She wouldn't understand. And what would you tell her? How do you tell her I'm the guy you think caused your father's death? Oh yeah, and I got hot and bothered with your sister. And because it happened a while back, I'm sure you'll see the humor there. Oh yeah, you like the great job and nice apartment too? I'm the guy that fixed that for you.*

He sunk down on the bed and rubbed his forehead. All of that would be reason enough for her to kick his ass. He groaned, recalling his complimentary description of himself. The fix it man. Yeah, you fixed it, bub. In the deepest recesses of his mind, he heard the nagging question that was never far away. What are you going to do? Damned if he had a clue.

He leaned over to tie his shoes and frowned darkly when a lace snapped. A sign of things to come? He stood up and then pulled a pair of loafers from the closet. If he didn't hurry, he would be late and he'd promised Lauren he would be early. Another lie. He grabbed his jacket from the bed and headed for the door.

He stopped in the entry hall to pick up the gifts he was taking with him. A good bottle of brandy for Adam, flowers for Raini and his gift for Lauren. That was the one thing he felt good about. It was the clearest statement of his feelings that he dared give her.

When he reached the lobby, he exchanged a few words with the doorman and handed the man a generous tip before stepping outside to wait for his taxi. Snow fell from the gray skies and had covered his hair before the hack pulled up to the curb. He climbed in and settled back with a grimace. The damned flowers were probably going to turn black before he got there.

By the time he arrived at Raini's apartment, he had cold feet and it wasn't from tromping around in the snow. He paid his tab and walked resolutely into the building to push the button for the elevator. While he stood at the apartment door, he gave thought to turning around and leaving. But Lauren was waiting so he pressed the doorbell. Lauren opened the door.

"Hello gorgeous," he said. His anxiety went south when she smiled at him. "Sorry about the early thing. It's snowing and I broke a shoelace." Okay, stupid. She's looking at you like you've flipped out. But that smile of hers always makes you crazy.

"It's okay, Raven." She took his coat and shut the door before taking his hand to lead him in to the entry hall. "You're here. That's all I want."

He shot a glance around before drawing her into his arms. He pressed a soft lingering kiss to her lips, and then deepened it as he drew her close.

When he lifted his head to smile into her eyes, she laughed softly.

"Since you're in front of me, I can't imagine what's poking me in the backside."

Somehow, he'd managed to not drop the things he held. He grinned and placed his special offering in her hand.

"What's this?" she asked and examined the fabric of the gift box.

"Merry Christmas, baby." He glanced from the box to her face. "You like opening gifts early. Go ahead."

He loved the sparkle in her eyes while her slender fingers plucked the silver cord from the blue velvet container. His heart hammered against his ribs when she lifted the lid and gasped softly.

"Raven. You angel," she whispered and took the fine gold chain from its bed of white silk. "What does this beautiful thing signify?

That you really love me?"

"Damned straight," he murmured. He touched the Burmese ruby that had been expertly cut to look like a full smiling moon. "It's to remind you that every time we make love, we set the moon on fire."

"You're the sweetest man alive and you love me," she said with a teasing smile. She held the fine piece of jewelry up to gaze at the star fashioned from a blazing white diamond. "And the star?"

He took the necklace and fastened it about her throat, kissing her nape before she turned to face him. "I wanted to give you the moon and the stars, but this was the best I could do."

She lifted her arms to hug his neck. "Everything you do is the best, Raven." She whispered against his mouth. "I love you so much, my darling."

She patted his chest and stepped away from him to take a box from the hall table and then handed it to him. "Merry Christmas, Raven." She tapped the silver wrapped box and sighed. "I'm afraid it's not as grand as your gift to me."

He tore the paper off and opened the box. Inside was a tasteful white silk neck scarf. "Thank you, baby. It's exactly what I need." He was hit hard by the glow in her eyes.

The sound of laughter and music drifted out from the living room. He reluctantly let her lead him away from the sweet private moment they had shared.

"Sounds like the party is in full swing."

She patted his rear and laughed. "I hope you're ready to listen to bad jokes and be pinched by the ladies."

He chuckled and followed her, taking the time to look at what she wore. Some kind of burnished gold lounge outfit that made her look like an exotic princess. He grinned when he saw the glimmer of a gold toe ring on her right foot. Strappy three-inch heels in a snowstorm. What a woman.

Before they went in to dinner, Raini and Adam asked for everyone's attention. They were holding hands and smiling like teenagers.

"Everyone, and especially my sister, Lauren, we have something wonderful to share with you. We couldn't think of a more appropriate time for this." Raini clung to Adam's arm. "We're expecting our first child next summer."

There was silence for a moment, before everyone rushed to congratulate the expectant parents. Victor's smile dimmed when he caught Lauren's pained expression.

"What is it, Gorgeous?" He turned her away from the noisy

group. "What can I do to make it better?"

"I'm fine, Raven. Just stunned." She dabbed the corners of her eyes and smiled. "I have to go tell my sister how happy I am for her."

She left him to embrace her beaming sister and brother-in-law. Victor gave a baffled frown at Lauren's reaction. When she came back to stand beside him, there was a new set to her dainty chin. She touched the gems at her throat and smiled sensuously up at him.

"Raven. The second the opportunity presents itself, we're going to my place and set the tree on fire with our lovemaking."

Victor shook his head. The rapid transition from tears to seduction was amazing. How did women change moods like they were pantyhose? Lord help him. How was he going to top all the things they had done before? But he sure as hell would try.

Chapter Nineteen

Lauren pushed the alarm button into the off position and slipped out of bed. She hadn't slept well even though Victor had spent the night. Being restless and dissatisfied was becoming a constant malady in her life, and she didn't have a clue why she was in such a funk. *You should be happy as a lark, but you're not. Post holiday blues, maybe? Stop avoiding the truth. The job you coveted for so long is far more demanding of your time than you were prepared to give. Plus, Victor isn't the carefree man you dreamed up. He's out of town on business trips too often and the most needling thing is Raini positively blooming in her pregnancy. You should be ashamed of your jealousy over her pregnancy, but you're longing for the same kind of happiness she has been blessed with.*

She slid a speculative gaze over Victor before moving around to the foot of the bed. Love for him rushed through her like a comforting balm. Her gaze traveled up from his nice big feet to his hairy calves. She reached out and slid her hand up the hard muscle of his thigh. He stirred and rolled over onto his belly, groaning before pulling a pillow over his head. She tickled the bottom of his foot.

"Let's make a baby." She didn't think he had heard her until he rolled onto his back and sat up to stare at her.

"What?" His forehead furrowed and his eyes narrowed.

"A baby." She picked up his shirt and slipped it on.

"That's what I thought you said."

She undulated her hips and caressed her breasts and stomach. "Get ready to sow seed, mister."

He lay back against the pillows and observed her sexy antics; following her seductive hip gyrations and exhibitionist way she opened the shirt to display her body for his pleasure.

"What are you doing?"

"This is the fertility dance." She worked her hips in the best tradition of belly dance and smiled seductively at him. "I think I'm fertile now. Let's play farmer in the dell."

He caught her in his arms when she flopped onto the bed with him.

"You're not serious about this, are you?"

She looked down at his full erection and laughed softly. "Aren't you?"

"I'm hard, but that's the way I stay around you."

"Let's make use of that beautiful thing."

He caught her chin in his fingers and tipped her face up to kiss her mouth. "This baby thing. Let's talk about that first."

She heard something unusual in his voice. Refusal of something she wanted. "I said, I want a baby. Are you telling me that you don't want to have one with me?"

"I didn't say that."

"It couldn't have been clearer. Either you love me enough to get us pregnant or you don't." She pulled away and glared at him while fighting back the hot tears burning her eyelids. "You don't believe I'm qualified to have your child."

"Damn it, Lauren. That isn't true." He exhaled roughly. "Have you thought about what you're saying?"

"Apparently a lot more than you have." She pulled out of his arms and slid off the bed to skin his shirt off. "You're not the only man with the right plumbing to make this happen." She bit the tip of her tongue, instantly regretting the reckless statement. But it was too late.

He got to his feet and stood with his hands on his hips, looking at her with a dark scowl. "You wouldn't do that."

Her chin quivered and tears welled in her eyes. "No, I wouldn't." She stalked off to the bathroom and started the shower. He followed her. "Don't worry. I'll go back on the pill, Mister Raven."

"Back to Mister again," he muttered. "Listen, pussycat."

She waved him off. "Can't hear you over the shower."

He reached in the stall and shut the water off. "I'm sorry if you think I don't understand what you're feeling."

She turned the water back on. "You don't and if you say anything about it being that time of the month, I'll give you a vasectomy."

He went to the vanity to begin lathering his face and watched her in the mirror. "Want me to shave your legs?"

"Oh. Now I have stubble?"

"No, I just want to play with your legs." When she didn't answer, he laid the shaving brush down and turned to face her. "I'd rather you screamed at me than give me the silent treatment."

"Reminiscent of your former wife, I suppose."

"No. She yelled her bloody head off which is what you're dying to do." He strode to where she stood stiff with resentment and picked her up. "We're going in the shower so you can sound off."

He laughed as he carried her under the spray. She lay back like a sack of potatoes until he set her down, then she backed up against the tile wall.

"You'll turn blue before I yell."

"You're hot. Why not let it out? Tell me what's going on in that beautiful head of yours."

"Okay. You're gone too much."

"I have to travel."

"My apartment's a mess."

"It's a great place."

"I'm not doing a damned thing at work."

"Take some time off."

"No. You take some time off."

He touched her cheek and studied her face with a crooked smile. "Let's talk about the baby."

She lowered her gaze and watched rivulets of water run off the bronzed muscles and down to his hard belly. She had an ache in her soul that nothing would satisfy except having something permanent with Victor, and he didn't feel the same way. She tapped his lips with her fingertip.

"Just a passing fancy, Raven. I've already forgotten it."

He narrowed his eyes and shook his head. "No you haven't. Let's talk this out."

"I said--subject's closed." She took the fastest shower of her life and slapped his hand when he tried to wash her back. He was in no hurry and it made her angry to know he wasn't upset. She had raved like a fishmonger and he hadn't lost his temper. That caused her more distress because she didn't really know what he was feeling.

She raked her fingers through her dripping hair and looked at him while he lathered up a second time. *Get out before you start doing that for him. He's not deserving of special attention.* She slid against his solid body on her way out of the stall. "And don't think that was a ploy to get you in the mood."

"Last thing on my mind."

The sweater she dragged over her head caught in her damp hair and she cursed under her breath. The object of her anger was stuffing his shirt in his pants and brushing his hair while casting an occasional glance her way. For a few seconds, she had thought about slapping his face for the offhand way he'd treated her idea. She bit her lip and drew in deep breaths to stop the trembling in her stomach. She wouldn't get over this blow for a long while.

They dressed in silence until he laughed. She secured the last button of her jacket before quizzing him.

"There's something funny going on, Mister Raven?"

"Only if you see the humor in someone wearing two different styles of shoe."

She thought he was talking about himself until she saw she wore one navy pump and one open-toed black platform. "Well, at least you didn't let me go out like this."

After she had matched her shoes, she went to the living room where he waited. He smiled at her and picked up his coat before leaning over to kiss her cheek.

"I want to say something before we leave each other today. I'm proud you want to have my baby. It's the compliment of a lifetime."

She ducked her chin and grabbed her sketch case and handbag. "I'm going to be late--again."

He opened the door and grinned down at her when she walked past him and out into the hallway. "You look mighty fine this morning."

She waited until he had locked the door before answering him. "You would too if you'd shaved both sides of your face."

* * * *

"Yes, of course I still love you." Lauren turned her chair away from the open door of her office and smiled. "You big dummy." Her heart swelled in her breast as the sound of Victor's laughter warmed her soul and kissed her ear through the phone line.

"So. You're willing to sit with Rachel tonight? I know it's short notice, but Annie has a cold and Rachel has begged for you to stay with her instead of her usual stand-in sitter. It's a quick jump to Chicago and I'll be back early in the morning."

Lauren felt her heartstrings being plunked by a six-year old con artist. The conversation that had passed between her and Victor that morning no longer made her angry. She'd had no right to spring something like that on him.

"Raven, I ... umm. About this morning. It must have been PMS and I'd love to stay with Rachel." She heard his soft exhale.

"Rachel will be excited. Uh ... what happened this morning? I wasn't expecting that and I didn't handle it well."

"I'm just full of surprises, aren't I?"

"Just one of the many reasons I love you, pussycat." He hesitated before further probing the subject. "Would you want to have that conversation again sometime in the future?"

She chewed on the eraser of her pencil and let her shoulders slump a little. "Don't try to humor me, Raven. I told you I'm premenstrual."

He made a choking sound and then chuckled. "Rachel and I will pick you up at your apartment." After a half second of silence, he laughed. "Are you ready for this?"

She laughed and made kissing sounds into the mouthpiece. "You can't scare me. How much trouble can one sweet little girl be?"

* * * *

After Victor had left for the airport, Lauren began to doubt her sanity. *What was she doing chasing after a six-year-old with energy to burn?*

"Rachel," she wheezed. "Stop running around the house and I'll play dolls with you."

The answer she got was a saucy 'no' accompanied by a giggle and a request.

"I want candy." Rachel stopped running long enough to issue her demand.

"Where is it?" Lauren was willing to resort to anything for a peaceful resolution.

"The top shelf in the cabinet over the refrigerator." Rachel ran ahead of Lauren. "I'll show you."

"I figured you'd know where it was."

"I always get as much as I want."

Lauren gave the little girl a dubious smile. "Someone told me that you get two of whatever is up there."

When Lauren pulled the box of treats off the shelf, she knew the rambunctious child had suckered her when she saw the size of the candy bars.

"I think we should share one of these. Don't you?"

Rachel's face crumpled into a pre-tear expression, but she quickly straightened her face. "Okay."

Lauren cut one of the bars into pieces. She wondered if she was doing the right thing. "How about some milk with your candy?"

"No, I want a cola."

"No."

Rachel looked aghast at Lauren's firm refusal.

"Rachel. You're not going to cry, are you?" Lauren didn't think she could handle tears, especially if she was the cause.

"Not if you'll play house with me."

"Deal." Lauren watched Victor's child with interest. She was taken with the daintiness of Rachel's fingers and the chipped red polish on her nails. "I have an idea. Let me give you a manicure."

"I want lipstick too."

Lauren decided her charge was going far in life. She was never at a loss for an answer or an alternate demand.

"All right, but just a little." Lauren wiped chocolate from Rachel's hands and face. "First, you need a bath."

"I'm not dirty."

"No bath--no manicure and no lipstick."

To Lauren's relief, Rachel took her hand and led her into an ultra feminine room that shouted 'spoiled female.' She had seen Rachel's room before, but tonight a mountain of stuffed animals and dolls concealed the pink down comforter. Lauren shook her head in wonder while gazing at the wall shelves stuffed to capacity with Barbie dolls, games and tea sets.

While Rachel was getting a nightgown, the open doors of triple wall closets drew Lauren's attention. There were double racks of dresses in every shade and fabric plus a closet of shoes. She grinned when she realized there must be at least fifty pair of shoes and boots in the closet. The child was a shoe fanatic, just like her. She turned her attention back to the little girl.

"Ready for your bath?"

"Um hum."

Looking at what Rachel held in her hand, Lauren grinned. "How about panties?"

"Oh yeah." Rachel giggled and opened another drawer to drag out a pair of pink polka-dot panties. "Now I'm ready." She began stripping off her clothing as she ran for Victor's bathroom. "Don't forget my bubble bath."

After the water was drawn and Rachel played in the tub, Lauren sat on the floor to make certain nothing went wrong. Bath time was declared over when Rachel began to splash her with water. Getting the little girl dried off proved to be harder than Lauren had anticipated and she finally wrapped her in a huge towel to stop her wriggling.

"Now you little rabbit." She gave Rachel's damp hair a final swish of the towel. "Let's get you dressed and then you get a manicure."

"Can I have a coke?"

"No."

Rachel grew silent while she was being dressed, but was apparently not upset. She threw her arms around Lauren's neck and smiled at her.

"I love you, Lauren."

"Well ... I love you too, Rachel. Who wouldn't adore someone as sweet as you?"

"I love Daddy." Rachel sat remarkably still while her hair was being brushed. "He loves you too."

Lauren smiled at her charge's comment. It was completely unexpected and endearing.

"You look like a princess, Rachel. Let's do your nails now."

"Then can I have a coke?"

"No."

"Okay."

While Lauren worked on Rachel's tiny nails, she caught the distant flash of lightning through the bedroom window. Rachel jumped when a clap of thunder followed the lightning.

"We're safe in here, honey." Lauren didn't like storms either and understood the child's fear. "I'll close the drapes and it won't bother us."

"I don't want to stay in here." Rachel scrambled off the bed and scampered out of the room.

Lauren hurried after her. She panicked when she couldn't find her. She flipped on the overhead lights in the living room and darted a worried glance around the room. "Rachel."

"I'm here."

The small and muffled voice had come from behind a sofa where she huddled with a rag doll.

"I'm here, sweetheart. Don't be afraid." She crawled over the back of the sofa to hug Rachel close. *Now what was she supposed to do?* A memory from her childhood set her into action.

"Let's play camp out. Stay here and I'll set up our tent."

She hurried around the apartment and gathered up blankets, pillows and a flashlight. She was out of breath by the time she had assembled a tent from kitchen chairs and blankets.

"Okay, honey. Your tent is ready."

Rachel peered around the corner of the couch and then ran for the shelter Lauren had created. She flopped on the pillows and smiled happily at Lauren.

"I'm hungry now."

"Let me look at the list your daddy left."

"No. He won't care what we eat now."

"All right. I'll find something for you."

Lauren checked the list that Victor had left on the refrigerator door. She groaned softly. Rachel's bedtime was eight o'clock. It was past nine and there she was making snacks. She piled a plate high with snacks and tossed a bag of popcorn in the microwave.

Hearing a shriek coming from the living room set her into high gear. She took the half popped corn from the microwave and loaded it on top of the other snacks. Grabbing two bottles of coke, she scurried back to reassure Rachel.

Crawling under the makeshift tent, she set the plate of snacks down.

"Look. Goodies." She saw the disappointment on Rachel's face. "The carrot sticks are good and the apple wedges are yummy." *Hog wash. She knows you are being ridiculous.* Lauren relented and handed Rachel the popcorn and a coke. "How's that?"

Rachel's smile was reward enough for her efforts. What harm was there in a little popcorn and a coke? Time would tell, she thought as she watched Rachel guzzle her drink. List, smish, she decided. She was winging it and took a long drink of her own cola.

"Aren't you sleepy?" Lauren was hopeful.

"Uh uh." Rachel crawled out of the tent. "I'm not sleepy. Are you?"

Lauren knew she had to be tougher or the child would stay up until midnight. "Sleepy-peepy. You should have been asleep long ago." She picked Rachel up and carried her to her room. After removing the toys from the bed and several requests for water, she tucked Rachel in for the night. She kissed the yawning little girl and prayed silently that the night was ending as it was supposed to.

She left the door to Rachel's room ajar and headed for the guestroom. She quickly got into her pajamas and prepared to settle down in the comfortable bed with one of the magazines she had brought with her. The photos began to blur and she yawned before losing the battle against the need to sleep.

She jumped when the magazine she had been reading slipped from her fingers and tumbled to the floor. When her eyes fluttered open, she saw Rachel peering into her face. She sat up to help her onto the bed.

"What is it, honey? Can't sleep?"

"It's still making lights outside." Rachel rubbed her cheeks and fussed with her hair. "Do you have room for me?"

"Always," Lauren said. "Get under the comforter. You have to get some sleep."

Rachel scrambled in beside Lauren and snuggled down like a soft kitten. While she was tucking the sleepy child in, Lauren noticed a familiar scent permeating the air. Raven's scent.

"You've been in your daddy's room and his cologne."

"Um hum."

"It's too masculine for you, Rachel."
"Um hum."
No doubt there was a lengthy explanation for her to be reeking of men's cologne, but that would have to wait. The little imp had fallen asleep.

Chapter Twenty

Victor stood with his hands on his hips and looked around the quiet living room. What was this? He dropped his briefcase on the coffee table and then inspected the makeshift tent. Squatting down to peer under the blanket, he took in the scene and shook his head. Empty soda bottles and a crumpled popcorn bag. Party time, he thought with a grin.

He followed the trail of doll clothes and manicure implements to his bathroom. It was obvious a female had bathed in his tub. Lacy undies and an empty bubble bath bottle had been discarded onto his bathmat. His hair dryer had been strung over the doorknob and two pink barrettes had been clamped to the roll of toilet tissue. The crowning touch was a Barbie doll perched over the toilet bowel.

His princess must have led Lauren on a merry and exhilarating chase from the looks of the place. Since it was so early, he thought about catching a nap before Rachel woke and seized the day. Before he made it to his room, another idea set off skyrockets in his brain. Lauren. She was in the guest room, warm and sleepy and smelling like heaven. His head spun with a myriad of mind-bending visions of sexual adventures with his lovely Lauren.

When he pushed the open to look inside the guest room, his randy thoughts were instantly squashed. What he saw was breathtaking in its sweet simplicity. Lauren appeared perfectly comfortable even though Rachel's foot was pressed to her cheek. He wanted to straighten his daughter to a more comfortable position for both their sakes, but opted to leave them alone.

Just as well, he thought with a soft chuckle. He needed sleep and it appeared the ladies had put in a late night. He went into his room and wasn't surprised to see the top of his cologne bottle lying on the floor. His little angel had been busy while Lauren's back was turned. He shucked his clothes off and crawled into bed for that longed for forty winks.

* * * *

The sound of female laughter gently greeted Victor when he woke and shook the weariness from his bones. Lord, how could they be so full of vim at this hour of the morning? He looked at the bedside clock before tossing it into a nearby chair. Two females? How could he have forgotten? Lauren was out there in his kitchen. Get up man. They're having another party without you.

He showered and dressed in a hurry and was still working on his tie when he looked around the kitchen door. Rachel and Lauren sat at the counter sharing a bowl of cereal. He noticed the box of cereal had been dumped into a large bowl. Rachel must have wanted the toy at the bottom. He groaned softly when Rachel helped herself to a sip of Lauren's coffee. He liked the way Rachel glowed with happiness because of Lauren's attention. *Oh brother, don't we all.* The fact his daughter was dressed and spit-shine clean was a relief. He didn't look forward to a tussle with the little girl. Trying to feed her and get her into her uniform was a daily war. Things were definitely looking up today.

"Good morning, ladies."

Both Lauren and Rachel turned to smile at him.

"We're not ladies, Daddy." Rachel handed the empty cereal box to him. "We're girls."

"I know. I'm seriously outnumbered here." He took the stool next to Lauren. "But I like it." He gave her a devilish smile.

"I'm sure of that," she said and lay her hand on his thigh beneath the counter. "Why didn't you wake me?"

"Believe me. I was going to, but you had a foot in your face when I ... looked in on you." He covered her hand with his and squeezed her fingers.

Lauren touched her knee to his, smiling sweetly into his expressive eyes. "I should make you a man sized breakfast to make up for that."

"It'll take a lot of breakfasts to smooth this over." He laughed and kissed her cheek. "I'll grab something at work. Anyone want a ride this morning?"

"We both do, Daddy." Rachel skipped from the kitchen to get her coat and gloves from her room.

"How about you, baby?" he asked and pulled Lauren into his arms for a hard kiss.

"You can drop me off at the office after you get Rachel to school. Okay?" She grinned at him and touched his collar. "Don't forget to put a jacket on. Oh, and make sure you've shaved both sides of your face."

"You know. I could get used to taking orders from you." He reached around her to pick up her cup. He grinned at her after drinking the last of her coffee. "You do it in such a cute way."

"Don't get too used to it, Raven." She picked up her handbag from the counter. "I'm usually a bitch in the morning."

"Yes, and you snore."

He knew the desire to pinch him was hitting her hard, but she wouldn't do anything to upset his daughter. Was it any wonder he loved her so much. Watching her get Rachel bundled up against the cold made him think of something else. The baby thing. He mentally shook himself. He figured he'd completely messed up with her. *You messed up a long time ago, you fool and now you can take the low road and keep lying or spill your insides. You know she'll drop kick you out of her life ... so, you'll keep quiet and keep adding ammo to the explosion. Not if it happens, but when.*

* * * *

She couldn't believe how lonely her apartment felt. What was wrong with her? Lauren dropped onto the couch she had bought even though she didn't really like it. That seemed to be the path she followed lately. She was settling, and the idea irked and frustrated her.

She kicked her shoes off and propped her feet up on the coffee table she detested almost as much as she hated the couch. But at the moment, she was too beat to care much that her plans for decorating were dead last on her list of things to do. Tears that had threatened to spill for several weeks began to flow and she let them. Facing the truth, she put a name on her down mood. She was lonely and completely disorganized. She wanted to be with Victor and Rachel.

Admitting to the problem only made it worse. *It's your own fault, woman. You were the one that could handle the situation, remember? You didn't need love and a steady diet of one man. If you didn't feel so horrible, you would laugh at yourself.*

Disgusted with her self-pity, she got to her feet and walked around the cluttered living room. Cripes. What a mess. She began gathering up upholstery samples and piled them in a corner. The end of her patience came after she stumbled over a roll of drapery material. And now, the insistent ringing of the doorbell pierced the air.

In her rush to get to the door and end the intrusive ringing, she tripped over a box of tile. She clenched her teeth and peered through he peephole before throwing open the door. "Victor."

She was in his arms and crying like a baby, clinging to him while he closed the door behind them. Wrapping his arms around her in a comforting, protective way.

"What's happened, baby?" He tried to see her face, but she pressed closer to his chest. "Tell me what's going on."

Whatever she said was garbled against his neck and her arms

clung tighter. He didn't ask any more questions, only held her to murmur soothing words. Having composed herself enough to speak, she took the handkerchief he offered and blew several times before speaking.

"What a greeting, huh?" She kissed him firmly on his mouth. "I'm so glad you're here tonight."

He wiped a tear from her cheek and hugged her protectively. "Miss Rose. You need some coddling." He grinned down at her. "Care to coddle?"

She laughed and then immediately burst into tears again. "I don't know what's wrong except maybe the fact I...." She moved away from him and twisted a swatch of fabric into a knot. "I'm not handling anything like an adult would."

He gave her the space she needed to pace back and forth in front of him. When she dabbed at her eyes with the swatch, he reached for her and pulled her into a hard embrace.

"This isn't working out," he said decisively.

She pushed on his chest and leaned back to gaze into his eyes. "No, I guess it isn't." Her heart froze with fear. What was he telling her? "I'll get this place straightened out and you'll like it then."

"To hell with the apartment unless you simply have to keep it." He kissed her mouth and nuzzled her cheek. "I think we should stop this. I want to go to bed with you at night and wake up to find you beside me every morning."

A tremor of disappointment that assailed her was hard to disguise. "You mean, live together."

"That's the usual arrangement for a married couple, isn't it?"

He was proposing and his voice poured from his mouth like orange blossom honey straight to her heart. She could only offer a fresh round of tears. When she managed to lift her head and meet his perplexed gaze, he jostled her gently.

"Well, don't cry, pussycat. You're making me nervous." He rocked her in his arms. "Do you think you could pull me out of the fire, Lauren? I haven't heard your answer."

Her hand shook when she took his to press it against her trembling heart. "I love you Victor Raven, so much I can't breath while you're away from me." She leaned against his tall frame and inhaled deeply to steady her frayed emotions. "Just try to get out of this one, Raven. I'm going to marry you."

Chapter Twenty-one

Lauren had just wrapped up an impromptu meeting with Steve and several of the designers when she looked up to see Raini walking through the door of her office.

"Raini. How nice." She hurried to greet her sister and led her to a chair near her desk. "What brings you downtown?"

Raini sat down with a sigh and rubbed her lower back. "I came in for my checkup and thought since I was in the neighborhood, we could have lunch together."

"A marvelous idea, but are you sure you're up to it. You look pooped." The few strands of blond hair escaping the chignon at Raini's nape gave her a certain regal look of dishevelment.

"I'm a little weary of the pregnant look." Raini patted her rounded stomach. "I'll be quite happy when this child decides to make its debut."

Lauren smiled and thought of her future brood. "I can't wait to be pregnant."

Raini laughed and took the cup of tea Lauren poured from a carafe on her desk. "Let's have your engagement party first and then the little Raven's. By the way, have you decided on the gown?"

"Yes and it wasn't an easy choice. I'm going with the champagne silk with puffy sleeves and tons of caviar beading. What do you think?"

"I think it's perfect for you." Raini put her finger into the soil of the plant on Lauren's desk. "I believe that plant is barely clinging to life."

Lauren shrugged and grinned. "I'm no gardener, that's for sure." She sipped her tea and quieted for a moment. "I've been getting a lot of hang-up calls and my caller ID says they're from a cocktail lounge."

"If it worries you, I think you should inform the authorities. It could be a stalker." Raini shuddered and laid her hand on Lauren's arm. "It does bother you, doesn't it?"

"Yes and no. I'm just a little fearful everything will end."

"You have nothing to worry about, dear." Raini looked around at the room's plush amenities. "You've done well for yourself, little sister."

"Better than I could ever have hoped for." Lauren steepled her fingers beneath her chin. "I have to tell you, sister mine, that I am so happy you handled most of this party tonight. I swear I am getting brain fried with all the stuff I have going on."

"Yes." Raini smiled knowingly. "I saw your employer leaving and figured you were creating a storm of some kind."

"Steve just informed me that a movie studio has asked to contract me to design the wardrobe for their period film coming up."

Raini raised her brows and looked astounded. "You accepted of course."

"Of course, and I can't wait to tell Victor." Lauren opened a drawer in her desk and rummaged around before pulling out a package of Ho-Ho's. "Hors D'oeuvres?"

The two women fell into gales of laughter and shared the rich treats before leaving for lunch.

* * * *

Lauren was in a hurry to get to her apartment and appreciated not having to struggle with the lock when she got home. She stopped in the entry hall long enough to get her mail and then ran up the remaining steps to her apartment. She was surprised to see a bouquet of flowers had been left at her door. He'd been gone for a week and she had worked up a bubbling brew of suppressed desire. "My darling Raven," she murmured. *He really loves me.* She got her door unlocked and scooped the bouquet up to sniff the fragrant daisies and roses. Thinking of Victor, she searched for the card. There wasn't one.

A sniggle of worry slid up her spine. What if they were from that phone call person? A stalker? She darted a furtive glance around the hallway. *Don't be ridiculous. They're just flowers and lovely at that.* She chewed her lower lip while deciding on her next action. Nothing to think over. Decision made.

Grabbing the vase in both hands, she carried it to the trash shoot and heaved it through the opening. While she dusted her hands together, she listened to the flowers clatter down the chute. Oops. What if they had been from Victor and he mentioned them? She grimaced and began to regret her cowardly action. He probably wouldn't ask, but if he did, she would tell him the truth. He knew her and would understand. She hoped.

The need to hurry gripped her once she was in her apartment. She did a couple turns in the center of the living room floor before tossing her bag and sketch folder onto the sofa. She shivered with anticipation, knowing Victor would be unlocking the door soon.

She went into the bedroom to look at the gown she planned to wear that evening. Unconsciously, her gaze slid to the telephone on her nightstand. It irked her that she was fearful of looking at the caller ID list. She grabbed her robe and hurried back to the living room and glanced at the phone on the sofa table. Sure enough, there were messages. Before pushing the button to clear the calls, she checked the caller ID. Damn. There were three new calls from a cocktail lounge. No message, just that someone had dialed her number. That was ten times in three days. She was nervous and ticked off.

To hell with that. No more calls from the friendly cocktail lounge. One by one, she gathered the phones in the apartment and carried them into the kitchen, sparing only her cell phone. With a shrug, she dumped them into the dishwasher and shut the door. She was proud of her courage when she took the time to contact the phone company and her number would be changed immediately. That meant dozens of calls to make giving out her new number, but that could be put off for a while. She was feeling confident and looking forward to the evening.

A glance at the grandfather in the hallway sent her into a flurry of action. Fill the ice bucket, light candles in the bathroom and spray perfume on the bed. Before she left the bedroom, she draped a silk scarf over the lampshade and dropped her ultra long strand of pearls on the pillow Victor normally slept on. Atmosphere was everything mixed with a few surprises.

She was fluffing the sofa pillows when she heard a key scrap in the lock. Inhaling deeply to calm her pounding heart, she went to the entryway to wait. Her man was home.

* * * *

Later, Lauren smiled in the semi darkness of her bedroom and tightened her thighs around Victor's waist. "You know you'll have to give me sex anytime I want it after we're married." She laughed deep in her throat when he gripped her buttocks in his hands.

"Making demands already," he growled against her damp throat. "I have a few of my own."

"Such as," she teased while locking her fingers deep into his rumpled hair.

"Would you mind very much, getting on top?" He collapsed onto his side and laughed. "Don't grin at me like that. I'm practicing for my role as your husband."

"You devil," she purred and slid her hand between their heated bodies and clamped her fingers around his erection. "I'll be glad to ride for a while."

Being in the dominant position pleased Lauren. She straddled him and leaned back like a bronco rider. "I'm taking my time with you, Raven." She licked her lips and rocked against his hard length. "Scream when you've had enough."

"There's never enough." He groaned and worked his hips. "Ride 'em cowgirl." He smiled in a sensuous way and lifted her up with the power in his strong back.

She leaned over to gaze into his eyes. "I'm wearing your favorite spurs." Lauren thought her heart would burst with the surge of the love she felt for him. "I'm crazy for you, Raven. Completely mad for you."

He lifted his hands to touch her elegant neck and shoulders, sliding his palms over the satin flesh of her thighs and stomach. "You're my forever, Lauren."

The string of pearls caught her eye and she reached for them and drew them over his face and chest. His deep chuckle teased her intimate places and changed her method of seduction. "Never resist me, Sir Goodnight. You'll only suffer for the attempt."

She wrapped the strand of pearls about her neck, and then looped it around his ridged sex. "If you move, it might be painful."

He arched a brow and surveyed her handy work. "You sure you want to do that? You know I can't lie back and enjoy it."

"Try."

She smiled down at him sensuously, fluttering her lashes like fine silk fans and worked her shoulders to set her breasts dancing over his smiling mouth. The tensing of his thighs urged her forward and she slid onto his steely member and began her rhythm of deep delicious motion and rotating her hips, to and fro, side to side until a flash of white-hot heat burst upward from her groin. His hands on her breasts eased the pain that followed her volatile climax. She gasped with pleasure while he squeezed her nipples, rekindling the knife edged delirium. She rocked harder against him to catch the sunburst of hot pleasure he had built with his deep upward thrusts into her. She joyfully fell forward onto his wonderful chest and let him roll over with her to complete his quest for completion. The strand of pearls was scattered over the rumpled sheet.

After their rousing sex, Lauren was exhausted and lay back to eye Victor with some amusement.

He touched the back of his head and turned to look at her with a wry grin. "Where are the phones? I told a colleague I'd contact him this evening."

"They're being washed." She spread her legs and lifted her arms in a full luxurious stretch. "Stop looking. You'll never find them. Besides, I have something to tell you."

"Okay. You talk while I make my call."

"I have to have your full attention." She slid off the bed and did her most provocative shimmy for him. "I, you sexy devil, have been chosen to design the wardrobe for a period film. What do you think about that?"

He grinned at her obvious delight and caught her in his arms when she ran to him. "That's great news. You've earned it."

She stood before him with her arms spread wide and smiled at him. "I think I've been given too much--the most awesome man in the world. What else could a gal want?"

"Sounds like you have it all, Gorgeous. And it's my life's business to never disappoint you."

She hugged him and kissed his mouth. "I think we had better start getting ready for the party. Raini would never forgive us for being late."

"Okay, Beautiful, but I still have to make that call." He held his hands out and gazed at her with a bemused smile.

"In the dishwasher." Lauren went into the bathroom and then came back out. "I know you're going to ask why so I'll just tell you now." She opened a fresh bar of soap while she talked. "Too many hang-up calls and some from a cocktail lounge that I've never heard of." She grinned at him. "And that's why the phones are in the dishwasher."

Concern was etched on his face. "Are you worried, about the calls I mean?"

"No. Just ticked at the loon doing all the calling. I've called for a number change and will have it by tomorrow morning."

"As long as you feel comfortable with the situation." He took his cell phone from his topcoat pocket to look at it for a moment and then tossed it onto a chair. "Hell with that. It's bath time."

While they showered, Victor washed her hair and tickled her until she shrieked with laughter.

"Stop it, you." She bumped him with her hips and tried to sound serious. "Now, I mean it. We have to stop."

She stepped out of the fine spray, leaving him to finish without her. The gown she had chosen to wear lay on her bed, beckoning her with its velvet bodice and sweep of sleek satin skirt, all done in rich hues of plum. She dried off in a hurry and sprayed herself liberally with CoCo before slipping on her undergarments. She looked up when Victor gave her a wolf whistle.

"Help me zip, will you handsome?"

Victor was quick to oblige her, smoothing the sleek bodice over her arms and back, then zipping it snuggly in place. "You look good enough to eat." He nuzzled her shoulder and licked in lazy cat laps until she caught his face in her hands.

"Get dressed, tiger." She stepped into her slippers, loving the soft glove fit of the plum colored satin shoes. "I hope Rachel likes her dress."

Victor laughed and glanced her way while brushing his hair. "Jonelle assured me Rachel is crazy about everything you do. Including the dress you made for her."

"That's encouraging. And that's all Jonelle had to say about me?" Lauren arched her brows and gazed at him. "Never mind. I don't think I really want to know."

He put the brush down and pulled her into his arms. "Do you know how much I love you?"

She cupped the weight of his sex in her hand and smiled sweetly into his eyes. "A great big bunch. Now, tell me if I have my boobs straight in here."

She adjusted her breasts into the built in bra and waited for his comment.

"I think the left one is higher than the right one."

"You think?" She lifted her arms and purred deep in her throat while he worked her breasts up into position. "Are they okay now?"

"Most succulent melons I've ever seen." He tilted his head to one side and gazed reverently at her blooming bounty. "Do we have time to mess around again?"

"We have twenty minutes to get to the hotel."

"Not enough for what I had in mind."

She kissed his mouth and whispered. "Show me when we get home."

* * * *

The ballroom of the hotel was ablaze in splendor beneath crystal chandeliers and candlelight and was decked out royally with its bowers of white roses and pink lilies, which draped from every stair rail and widow sill. Each table was graced by a saucy arrangement of scarlet roses and cattails. Beautifully dressed couples filled the dance floor and enjoyed the music provided by a wonderful orchestra.

Lauren took in the dazzling scene and clung to Victor's hand while they greeted their guests. She had seen some curiosity in more than one gaze, but it didn't bother her. She was too happy.

Raini was in her element, making certain nothing went askew and every guest received the very best that was available. She joined Lauren to watch Rachel stepping on Adam's patent leather shoes out on the dance floor.

"This is so beautiful. Just look at Adam charm that little girl. Practicing his parenting skills...." Raini's smile faded abruptly.

Lauren was perplexed by her sister's change of emotions. She had been glowing, and now she appeared anxious. "What's up, Raini?"

"Nothing. Everything's fine."

"Is it potty time?"

Raini shook her head and appeared to be battling a war against tears. "Have you seen the lovely candied fruits? I know how you love them." She grasped Lauren's arm and tried to move her away from the ballroom entrance.

"Okay, sis. What's going on?"

"I'd rather tell you in private."

There must be a serious issue at hand for Raini to be stressed out. Lauren put her arm about her sister's waist. "I need to check on my mascara. Lead the way, sweetie." She gave Victor a crooked grin and inclined her head toward Raini. "We're taking a time out for the mother to be."

He smiled indulgently and winked at Lauren. "Go right ahead, ladies. I think it's time I took charge of Rachel." He kissed her knuckles and then strolled off to relieve Adam of his babysitting duties.

Lauren's gaze followed him, and she sighed rapturously under the weight of romantic bliss that mantled her soul. She followed closely behind Raini, keeping up a stream of happy chatter until a commotion around the orchestra section caught her attention.

She couldn't believe fate was so damned cruel and she was the butt of the worst joke in history. Justin. He was on the dais, attempting to wrestle the microphone from the orchestra leaders hand and high stepping like a cocky rooster.

She was stiff with outrage and disgust. "What--is he doing here?"

Raini shook her head. "I have no idea."

"You invited him, didn't you?"

"Certainly not. He made the decision on his own. And how dare you think I would do something like this."

"It has your fingerprints all over it."

Lauren shook with fury and desire to claw furrows on Justin's face. "Well, you just ask him to leave before he ruins everything."

Lauren knew it was too late to save face when Justin took control of the mike and began dancing around on the dais. He sang a few bars of 'Dancing in the Dark' before hiccupping over a drunken laugh. She clenched her hands into fists. The bastard was set on ruining her life.

It seemed an eternity passed before Adam hurried to her side and took her arm. "I've sent for security to handle him, honey. Just relax."

The muffled laughter and comments from the crowd hit her like a slap in the face and she shook with anger. "I'm going to knock his block off."

Adam gripped her wrist, stopping her forward motion. "Give me a second here and the problem will be taken care of." He guided her to the edge of the crowd. "I'll see what's keeping them."

She could see Victor dancing with his daughter and wanted to cry out to him to help her, but she couldn't speak. Justin's voice burned her ears; his slurred words were indistinguishable from his laughter. When he said her name, she stiffened against the coming assault of humiliation.

It was obvious Justin had already drunk too much, but he was downing a large snifter of brandy and swaying like a palm while the orchestra played light jazz. He pointed a finger in her direction and grinned from ear to ear.

"Ladies and gentleman." He hiccupped loudly. "Just want to toast the future bride, my ex-fiancé. Yeah. I was a fool and walked out on her so Victor slips in and takes my place." He grinned and then scowled. "She doesn't know about him yet so I've got to tell her." He waved at her and rocked back on his heels for a second. "Hullo, beautiful. That guy you think is such a stud is a liar honey. I tried all week to call you, but you didn't answer."

Lauren's heart was pounding under the assault of total disgrace. She shivered and knew what it was to desire to become invisible. She had no choice but to stand and listen to what the drunken fool was saying.

Justin showed amazing agility and dodged security officers' attempts to lead him off the dais. His ranting continued. "Baby, listen to me. You don't want to sleep with the man that killed your father and screwed your sister." He made some disco like moves and then began his tirade once again. "Hate to tell you, babe, but you're bought and paid for. Like a call girl. The apartment, the job. You're nothing on your own. Nothin'." He laughed crazily. "Don't come crying to me when he dumps your sweet ass for someone else." He ended his speech with a last hiccup.

Lauren spotted Victor on the dance floor. He was hurriedly giving custody of Rachel over to Adam before striding toward her. Lauren's lips worked in an attempt to speak and her gaze frantically searched his face for reassurance. "What is that mad man talking about? You didn't tell me you knew him on such intimate terms."

Victor's expression revealed his worry. He put his arm around her waist and leaned forward to whisper in her ear. "I'm sorry for the disruption. Let's go out in the hall and discuss this."

"Then, it is true?" She was afraid she already knew the answer.

"He's speaking out of jealousy, Lauren. He's potted."

"I know he's drunk, but why would he say those things? Why does he know more about you than I do?" She spurned Raini's hug and turned back to look into the face she called her most beloved. "How could you do--this? Why?"

Victor paled and reached for her hand. "Lauren."

"No. No more. Just the truth if you can manage that." She gathered up the excess length of her gown in her shaking fingers and glared at him.

"The truth is I love you more than life and I want to get straight with you."

"Not good enough, Raven. You can't possibly know how rotten I feel, knowing you treated me like a psychotic. You never loved me. I'm a novelty you would have tired of. What about my heart? Did it make you feel macho to crush it beneath your foot?"

She was alone in her desolation, suppressing a sob of anguish when a shower of rose petals swirled about her and fell about her feet. The lovely display seemed to mock her in its splendor. Anger at her sister loosened her tongue.

"Raini. I can understand you not telling me about the affair you had. Sisters don't always share secrets. But I'm mad as hell you didn't tell me he was a man with no principals, the man that hurt my father so badly."

Victor tried to appease her with a quiet suggestion. "Let's go home and talk this out."

She looked at the ceiling before lashing out at him. "I told you, too little too late. You couldn't explain this to me months ago, the part you had in my father's life. You make me feel like dirt. Damn you all. You disgust me."

She kicked the rose petals aside and sent an incendiary glower to the dais. Justin's drunken laughter echoed throughout the suddenly quieted ballroom. Getting a better grip on her skirts, Lauren paused long enough to stab Victor with a glare. She ground out her last words to him in a raspy whisper.

"You had better be grateful that your daughter is here because I want to scream that you are a son of a bitch."

She stalked off across the floor to step up on the bandstand. An ominous silence settled over the noisy crowd while she faced Justin like an angry zephyr. He smiled at her through a sodden daze and held his arms out.

"Hello, Lauren." He hiccupped and grinned crookedly. "I knew you'd want me back. You had to hear the truth about that bastard."

She took a step forward and shuddered visibly in her disgust. She drew her fist back, taking dead aim on his chin. The impact made a satisfying thwacking sound and the sight of his eyes glazing over was balm to her soul. She didn't flinch when he toppled over onto the drummer in a crash of cymbals. There was a collective gasp followed by wave of hushed comments from the onlookers.

She whirled to find Victor gripping her elbow and wearing a bemused expression.

"Nice shot, baby."

"It should have been you."

Her one thought was escape and she rushed madly for the hotel lobby. Victor followed after her, pushing his way through the milling crowd. In the background, Rachel was wailing and the sound broke Lauren's heart. She flung a heated comment over her shoulder at Victor.

"Leave me alone, you. Take care of Rachel." She paused for a split second and wondered where her handbag was. It would be too humiliating to go back for it. She raced blindly for escape from her crushing pain of her latest disgrace.

"Lauren, wait."

"Leave me alone, you son of a bitch." Her voice had broken and tears glistened like frost on her cheeks.

"Lauren. Stop running from me. I won't let you go."

"You don't have a choice." Her heart splintered anew when she looked into his face and saw the only man who would ever be in her heart. Why did she have to do something crazy like falling in love with him? It hurt so much and she couldn't bear anymore.

He managed to keep his hands to himself while he pleaded with her. "You don't have a choice either. You love me. Remember?"

"That was before I knew you were a despicable liar."

She ran out onto the sidewalk and looked for the doorman. Victor kept pace with her as she walked back and fourth at a furious gait.

"Come with me Lauren and we'll talk about everything. Please, come inside. You're getting soaked."

"Go to hell, Raven." She waved frantically at a passing taxi.

"Lauren. What are you doing? You don't have your handbag."

She looked over her shoulder to slash him with her angry gaze. "Then I'll walk."

The cab pulled up to the curb and she reached for the door handle. He covered her hand to stop her. "For God's sake, Lauren, I'm coming with you."

"No way in hell."

She flung his hand aside and opened the cab door and scrambled inside. Victor found his money clip and handed the driver several large bills and spoke to the stoic faced driver.

"Take her wherever she wants to go." He leaned inside the cab and touched Lauren's arm. "Have the courtesy to call Raini when you get wherever you're going."

"You just take care of what concerns you and that isn't me or my sister." She leaned forward to speak to the driver. "Please go."

"Where to, ma'am?"

"I'll let you know when I do."

She lost count of the times the cab cruised by her apartment building and it didn't matter. The driver finally stopped asking, "Where to?" She figured he had seen everything in this city. She looked down at her rumpled gown and mud-spattered shoes. Complete ruination, exactly like her life. She caught the gaze of the driver in the rearview mirror and grimaced. It was pointless to keep riding around the city like a lost cat. She finally gave her address to the driver and sat back to stare out the window during the rest of the ride home.

It wasn't until the taxi was pulling away from her apartment building that she realized she had made a terrible blunder. No handbag meant no key. The weight of her emotional upheaval hit with devastating force. She moaned in utter dejection and the morose sound wavered in the cold night air. Clutching her stomach, she crumpled on top step of the small portico and gave into the sobs that assailed her heart.

She used the skirt of her demolished gown to muffle the sound of her crying and squinted against a slash of approaching car headlights. She huddled against the door to escape being seen. The car stopped at the curb and the driver got out.

"Lauren."

It was Victor and the son of a bitch was wearing a nice dry

raincoat. She turned away from him, drowning anew in her hurt. He was shucking off the coat and draping it around her. She wanted to die in her twisted fury of emotions. Love him; hate him. So hurt by him. Her tattered heart cried out to him and his strength but her pride spurned all feelings of tenderness.

"Lauren. I remembered you left your handbag. I'll open the door."

She heard his voice and saw him work the key in the door, yet she felt far removed from him. He had cut out her heart and now he was back to rip her apart again. The door opened and she got to her feet and swiped his coat from her shoulders. She yanked her handbag from his grasp and walked into the warm foyer. Trying to slam the door in his face was wasted effort.

"Not yet," he said evenly after catching the door against his palm. "We have to talk and we can't as long as you keep shutting me out."

She ignored his words and started up the steps to her apartment. When he lay his hand on her arm, she gave him a hard glare. "You're still here?"

He caught her about the waist and held her fast. "Wait, pussycat." His voice was edged with quiet resolve. "You know you're killing me, don't you?"

Her body and soul screamed out for him and his way of making things right, but this time it couldn't happen. "That's supposed to touch my heart? You had no mercy on me." Her back stiffened under his touch. "Make sure the door is closed when you leave."

For one more second, she stared down into his midnight blue eyes before going up the steps. He stood firm, not budging under her lethal glare. He lifted his hand in a farewell gesture.

She clenched her teeth to stem a scream of outrage and managed to speak in a normal voice. "This isn't just a little spat, mister. We are so finished. Have the decency to leave and forget we ever had the misfortune of meeting." When he didn't instantly react, she gave in to her seething anger. "Get out!"

"I'm going, baby." He picked his coat up off the wet floor before opening the door, looking up at her once more before going out into the rainy night.

She wept bitterly. Nothing in her life had prepared her for such pain. She was physically ill and rushed inside her apartment to hide from the cruelty outside her door.

Victor had walked out of her life and taken everything with him.

Chapter Twenty-two

Lauren looked around her bedroom and realized she hadn't been out of the bed for anything other than necessary needs and personal hygiene for several days. The mangled gown she had worn to the fateful party lay in a soggy heap on the entryway floor along with her soiled slippers.

She got out of bed and headed for the kitchen, stopping long enough to give the clammy lump of clothing a hard kick. A second later, the doorbell rang. Her first inclination was to scream at whomever it was to go away, but she didn't. Maybe they would go away on their own. Damn. They were still in the in the hallway and obviously knew her.

"Lauren. Let me in." Raini's cultured voice was unusually loud.

"You have something more to say, Raini?" Desire to see her sister and resentment toward her merged in a jumble of painful twists in her stomach. "Just go away."

"No! I have plenty to say young lady, and I will not go away."

Lauren knew she would stand out in the hall until one of the other tenants called for security. "Call me."

"No. I have to see your face while I'm talking to you."

The urge to yell obscenities at her sister was hard to stamp down, but Lauren swallowed her anger and pride and opened the door. Raini walked in, looked around the entry hall, and craned her neck to see into the living room.

"He's not here and never will be again." Lauren crossed her arms at her waist, feeling ill and depleted of the desire to live.

"I had to see you, Lauren, to make sure you were all right. Won't you come stay with me for a while? We need to be together."

Lauren dragged a quilt off the bench in the entry hall and snuggled into its comforting softness while walking toward the living room.

"I turned in my resignation at the Christopher Company and I'm thinking of subleasing the apartment." She sat on the couch and curled up in one corner. "I'm going to spend some time in the summer house in the Hamptons."

"Please don't close me out of your life, Lauren."

"I have to get away. This has been too much to bear and it comes back to haunt me every day."

Raini got up and went to stand in front of her sister. "I can never apologize profusely enough to you, Lauren. But let me try to make it better."

"That's impossible." Lauren rubbed the corner of the quilt against her cheek and gulped back a jolt of despair when she thought of Victor. "I want you to explain to Rachel that I love her and will see her again."

Raini brightened. "When may I tell her you'll see her?"

"Lie to her. That shouldn't be too hard. Just whatever it takes to make her feel good."

Raini sighed heavily and touched her forehead in a show of defeat. "You're suffering a lot more than I expected, Lauren. I can't say how deplorable we all feel about it and want so much to be in your heart again."

Lauren was afraid of what the answer to her question would be, but she had to ask it. "Did you love him?"

Raini appeared nervous and hesitated in answering.

"Your affair." Lauren bunched a pillow against her chest in preparation of severe pain. She winced realizing she would never be prepared for what her sister would tell her.

"Immediately after his divorce and before I met Adam, we drifted together as friends or companions I suppose." High anxiety colored Raini's fair complexion.

"Go on." Lauren stared at her sister in an attempt to detect signs of dishonesty. "How serious was it?" She wanted to snatch the question back. "Please don't tell me. I couldn't stand it if he loved you."

Raini's eyes widened and she laughed. "Don't you know he could never have loved me? It just happened that we were both unattached at the same time. A convenience you might say."

"Stop." Lauren threw the pillow on the floor. "I don't want to hear anymore."

"Lauren, we didn't have sex." Raini peered at her sister with a hint of a smile.

Lauren couldn't reply for a second. Hearing that Victor had not been in bed with Raini was strangely dissatisfying. She could have forgiven a past fling, but his long history of lies was unforgivable. Raini interrupted her thoughts.

"You should know that wasn't because I refused. To him, I was a friend."

Raini's innuendo comment was completely alien to her personality and a grin tugged at Lauren's mouth. "I'm not touching that, sister dear."

She got to her feet and went to look out the terrace door. "Nice and gloomy. Very fitting."

"Come stay the weekend with me. We'll both feel better."

A quiet fell over the room. Lauren shattered it when she asked, "Why did you hide the fact that Victor bought Dad out? That really hurts me more than I can tell you."

"I don't know why." Raini went to stand near Lauren and smiled weakly at her. "Yes, I do know. At the time you were hysterically screaming threats about the buyer and calling them headhunters and killers. You didn't seem like a good risk to confide in at the time."

"Okay, you've semi cleared yourself." She walked Raini to the door and kissed her cheek. "You had better leave before I forget I'm not angry with you any longer."

Raini hugged Lauren. "Thank you for telling me where you're going."

"Sure, sure. Just keep this as good a secret as you have everything else."

Touched by her Raini's words, Lauren couldn't remain cold. "You can call me when I get to the Hamptons. You will keep that our little secret, won't you?"

* * * *

Victor was on his feet and running before the sound of breaking glass had faded away. His heart pounded furiously as he ran toward Rachel's bedroom. He collided with the wall as he cornered, trying to get to her room.

"Rachel!"

"Daddy." The shriek of fright had come from his ashen-faced child. She stood in horrified fascination of the shards of glass scattered over the carpet. Bottles and hairbrushes, hair rollers and a full compliment of feminine stuff lay in a jumbled heap near her dresser.

"You okay, honey?" He hoped he sounded calm because his hands were shaking furiously just like his knees. "Have an accident?"

"Um hm. I was trying to cornrow my hair like Lauren does it." Rachel cast a fearful glance about the room and began to wail. "I want Lauren. When's she coming home?"

She held her arms up and Victor drew her close. He was too close to tears to say anything. All he could do was silently try to sooth his daughter's aching heart. After regaining a semblance of control, he carried her into the living room.

"You stay put while I clean things up. Okay?"

"Okay." She rubbed her eyes and yawned before giving him a tremulous little smile. "Is Lauren mad at us?"

His stomach hit his backbone with a killer shot of dejection and a desire to runaway from the hurt. His daughter had been deeply affected by his total disregard for anything or anyone but what he had wanted. He gave her his best 'nothing's wrong' laugh.

"She's just mad at me, honey. Never at you. Do you understand?"

"What did you do, Daddy?" Her eyes were droopy with the need for sleep.

How was he to answer that without running his head into a wall? He had to try. "Some really, really dumb things. I would love to make it up to her."

"Go get her, Daddy. I want Lauren."

She began to cry again. He picked her up to hug her close. She wailed louder with every breath and Victor walked the floor with her like he had when she was an infant.

While he paced the floor with Rachel, he was reeling from the knockout punch life had thrown him. It was unbelievable to see the mess he had made of paradise. Shifting Rachel in his arms, he admitted to himself that he'd always known something explosive was going to come about in his Eden-like relationship with Lauren. If he lived to be a thousand, he would never know the answer to the riddle. Why hadn't he just told her all he knew and risked her anger? She was the first woman that he had been afraid of losing. He had taken the coward's way and now, he and a lot of other people were paying for his sin.

He became aware that Rachel had drifted off to sleep when her arms and legs dangled from his embrace. He carried her to her room and tucked her in for the night. Looking at her serene little face, he sighed heavily. Sleep, if it came at all, would be minimal for him.

A picture on Rachel's dressing table caught his attention. His heart thumped mournfully in recognition of his beloved Lauren. In the photo, she was hugging Rachel and smiling as only she could. Christ, he was dying to be with her. He carefully set the picture down, cleaned up the mess and walked out of the room.

The liquor cabinet seemed to be calling his name and he answered by pouring himself a tall scotch. He carried his drink out to the terrace and leaned on the railing to look at the glittering lights below. Not long ago, a lifetime ago, he had held Lauren in his arms in this shadowed place and tasted ecstasy on her lips. Without her, he had no direction to steer his life toward. She wouldn't leave his thoughts. Loneliness and the nightly sensual dreams were not a replacement for her scintillating passion.

He tossed the remainder of his drink in a potted corn plant and paced the length of the terrace a few times before he turned on his heel and went back inside to pick up the phone.

He sat on the arm of his favorite couch and stared at the keypad. The situation he had caused weighed mightily on his heart. He had to set things right. Three lives depended on his ability to do that. He would fight to win her back. He loved Lauren too much to stand by and do nothing. Sure, she would say she hated him and never wanted to lay eyes on his rotten carcass again, but she wouldn't mean it.

He heaved a mammoth sigh. Hell, Raven, you're scared to death of the possibility she really doesn't want you. Too bad, man. He had to take the chance that he could show her that she loved him. There was the major problem of finding her and only one person could tell him.

He punched in a phone number with shaking fingers and hoped his voice didn't. "Hello, Raini."

Chapter Twenty-three

Three weeks of absolute, stone cold solitude and Lauren still couldn't think of anything but how much she loved Victor. She was two hours away from what her heart longed for and five minutes from the nearest Ben and Jerry's. She soon became disgusted by her eating binge and mooning into an empty ice cream carton. She needed another way to fill the gnawing hunger in her soul. The house in the Hamptons was set well back from the beach and surrounded by an iron fence. As time wore on, she began to long for the comfort of human companionship.

After a night of fitful sleep and hearing strange noises and a day of looking out the window, she was eager to hear the sound of cars and laughter. She pulled on a comfortable pair of faded and frayed Levi's and a stretched-out purple sweatshirt, hurrying to get to the mini mart before it closed for the evening. She grabbed a pair of deck shoes that had seen better days and ran a comb through her hair. No time for a clasp today. She was in a hurry to commune with whatever wanted to talk. Snagging her handbag off the coat rack, she hurried out the door and headed for the trail that lead to the small shopping village.

She stopped long enough to look at the playhouse that had been built beside the garage. That was where Raini had held court surrounded by an all male realm and Lauren had experienced her first kiss. What was wrong with her? A shot of desire streaked through her like warm cognac at the thought of Victor's lips touching hers. She grumbled at her horrible weakness and admitted she was a poor excuse for an independent woman. She was a blubbering female with a hearty sexual appetite and her mate was untouchable. Well, too damned bad.

She just might look into that cloister thing after all. Who was she kidding? Certainly not herself. She wanted sex and she wanted it with Victor. *There, you have become an honest woman and that part of your body hasn't gotten the message about him yet.*

As she walked away from the childhood toy, she knew her energy had to directed to more productive things, like working on that mass of sketches that hadn't been touched in three weeks. And there was that cute little pinafore she was making for Rachel. Another jolt of loneliness rushed around her until she became dizzy.

A fresh supply of Double Chunk Marshmallow topped her list of things to do, she thought and walked away from childhood memories. She frowned when the thought of the rich dessert made her stomach churn. There was nothing in the house for maladies of the stomach. Nothing to do but make a trip to that really expensive combo market variety store with its lovely soda fountain.

The tiny bell over the door signaled the storekeeper she had walked in and a face from her past smiled at Lauren from behind a glass showcase.

"Hello Mrs. Migillicutty." Lauren grinned to herself, recalling how difficult it had been to pronounce the woman's last name at the age of four.

"Hello, dear." The woman didn't stop arranging the baked goods, but continued to speak. "Look around and I'll be right with you."

The well-stocked, overpriced store was timeless, smelling of magazines and saltwater taffy. There was still a soda fountain with polished chrome fixtures. The sparkling glassware behind the counter took her eye as she sat down on a stool. Mrs. Migillicutty came to the soda fountain and polished the green marble counter while speaking to Lauren.

"What can I get you, dear?"

Lauren patted her stomach. "Bromo I think." She choked a little when the smiling woman chuckled and issued an observation.

"If you're expecting, you shouldn't drink that."

"Pregnant. Why on earth would you say that?" Lauren smiled wryly and took the fizzing brew to gulp it down. The smile was brief when she considered how often she was nauseous and where were her birth control pills?

"Your color is high and your eyes have that particular glow." Mrs. Migillicutty's face was sweet and she peered at Lauren as if she were knowledgeable on the subject. "I've seen many a young mother-to-be come in here and you can't fool me." She glanced around the store. "Where's your young man. He's a good looking fellow."

Lauren laughed good naturedly at the woman's obvious mistake. "I'm here alone, Mrs. Migillicutty."

"Well, he said he was with you. Even bought a trunk load of groceries and fresh vegetables from the Farmer's Market. Real nice looking too."

"Mrs. Migillicutty. I think you have a crush on my mystery man."

"That's a fact, honey." The silver haired woman smiled and

fanned her face with her starched apron.

"Thank you, Mrs. Migillicutty." Lauren forgot about the Double Chunk Marshmallow and left the store in a quagmire of emotions. Could it be Justin? He could be up here at his parents' place. No. He didn't like the solitude. Only one other man she knew would dare bother her in the state she was in. Victor Raven.

It made sense to her. He was pushy, arrogant and a liar. He was there and going to try to weasel his way back into her life. It wasn't going to happen. God help me, she prayed as she jogged back toward the house, it isn't going to happen.

* * * *

Her suspicions had been completely founded. When she got back to the house, she peeked around the trunk of a huge pine tree to survey the front of the place. Damn it! There was a huge, to the point of being vulgar, RUV parked outside her door, black as night, tall at the roof and spit shine clean. It was Raven all right, and she was outside and he was inside looking through her stuff. How had that happened?

Her imagination took flight. Looking through her stuff, handling her things like he always did. His big hands were so strong and there was magic in them. A surge of heart-pounding delight rocked her to the soles of her battered deck shoes. She stood motionless for several minutes, letting her purse slip to the ground and stared at the window he had just looked out of. Something cold gripped her throat. Cold, cruel reality. Face it. You're excited and weak.

Yanking her purse up onto her arm, she squared her shoulders and stalked off toward the house, chin held high and she hoped, fire in her eyes. She couldn't wait to toss him out on his can. When her foot hit the last step of the veranda, she hesitated. Her bravado melted and she was absolutely flustered.

She withdrew her foot from the landing and stepped back to slink off to the kitchen door where she would have the advantage of surprise. A strange stiffness clamped around her legs and she stumbled into a hedge. After righting herself, she opened the door and peeked inside before going in. The way was clear and she managed to close the door with out alerting her him of her presence.

She froze, and then became angry. There was music sweeping into the kitchen from the great room. What the hell was he doing? Throwing a party? What the hell was she doing? This was her house. She tucked her chin like a prizefighter and walked resolutely to the doorway of the great room.

The angry shout died in her throat, silenced by the joy that rose up in her heart just to see him standing at the window with his hand braced on the sill. Good God, he was beautiful--tall and broad shouldered with the crispest black hair she had ever touched. A tiny sniggle of sensibility tickled her ear and forced her to say something.

"Cat burglar one of your corporate titles now?"

She just knew her heart had stopped pumping when he swung around to smile at her. *Oh, dear Lord, don't let me like him.*

"Hello there." He looked at her with a half smile and his gaze traveled over her like a slow caress.

"When you get through looking at me like an idiot, take the first exit out of here." Her lips were numb and her breasts were swelling. Oh, Lord, she was going to cave just like she always did. "Well?"

"I-It's just that I've never seen you with your hair so windblown and dressed in such a cute outfit." His grin was slow and easy and his gaze touching all of her. "You looked like a twelve year old at first glance."

She tossed her handbag onto a chair by the door and gave him a withering glare. "So far, I'm messier than you remember and can be mistaken for a twelve year old. Cute. Very cute." She crossed her arms over her breasts and grimaced at their tenderness. "The door opens the other way."

"You're looking great." He ignored her invitation to leave.

"You don't want to get caught out after dark. Prowlers are not popular here." She didn't think a look at him would lead to anything to weaken her resolve to hate him. She couldn't have stopped herself anyway so she openly stared at him.

He leveled a penetrating smile on her and stepped closer to her. "I've missed you."

"Of course. You haven't had your patsy to play connect the dots with you."

"You miss me?"

"Like the plague."

"Which is my room?"

Her jaw went a little slack and her eyes rounded with indignation. "You're not staying here."

"Don't think you will be able to stay out of my room?" His grin was pure challenge. "I'd be proud to let you get under my blanket."

Why did his damn voice nuzzle her ear and lull her into some kind of goony bird trance. She blinked and managed to sneer at his suggestion. "Forget your little black book?"

"You name's on every page."

She sensed him getting closer to her, but she couldn't move. She turned away from his appraising but warm smile.

"Just leave. I can't pretend you're not here." She was a blink away from tears and that meant she was a weakling and still wanted his love, his arms around her and his ridged shaft inside her. She heard his step behind her.

"I can't leave without you, Lauren."

"You're being a jackass, Victor."

"Victor?" He exhaled roughly. "This must be a definite turning point in our lives. You said my name."

"It means nothing. Only that I no longer see you as an equal to honored bird."

His fingers skimmed the sensitive skin of her wrist when he captured her hand. "Truth is, baby, we love one another much more than ever. Isn't that what you really feel?"

She pulled her hand free of his big comforting paw. "How I feel about you doesn't matter. Nothing matters. Maybe one day I'll feel nothing for you. Do you understand that?"

"I'm afraid I do and it's going to be tough changing your mind." He slid his into his pants pockets and looked away from her. "Okay. It's going to be a long and silent night."

She couldn't help it if her heart skipped rope and smiled madly because he was inches away from her. Her words didn't reflect her inner feelings. "Since you invited yourself--fend for yourself."

"To be with you, any sacrifice is worth making."

"You sanctimonious bastard."

She wanted to scream at him when his chuckle followed her up the steps and down the hallway to her bedroom.

* * * *

What was he doing down there? She had listened to the sounds Victor made for several hours until her curiosity forced her to get out of bed and hurl an insult from the upstairs landing.

"I hope that's sounds of your packing."

He was evidently ignoring her because the expected comment didn't rise up to meet her ears. She leaned over the railing to crane her neck, but he was nowhere in sight. Damn. He was doing something down there and she wanted to know what it was. No, that was a lie. She wanted to see him. Jamming her hands into the pockets of her robe, she huffed back into her bedroom. The phone on her nightstand took her eye. Why not? It was a safer way to converse with him. She heard his cell phone ring a dozen times before he answered.

"Hello, baby."

"Why aren't you gone?"

"When are you coming downstairs?"

"When you're gone." His soft laughter teased her earlobes and warmed her heart, but she had questions and he damned well better answer. "I know about your affair with Raini."

"That's good. No secrets there. Right?"

"She thought you were pretty hot--once."

"I love you, Lauren."

"You bought out Swanson's and you were real creative in making a place for me at Christopher's. I hate you for that."

"You truly underestimate yourself, Lauren. I'm sorry, but you wouldn't have gotten that job if you hadn't been a topnotch designer."

She chewed her lip and walked to the open door of her room. He was just buttering her up for the kill. "The miraculous quick sale of my home in Malibu, no haggling over the price. You again and I hate you for that."

"I love that house and wanted to keep it in the family. I'm just a born son of a bitch."

"The first pearl of honesty from your black heart, Mister Raven."

"I have been nothing but honest with you, baby. Maybe slow in filling in all the spaces."

"The unbelievable quick find of my sumptuous apartment was due to your benevolence again."

"I couldn't have found a better tenant." He chuckled. "The price was fair wasn't it?"

"You're smarter than I thought." It was time for a bit of payback. She scraped the phone over the pebbles in a Japanese sand painting. Lifting the handset to her ear, she heard his rich laughter and allowed a smile to whisk over her mouth.

"Okay. You got me. Think you could come downstairs and have a drink with me? The fireplace is cozy."

"In your dreams." She was trying to belt her robe about her waist when the table lamp flickered and went completely off.

"Raven." His name slipped from her mouth without her notice as she felt her way along the wall to get to him.

"Don't move, Lauren. I'll try to get the lights back on if I can find the fuse box."

"No, don't leave me up here in the dark." Her eyes were rounded and her legs were wobbling in her fear. She whimpered against the sleeve of her robe. "Raven."

"Lauren." His voice was so near, all she had to do was reach out and touch him. She snatched her hand back after feeling the warmth of his bare chest. The phone dropped to the floor when he reached out to firmly grasp her shoulders.

"I've got you," he murmured and pulled her close.

"No ... don't. I don't want to...."

"I insist. I'm taking you downstairs." He laughed and lifted her up in his arms. "The fireplace offers some light."

"If I wanted light, I could find it." She pummeled his chest and shoulder while he ignored her clumsy attempt to inflict pain on him. She tried to beat back the longing to be crushed in his embrace while her blood bubbled dangerously and his scent of sea washed heather teased her erogenous zones.

At the foot of the stairs he let her slide down the entire length of his frame to stand on her feet. She bit down hard on her lip to silence the little sigh of pleasure that touching him had shot through her senses to her.

"Something wrong, Lauren?"

"No. I'm fine." He hadn't removed his hands from her arms and his nearness made her want to climb his big tall body and take his breath like he was doing to her.

"Are you sure?" He put his arms about her waist and exhaled roughly. "I think you're trembling."

She couldn't respond with a snappy insult under the onslaught of chaotic emotions centering at the fork of her legs. He was stealing her strength and she didn't care. She let her body warm against his, relaxing her legs, allowing him brush his long fingers against her moist center and finally, blessedly slip them inside her.

He knew how to render her helpless and wanting with his caressing and teasing, slowly changing her into a moaning Jezebel. The flicker of desire leapt into a raging torrent and she was no longer content with only preliminaries to intercourse, she thrust her hips hard against his hand and grasped his engorged shaft. Her breathing had reached a dangerous rate and her heart hammered wildly in her chest. Opening the placket of his lounge pants had become a form of wonderful things to do for Lauren, and she quickly pulled them down to leave him standing ridged and throbbing, ready for her pleasure. Her moan ended the foreplay and he gripped her waist, pulling her up to hold her fast against him. She rocked against him, dug her nails into his shoulders and silently begged him to hurry. He seemed determined to drive her mad, holding back, giving her one throbbing inch at a time and moving slowly in exacting thrusts of deliberate tantalization. She cried out in her ecstasy when he thrust forward and impaled her with his sleek length.

She could do nothing but loll her head to one side and let him suck the last vestige of resistance from her as she spin off into an inferno. He had called it up and it came, blood red desire that licked every secret place of her body, making her push herself against him and beg for everything he could give. Sweet fire rushed upward from her feet and spiraled about her until she sobbed in joyous release.

He held her up, holding her limp body against his until she gasped raggedly and relaxed against the wall. She swallowed hard, blinking in the last tremors of her climax, staring at his sweat-dampened face that glistened in the firelight.

"I haven't changed my mind," she said gruffly, shuddering when his hand accidentally brushed her breast.

"I know. I was horny; you were horny."

She smacked his hand when he tried to touch her hip. "It was just sex. Nothing more."

He shook his head and laughed. "It couldn't have possibly been more." His breathing was still labored and he shuddered in the echoes of a nitro blast.

She braced her hands against the wall and looked away from him, wishing he would move or have sex with her again. She licked her lips and told a lie. "Okay. I lost my head for a minute, but you still have to leave."

His grin was devastating to her libido. "Can't. My car's out of gas."

"Siphon from mine."

"Octane's too high. Car could explode." His hands were on his waist and his gaze was on her breasts.

She yanked her robe together and scowled at him. "What are you really doing here? It can't be for anything honorable."

"To get my woman."

"Look around. She's not here."

"I can wait until she comes back."

"Leave a message."

"Can't do that."

"I'm asking you to leave."

"And I'm not giving up on us, baby."

A glint of anger flashed in her eyes. "You're assuming I'm interested."

"Come on, Lauren. Let's make absolutely sure this is what you want. You love me, so stop kicking me away." He reached out to touch her collar. "Look at me and tell me you don't love me."

She lifted her chin and her gaze locked with his. "If you had an ounce of self-respect, you'd leave right now."

"You have no idea to what depths I would stoop to have you say you want me again." He stepped back, letting her walk away. "Lauren. Did I ever tell you that when I love something, I never let it get away?"

"We all lose things we like sometimes. Even you, big shot."

Chapter Twenty-four

He wasn't budging and she didn't trust herself and her hot-natured attraction to him. She would not allow it to get out of hand again. Lauren used every possible means to avoid Victor, but they were in constant proximity of one another. She never locked her door against him and he didn't appear inclined to violate her privacy. She wanted to rage at him, but he gave her no excuse to lose her temper.

He made coffee and mixed drinks and drank his while watching her and getting underfoot. He took up his place wherever she happened to be and observed her while she worked on the sketches she had foolishly committed herself to do.

"Do you think you could go watch TV or read a book?" Lauren turned away from his steady gaze. He didn't budge from his vantage point on the stairway and smiled at her. "Well, if you're going to sit there, I'm going to the library to work."

Victor stood up and held out his hands. "Let me help carry those sketch books."

"No thank you. Go find something else to do, like pack."

She despised her whining inner voice that repeatedly suggested they have wild and extended sexual encounters. It was a persistent nag even though she constantly reminded herself of how much she hated him.

"Hey." He waved his hand in front of her face. "Wherever you are. I'm going to take a walk on the beach. Want to come with me?"

Yes, thank you kindly, sir... Stop it. You're letting your hormones lead you by the nose. She chose to ignore him outwardly, but threw herself at him in a wild and wonderful dream. "Stop asking me to do things. Get it in your head, we are over."

"I'll bring back some driftwood."

"You are so dense." She gathered up her sketchbooks and pencils and walked away from his charismatic person, trying to appear graceful and unruffled.

"I'll see you later, honey."

There was laughter in his voice and fire in her gaze. "I'm locking the door and tossing your junk out."

She waited until she heard the door closing and then ran to the window to see him talking to someone on his cell phone. She ducked out of sight when he turned to face the house. His conversation was none of her business; she decided and went into the library, closing the door behind her.

Memories, sweet and sad slipped about the room and kissed her cheek as they drifted by the big teak desk where she had chosen to sit. This was where she had told her father she needed money for ballet lessons and that she was engaged to be married. She wondered what her indulgent father would say to her now. *Foolish girl. Leading with your heart.*

She idly tried the handles on the desk drawers, and found them all locked, all but the last one. She opened it and found two white business sized envelopes inside. Her hand trembled when she lifted them from the drawer and read the hand written names on each of them.

A letter for Raini and one for her. She smiled when she recognized he father's sweeping scrawl of handwriting. She lifted the flap of her envelope and read the letter addressed to her. She devoured his flowery little prose and she smiled when he reminded her of her promise to let him live with her and Justin when he became old and cranky.

She winced in remembered pain and wished for her father's warm guidance. There was a mist in her eyes when she came to the final paragraph and her heart thudded to a halt. One sentence held her gaze in blind fascination. It began with an airy explanation of the possible sale of the pharmaceutical firm and his other holdings and ended with the name Victor Stuart Raven named as the buyer. She didn't want to revisit that subject again and coming from her father, it would hurt even more.

Unable to stop herself, she read on through her tears and aching heart. She stood and walked to the door and opened it, carrying the letter in her icy hand. Her trembling legs carried her to the sun washed great room where she slumped into a pillowed bay window. She was overcome with disbelief and fast spreading shame.

The letter revealed her father's deep admiration for the young man and his reliability, fine reputation, and strong code of ethics. He had asked this young man to buy him out because of his failing heart and said how relieved and proud he was to have put his life's work under his fine guardianship. He would never regret putting all he owned in the hands of the young man with the good heart, and he wished he could have been his son. Victor Stuart Raven.

The words swam before her eyes. "Oh God, no," she whispered and crushed the letter to her breast. "What have I done?"

You've turned away the man you love because of foolish pride and belief in something that was never there.

How was she to ever make this up to the man that she had mistrusted and given no chance to right things? She had treated him like the dirt under her feet. *What you've done is probably lost the man that makes your heart beat and the sun rise.* Reason took over her spiraling thoughts and gave her a hint to her survival. No, she couldn't do that ... or could she?

The door at the front of the house slammed shut in a gust of wind and a scuffling sound caught her attention. She looked out the window and saw Victor loading his things into the super sized RUV he had arrived in. He was walking out on her and she had to stop him.

She brushed at her hair and moistened her lips as she ran for the door, almost colliding into him as he came back in. She hid the letter behind her back and smiled weakly at him. "Leaving huh?"

He brushed at a leaf that blown in and settled on her shoulder. "I got a call and I have to get back to New York, pronto. I was coming to tell you."

"It isn't Rachel, is it?" She reached up to lay her hand on his shoulder.

He gave her face a lingering gaze before shaking his head, "No. Thank God. Just business." He looked around and inhaled roughly. "You going to be all right here alone?"

"Absolutely." *Why are you being brave, you fool? Tell him you need him. Damn your pride and your fears.* "Raven."

"Yes?" he answered in a distracted way. He was searching for something on the hall table. "What is it, Lauren?"

"Do you think you could call me something besides Lauren?"

He chuckled and leaned over to kiss her cheek. "Of course. You'll always be my gorgeous scarlet rose and cattail baby."

"Tell Rachel I love her, will you." *Really clever, lady. He didn't get the hint and you're standing here with egg on your face.* "And you take care, okay?"

He hugged her so tight she couldn't breathe but managed to cling to his waist until he removed her arms from his body. "I'll take care of it all, baby. Lock the doors and go easy on the Ho-Ho's and Ben and Jerry."

His grin tore her heart to shreds and her blood barely crept through her veins. He got into his big car, waved good-bye to her and drove away.

She went into immediate depression and ran into the house to sob herself sick.

She lay in the window seat, numb with grief and wishing she was dead until the sun disappeared and the house had gone dark and silent. Dragging herself onto her weary legs, she went up to her room and took a shower.

Dressed in nothing but her floppy house slippers and one of Victor's forgotten shirts, she went to the kitchen to take her solace from the freezer. Double Chunky Marshmallow seemed to sicken her and she tossed it into the sink.

Her life was over and she had been the one that had killed it. Maybe she wasn't supposed to be happy like other women with their house full of kids and a husband that gave them grief. That all sounded pretty dreary until you couldn't have it. Grabbing a box of tissues, she sat down on the bottom step of the stairs that would take her to her lonely room. She buried her face in her hands and wept until there was nothing left but moans from a deserted heart. She remembered she had put her father's letter in the pocket of the shirt and she took it out to press it to her lips. No longer able to cry, she simply leaned against the stair rail and let images of a dreary future reel off before her tear reddened eyes.

She must have dozed off and the sound of the grandfather clock shook her awake. No, it hadn't been the clock. Someone was on the veranda, opening the door and there wasn't a light on in the entire house. And what had Victor said? Lock the doors. She hadn't done that and now she was terrified.

Too late to do it now, she rationalized. Grab something to defend yourself with. Her house slipper was the only thing available and she took it off her foot to grip it in her fist. She crouched low and waited for whomever it was to show their face in the entry hall.

Her heart lurched in her chest when the shadow of a giant loomed on the wall. Her eyes felt close to popping from their sockets, and her mouth had gone cotton dry. She tried to recall her childhood prayers but couldn't and screamed shrilly when the intruder stepped into full view.

Her eyes were squeezed shut and her body tensed in preparation of her doom. Someone grabbed her wrists and was shaking her.

"Lauren, baby. It's me."

Her initial fear flew away and was replaced uncontrollable jubilation. "Raven." She stood up, weaving slightly until her arms slipped about his neck, her rock of Gibraltar. The letter crackled in her pocket and she hurriedly took it out and held at her side, ready to dispose of it at the first opportunity. When her gaze went to his, her smile was radiant.

"Say, miss. That wouldn't be a gun behind you back--would it?" His discerning gaze traveled up her legs and nestled in her cleavage showing at the open front of her shirt.

"It's nothing," she said and gave the paper a twist of her wrist to send it off into the nearest corner. "Now, sir. Tell me why you returned to me." She twined her arms around his neck and promised herself he would never get away from her again.

"Seems like I forgot my own vow. You know, to never let go of something I love." He dipped his head to kiss her mouth and then smiled at her. "I made it to that little store in the village and it struck me that I had left something of mine behind."

"Raven, someday I have to tell you a secret. One that's better left alone for right now." She kissed his chin and pressed against him for warmth. "Truth is, I'm afraid to tell you."

"No, I'm afraid to hear it." He nuzzled her throat and squeezed her tighter. "Right now, I just want you, and the only thing I want to hear is what your pleasure is."

His soft laugh eased her fear and was sunlight in her precipice of doom. He had let her off the hook. She obliged his nudge to her chin and lifted her head to accept his kiss that reached her soul. She clung to him, kissing him with a passion she hadn't known before. Everything he did lifted her desire to be his, so high she felt the heat of the sun on her face.

A wisp of worry snaked about her mind when he made it clear he was interested in having sex and in a hurry, trying to ruin the moment. She should tell him about her newfound knowledge, but not now. There was nothing strong enough to separate him from her again. Lie, cheat, steal, she would do it all to be in his world.

She looked at his hand that cupped her breast and gave into the streamers of ecstasy that teased her into the first waves of a delicious climax. There was no way she could consider stopping him from touching her stomach and then the curls between her thighs. Not me, she agreed with her little demon of Eros.

"Do you still wear those nice short legged boxers, Raven?"

"Maybe. Put your hand in my pants and check it out."

She laughed and the sound of her laugh circled about them like sweet, warm smoke. "I believe your trying to get a free feel."

"Whatever it takes." He chuckled and placed her hand against his sex. "What do you think?"

"This will require closer observation." Her eyes closed and her smile sensual when she brushed her palm over the hot flesh bulging against the front of his slacks.

"I'm game, baby." He looked down at her with a villainous grin while she unzipped his pants. He gave out a low whistle when her hand dipped into the fly and her fingers teased his hard shaft. She moved her grasp up his length and then squeezed firmly.

"I do believe you're ready to do deep penetration, love." She laughed at his intake of breath when she opened her thighs and closed them about his ridged sex.

"Oh yes, ma'am. I do believe you're right." He picked her up and kissed her mouth roughly, growling against her lips. "I was wondering, madam. Have you adorned your bonnie body with a new piece of jewelry?"

She kissed him ardently and whispered against his seeking mouth. "Not a new piece, lover. Just the same belly button ring you admire so much."

"You don't really have one ... do you?" He laughed when she smiled slyly at him and pulled the hem of the shirt up to the top of her thighs. "Can you stop that for a second. I'll never make it to the top step."

"Raven. I believe I'm pregnant."

He raised his brows and grinned broadly. "Lets make certain."

He carried her up the stairs and to bed, kicking the door shut behind them.

Epilogue

Heaven opened wide it's gates and poured sunlight through the beveled glass windows of the church. Ethereal gold streamed over the bride and highlighted her face as she walked down the aisle on the arm of her brother-in-law. Her gaze was for Victor Raven alone, and her smile sent a message of her devotion to him.

He's yours, Lauren. There's no need to bring the letter up, not now. He need never know. You've kept it to yourself all these months. He need never know. Don't rock the boat. He may push you overboard for being a liar.

When Adam put her hand in Victor's and turned away to take a seat beside Raini, the moment of decision grew heavy on Lauren's shoulders. She met Victor's warm gaze and reached out to lay her hand on his chest.

"I have to tell you something, Victor." She had whispered and was afraid he hadn't heard her.

He leaned over to let her press her face to his neck and listened while she poured out her guilty secret.

"You have every right to walk away from me because of my dishonesty, but I was so afraid of losing you that I couldn't take the chance you would do exactly that." She gripped his arm, not noticing the petals that fell from her bouquet of white roses. "Do you understand what I did? I kept it to myself, hoping it would go away. That's how much I love you."

Victor cupped her cheek in his palm and chuckled even though there were tears in his eyes. "Lauren Kathleen Rose. I thought I was the only one with checkered past." He motioned for the perplexed minister to give them privacy and gave her a wicked grin. "I understand everything you did and all the worry you've gone through. We did what we did for love." Pressing a kiss to her ear, he whispered encouragement. "It all turned out very well if you ask me."

She smiled through her tears and kissed his hand. "I'll never ask for another thing if I'm with you."

He took his handkerchief from his pocket and dabbed her tears away. "The minister is waiting. The guests think there may be fireworks again."

She peered around his shoulder and found several hundred pairs of eyes trained on them. "I think that's why so many came for the ceremony." Her laugh was borne of complete happiness and her kiss to his lips one of daring proportion and elapsed time. "Let's disappoint them and quietly get married."

They held hands and took their marriage vows, falling in love all over again, with just one look.

Printed in the United States
47880LVS00001B/280-369